THE UNDERGROUND BOOK ONE

Chasing Rabbits

FROM USA TODAY BESTSELLING AUTHOR

ERIN BEDFORD

Also by Erin Bedford

The Underground Series
Chasing Rabbits
Chasing Cats
Chasing Princes
Chasing Shadows
Chasing Hearts
The Crimes of Alice

The Mary Wiles Chronicles
Marked by Hell
Bound by Hell
Deceived by Hell
Tempted by Hell

Starcrossed Dragons
Riding Lightning
Grinding Frost
Swallowing Fire
Pounding Earth

The Celestial War Chronicles
Song of Blood and Fire

The Crimson Fold
Until Midnight
Until Dawn
Until Sunset
Until Twilight

Curse of the Fairy Tales
Rapunzel Untamed
Rapunzel Unveiled

Her Angels
Heaven's Embrace
Heaven's A Beach
Heaven's Most Wanted

Academy of Witches
Witching On A Star
As You Witch
Witch You Were Here

<u>Granting Her Wish</u>
<u>Vampire CEO</u>

<u>Granting Her Wish</u>
<u>Vampire CEO</u>

THE UNDERGROUND BOOK ONE

Chasing Rabbits

FROM USA TODAY BESTSELLING AUTHOR
ERIN BEDFORD

THE CHASE

BRANDI BRIDGERS WAS a bitch in high school, and as I watched her sitting behind her desk with her 'holier-than-thou' attitude and her stylishly bobbed blonde hair, she gave me little hope she had changed. I rolled my eyes as she adjusted her neck-high white blouse. Her lips pressed together in a thin line as she scanned over my credentials. My resume dangled in her hand like it was something she found at the bottom of her drain.

"...come home."

My eyes widened, snapping up to look at Brandi. "What did you say?"

Brandi's lips tilted in a frown at my question. "I said, I'm not surprised you came home after all this time. Almost everyone comes home eventually. Really, Katherine, this is an interview, you really should be paying more attention."

"Sorry," I grumbled, too fixated on what I thought I'd heard. *Come home.* The words had plagued me for over a year now.

It started shortly after my twenty-first birthday. At first it was a whisper in a dream that I'd brushed off as being homesick, but then it bled into my waking life. I'd hear it in the breeze, or in my economics class. One time I swore my own reflection said it back to me. I had also been drunk out of my mind at the time, but it was hard to believe they were all coincidences.

So, here I was, back in my hometown, and the words were still taunting me. I was home. I couldn't get any more home than Iowa. I was even looking for a job. Not that I had high hopes for this interview, but with an English Literature Degree, there weren't many options available. I learned that painful truth back in New York; I should have been an accountant.

"I see here you were a library assistant in high school." Brandi's voice had a high-pitched, 'bless-your-heart' tone to it that grated on my nerves.

"Yes, Brandi. We went to high school together, you already know that." I crossed my arms over my black silk blouse, careful not to catch my thick copper hair on the buttons of my sleeves. My choice to wear a black shirt over a white one, like my mother had suggested helped to keep me from jumping over the desk to wring her grace's little neck. I didn't want to match Brandi in any way, shape, or form.

Brandi's brown eyes peeked around the side of the piece of paper, which held my meager life experience, bare to her over-accentuated eyes. "Katherine, as I told you before, I won't let our history together affect my judgment. No matter how offensive." She sniffed as her gaze returned to the paper as if her thinly veiled reference to my previous transgressions didn't affect her.

Like I had ever given two shits about what she thought.

Years ago, when I was an angry teen rebel full of sarcasm and black nail polish, I had the displeasure of going to school with Brandi and her swarm of over-medicated vultures. While everyone else in our class was trying to make as many memories as possible, I had spent the majority of it applying to every coast school I could afford. No place was far enough away from them.

So, when the miraculous day came and I got my acceptance letter to New York University, I didn't waste any time with long goodbyes. I gave Iowa a middle finger salute and made my way out of town screaming 'fuck you' to every innocent bystander I saw on my way down Broadway.

I probably should have been more selective of my targets, but how was I to know I would be sitting in an interview with one of the few people who actually deserved it?

My eyes narrowed at my captor, and I growled out, "Kat."

"What?" Brandi did not offer me her eyes this time.

"I like to be called Kat, which you also know."

For more than the first time – hell it was more like the hundredth time – I regretted coming to the interview. I would have turned tail and ran the moment I saw her, but my mother had gotten me the interview. If I left without even giving myself the chance to fail, I would never hear the end of it. I had to sit and swallow the half-assed insults to my person and abilities and hope to whatever deity was listening that I didn't get the job.

"Of course." Her voice still held a sickly sweet tone. "I'll make a note of it in your file." Her neatly manicured fingers gripped her pen as she scribbled onto a notepad.

I doubted she was actually making a note of it. It was probably a reminder to get her roots bleached again, or to tell the vultures about how Katherine Nottington had sloppily begged for a job. I am sure they would all have a good laugh over their next mani-pedi excursion.

"Well." She gave an exaggerated sigh. "You don't really have the qualifications we are looking for in a librarian. An English Literature degree is all fine and dandy, but you never learned the Dewey Decimal System."

"I completely understand, I will just–" I stood up, happy for the interview to finally be over.

"But." Her tone stopped me. "Your mother is a good friend of ours, and she contributes quite a bit to the funding of this town's community. It would be rash, not to mention unchristian like, to toss you out into the cold when you have been brave enough to come back to our – what was it you called this town?" She paused, pretending as if it were not on the tip of her tongue. "A prehistoric cesspool that didn't deserve the pavement it was built on?"

Why could she remember a nonsensical insult stated under the influence, but she couldn't remember I liked being called Kat?

My brow furrowed at her words. "So, I got the job?"

"You've got the job!" Brandi threw her hands up as she hopped out of her seat and enveloped me in a tight embrace.

My body tensed at the sudden intrusion to my personal space. She dwarfed me in her three-inch heels. My nose went smack to the middle of her neck where it was assaulted by her top-shelf perfume.

I had gotten the job. How the hell had that happened? I hadn't been pleasant. Hell, I had been snarky at best. I knew she didn't want me on her staff any more than I wanted to be there, but money talked, and if there is one thing my family had going for them it was money.

"Yay." I gave a small, half-hearted response.

"Let me introduce you to our team!" Brandi finally let me go and led me out to the main circulation desk where the other employees were waiting.

The 'team,' as she called it, consisted of two people. Two. And they seemed to have as much enthusiasm for Brandi's leadership as I did in being there. Yay just about covered it.

"This is David." Brandi pointed at a guy about my age who gave me a shy smile and then a nervous cough at Brandi's overshadowing presence. "He does most of the shelving, but he also works the desk with Mrs. Jenkins here."

Mrs. Jenkins was an elderly lady. She had dark-brown skin that contrasted nicely with the whitest hair I had ever seen. That kind of white hair wasn't seen in the city if it didn't come out of a box or a salon. I must have been staring, because the old woman's eyes narrowed into a glare.

"You got a problem?" Her voice was raspy as if she had smoked too much.

"Only on days that end with y." I gave a half smile at my own joke, and then frowned when her brow furrowed further before she barked out a laugh causing David and Brandi to jump.

"That's nice. I think we are going to get along just fine." She turned a sharp eye to Brandi. "I half expected another one of those prissy little chits you keep hiring." She glanced over at me with a crooked smile. "Couldn't stand them, with all their 'rules are rules' nonsense. Bah. Brandi here knows what's what."

"Yes, well," Brandi began, she seemed nervous with Mrs. Jenkins's attention on her. "We decided to take a chance and go a different direction this time."

The fact that the old lady ruffled Miss Prim and Proper's feathers made me instantly like her. At least someone in this place had a sense of humor. I needed some humor in my life.

Come home, the voice had said. I was home. So why was I still feeling like I had somewhere to be?

A WEEK LATER and nothing extraordinary had happened. I went about my mediocre life and the ever-present words that followed me were deafeningly silent. I was afraid to let my guard down, not that my mother would let that happen.

I found myself having my usual argument with my mother over my social life, or rather, the lack of a social life, of which I had become so proud. We had already gone over everything new in her life, so of course she had to start in on mine. My hands were busy washing dishes with anal-retentive detail as my mother harped in my ear.

"Katherine, I just don't understand why you won't at least have dinner with Kevin. He's a nice boy, and he has a job!" My mother's exasperated voice grated on my ear as I held my cell phone between my shoulder and face.

"Because, Mom, I don't want or need a boyfriend. I am fine on my own."

I surveyed the dish I was cleaning, making sure all the food had been rinsed off before putting it in the dishwasher. Nothing got on my nerves more than food stuck to a plate, but at the moment, my mother was riding in at a close second.

"Oh, yes, a twenty-two-year-old woman all alone in that big house— in the middle of nowhere—is completely fine."

I rolled my eyes at the sarcasm in her voice.

"It's Iowa, Mom. The whole state is practically in the middle of nowhere." I shoved the sleeves of my gray, NYU sweatshirt back up over my elbows and switched the phone to my other shoulder. "Besides, Crescent is only a few minutes outside of town and Grandma needs someone to take care of her house while she's off playing in Florida."

"And she told you to sell it and put it toward a house in town. There is nothing wrong with wanting to be independent, Katherine, but being a hermit is drawing the line. Isn't being a librarian seclusion enough for you?"

A snort left my nose before I could stop it. The fact that she disapproved of the very job she pulled strings to get me was astounding. Though, it shouldn't have been surprising, she was always the one who brought up her disapproval of my career choices.

She had been one of the ones who had griped at me to pick a sensible major, like accounting or, God forbid, political science. She never understood my love for the English language. I wanted to be an editor, or maybe even a writer. If I could ever buckle down and write something worth reading.

Lately, though, it seemed like I couldn't do anything right. This was probably due to my sister, Linda, also known as Miss Fucking

Perfect, who was getting married this month. My mom had it in her head that I needed to find a man and be more social, or I would be doomed to be an old maid by thirty.

"You don't want to still be marking single when you're thirty do you?"

I should have bought a Powerball with how right I was.

There were worse things out there than being single at thirty. I could be dying of cancer or be a drug addict. No, my mother cared more about how my being single reflected on her.

"I'm not secluded at the library," I argued, ignoring her question completely. "Plenty of people are in and out every day. Plus, there are other workers there, not just me. Mrs. Jenkins works there, and so does David."

"Ha! Hardly suitable companionship for a girl your age. A senile old lady who has probably been there since the library opened, and David is more of a hermit than you! Though, if you dated him, at least you'd be dating. And Lord knows you'd never have to worry about him cheating on you. He hardly has the looks to be picky."

David was a nice guy, even if he was not the most attractive. He had a slightly hooked nose and a pudgy build, but after a week of working with him, I found his hesitant smile and soft-spoken ways endearing. If I was looking for someone, and I was not, he had a lot of the qualities I would want. Too bad he was taken.

"I'll make sure to tell his fiancé you think so."

I almost dropped the dish in my hand when she gave an uncharacteristic chortle. "Even that spud has someone! Doesn't that tell you anything, Katherine?"

My knuckles turned white as I gripped the plate in my hands. It started to make a tiny cracking noise, and I put it down. My mother had that effect on me. We would start fighting and she would pick and pick at old wounds until they bled. Sadly, my dishes were always the ones to suffer.

I slammed the dishwasher closed as I took a deep breath. "You know what, Mom? If it will make you happy, I will go out with Kevin, but not this week." I waited for the comment that was sure to come because she wasn't getting her way.

"But if you don't go out this week, you won't have enough prep time to have him be your date to Linda's wedding."

Linda's wedding. Of course, that's what she was worried about. No way would it be about my happiness.

"I'm in the wedding, Mom. The groomsmen assigned to me will be my date." I yanked the hair tie from my copper locks and set to work on tying the messy bun again. "Besides, I'm busy this week."

"Oh? Busy with what? That old garden?" I could almost see her rolling her eyes even though we were on the phone. "You know nothing good ever grows in your grandmother's yard. I should know. I grew up there."

"Yes, the garden, and if you'd bother to come over you would see how great everything is growing. I even have a carrot patch–"

As if knowing I was talking about it, a loud crash came from the backyard signaling my trap had gone off again. Damn rabbits!

"I've got to go."

"But Katherine, what about–"

"I'll talk to you on Sunday at lunch. Love you, bye," I cut in hanging up the phone before she could answer. I dashed to the door, shoved my feet into my sneakers, and took off toward the sound.

I scanned the backyard for any sight of the little thief who had been plaguing me for weeks. I skipped going into the garden. I knew my trap would be empty like it always was and skimmed the trees for any sign of the white devil instead. My forest-green eyes caught sight of a white streak bolting for the woods behind the house. Not wanting to lose him, I took off into the dark.

"Where did you go?"

The green of the trees created a darkened gray, making it hard to see as they blended into their surroundings. The rustling leaves to my left drew my attention just as the dull white streak made for the clearing up ahead.

"There you are!"

My sneakers thudded against the ground as I chased after him, and the whispers returned. With each footfall they chanted. *Come home. Come home. Come home.* My heart beat faster in my chest and my bare legs seemed to catch on every single branch I ran past, leaving little scratches all over my skin.

I ignored the stinging in my legs and kept my eyes on the white coat that glared neon in the visible moonlight from the clearing. Though I had a clear view of him, he was still too fast for me to catch. I wasn't in the best of shape, and my short legs could only get me so far.

The wind picked up as I bent over to catch my breath. The words floated on the wind as it whipped bits of hair out of my bun and into my face. I glowered at the single section of blonde that had fallen, its contrast so different from the rest of my copper hair. A birthmark at the nape of my neck had caused the discoloration. I usually kept my hair down to hide it. The fact that I even let it show at home would cause my mother to start a tirade about how I should just color it.

I didn't really care about it, and probably should have given into her urgings, but I didn't see the logic in buying a box of hair color just for a single section. I wasn't so vain to think the expense was worth it, so it hung freely underneath my hair with none the wiser. Plus, it pissed my mother off, which was reason enough in my book.

Standing up, I noticed the rabbit had stopped next to the little pond my sister and I used to fish at when we were younger. It wasn't a very big pond, and to our dismay, it had more frogs than fish in it. It did have a great little hiding spot. There was a cave where water from the Missouri River trickled into the pond, and sitting right outside the cave, taking his time as he enjoyed my carrots, was the long-eared fiend.

He munched away at one with every confidence he had lost me. I took a moment to try to get the jump on him by moving across the field toward where he was sitting. Luck was not on my side, however, because as soon as I was about to sneak up behind him, he saw my reflection in the pool and panicked. He shoved the carrot into his mouth and darted toward the mouth of the cave.

"Shit."

The rabbit was more trouble than he was worth and a lot smarter than he seemed. I had tried everything to keep him out of my garden.

Animal repellent, traps, even wire fencing. It still didn't keep him out. He had somehow even cut a hole in the fence big enough for him to get in and out with my carrots.

No clue how he pulled that one off.

I once mused he was a runaway lab rabbit that the government had been doing experiments on him. As a result, he'd become a superfied genius rabbit. Though, if that were true, nothing short of a high-powered security system was keeping that rabbit out of my carrot patch. So, since I couldn't afford that kind of tech on a librarian's salary, I decided to take him out.

In order to not spook my prey again, I inched my way toward the cave's entrance. It wasn't very big. At ten years old it had been quite easy to go in and out as I pleased, but as a moderately chested grown woman, it was a tight fit.

I tried to be as quiet as possible as I sucked in my stomach. Think thin. I was as thin as a rod, as skinny as a Victoria Secret model. This wasn't making me claustrophobic whatsoever. Finally, I got through the entrance and blinked as my eyes adjusted to the dim lighting in the cavern.

The cave I remembered was usually pretty dark with only a sliver of moonlight coming through the opening, but to my surprise, it was brighter in the cavern than it was outside.

As my eyes adjusted to the cave an ominous feeling washed over me. Weird, neon-white painted symbols covered the walls.

What the hell?

My fingers traced one of the symbols, and I realized it was not paint at all. It was as if they were part of the wall itself. I didn't remember them being there the last time my sister and I had ventured into our little hideout. I would remember mysterious nightlights, wouldn't I?

As conspiracy theories started to circle my mind, a sneeze from the back of the cavern reminded me of my purpose. I turned away from the mysterious symbols and moved toward the sound. Every step I took felt heavier than the last, and a chilling thought came to mind—what if something, or someone, was in the cave?

With that disturbing thought, my footsteps became more cautious, and my eyes darted around. No one was going to get the jump on me. I had read enough horror novels to know I was a prime candidate for being abducted or killed by some lunatic with a skin fetish. I really should work on my sense of self-preservation.

More symbols started to appear on the walls the further back I got. In the front of the cavern they had only been on the sides, but as I progressed deeper into the cave, the symbols began to run all along the ceiling and the floor.

They were angled in the direction of something in the center of the back of the cavern as if they were being drawn in.

I followed the spiral of symbols until I ended up in front of a basketball-sized hole in the wall. That had definitely not been there before. Turning around in a circle, I searched the walls for any other changes. There was not really anything different, besides the weird nightlights and the hole, and there was no sign of the rabbit anywhere.

I gave the hole a wide berth as I contemplated what to do next. I knew the only exit to the cavern was the one I came through, so the rabbit must have gone through the hole. Then again, I could be in a horrible version of some mummy story, and the moment I stuck my arm in that thing, it was going to get eaten off.

I wasn't the bravest person. I didn't agree to work in a library just because I loved to read, and I'd admit, a little desperate. It was quiet, making it easy to get lost in one's thoughts, which I was known to do on a semi-permanent basis. There was also the seclusion from the lack of employees, which made it an anti-social's dream job.

Though, sometimes being so alone could have consequences, such as not being good with people, or more specifically, guys. I usually became either a stuttering mess or a sarcastic asshole when faced with an attractive specimen. That's why I liked working with David so much. He was plain enough I could be myself.

Mrs. Jenkins knew how I felt about men and people in general. She could be as bad as my mother when it came to me dating. I could just imagine what she would have to say about my hesitancy to stick my arm in that hole. "Dear, everything worth having comes with a leap of faith. Just hold onto your panties and take the plunge."

I had only been working at the library for a day when she said that to me. I had been so shocked; I had fallen out of my seat from laughing so hard. Yes, she was a little eccentric. She takes the whole 'I'm old so I can say whatever I want' a little too far, but she had a lot of great advice, and I already loved her for it.

I took a deep breath and let it out. "What the hell."

I stepped back up to the hole and placed one hand on each side of it. I bent at the waist and squinted into the hole to see what waited.

Darkness.

While the cavern was lit up with the glowing symbols, the hole was nothing but complete blackness. I couldn't see a damn thing. I blew out a shaky breath between my teeth, all that lead up and nothing.

"Fuck it."

I threw up my hands and moved away from the hole. That rabbit was not worth becoming some creepy crawlies food. Studying the symbols as I walked away, I made a mental note to dig into the language section when I got back to work in the morning.

"Does Mop think Lady is gone, does Mop?"

I turned an ear back toward the hole at the squeaky voice's question. I took large strides, well as large as my short legs would let me back to the hole.

Who was that?

"I don't know! Ye shouldn't have led her here in the first place!" A low rumbling voice growled in return.

I inched my face down to the hole and peered in again. Instead of darkness, there was a fading light coming from inside the hole. *Come home*, whispered against my face. I twisted around to look behind me. As usual, no one was there. Shoving down every part of me that screamed to just go back to the house and crawl into bed, I reached into the hole.

The warmth of the light engulfed my hand and tugged me toward it. I tried to retract my hand, but it was too late, it had its hooks in me. I remembered wondering if this is what it felt like to be sucked through a straw before everything went black.

THE BETWEEN

I LANDED WITH a hard smack. My head filled with miniature dancing cappuccinos. Coffee sounded good right now. I groaned at the damage my aching limbs had taken from the fall. Before I could assess my injuries, a door slammed shut behind me causing me to jerk up and open my eyes. I squeezed them shut again when piercing white light filled my vision.

My eyes! I was blind! I blinked a few times, waiting for my eyes to adjust. Okay, I guess I wasn't. I was okay.

It wasn't my eyesight that was the problem. It was the room, well not really. It wasn't a room but a big white space. Looking up, there was nothing but white. There was no way to tell how tall the room was, or from what I could see, how far it reached around me. There weren't any walls or windows. The only objects were four doors, one in each direction.

Someone seriously needed to rethink the décor.

The door closest to me wasn't anything extraordinary. It was made of plain old wood. I peeked around the edge of the door, and there was nothing. Besides the doorframe, there was nothing that would allow the door to stand on its own. There was no wall supporting it and nothing but more endless white space behind it.

I rattled the doorknob – locked.

Of course it was. Why wasn't I surprised? I beat on the door and shook the handle once more.

"Hello? Let me out!" I banged on the door harder and twisted the handle until my hand began to burn. My eyes darted around the room searching for another way out, but all I saw were doors and endless white.

I fought the urge to scream as I pulled my hair. What am I going to do? There was no one here and no way out. No one at home even knew where I was. They'd think I'd been kidnapped or was dead. I had to get out of here!

I considered the other doors and took off toward the one to my right. I jiggled the knob and banged on it but found it to be like the other one – locked.

Before I could think about it, I ran to the next and found it locked as well. I kicked the door and turned my gaze to the last remaining door.

It was more beat up than the other ones with scarring all along the surface. My hand moved to try the handle only to find it was missing.

Great. I wasn't going to get anywhere with this one.

I turned around in a circle and stared out into the white void. Good going. I was stuck in what was probably someone's bleached butt hole with nothing but doors to taunt me forever.

Just when my eyes were starting to strain from the blinding white light, something moved in the distance.

"Hello?" I stepped around the door, but before my feet could move in its direction a voice squawked at me from behind.

"I wouldn't go out there if I were you."

I whirled around. In the center of the room, where nothing had been before, was a circular reception desk. Behind the desk was some kind of bird. It wore a fuchsia-colored dress with a loud floral pattern. But unlike any bird I'd ever seen, it had not one, but two heads. One of the heads wore glasses on the brim of its beak, which it used it to tap away at the keys of a keyboard. The other one was watching me as if waiting for an answer.

"When did you get there?" I cocked my head to the side, looking back and forth where nothing had been before.

The head squawked and shook its head. "We've been here all along. You just haven't been looking hard enough."

"Oh." Well, that made no sense whatsoever. I looked from the two-headed bird and back out into the white void where the black spot had disappeared. "Why shouldn't I go out there?"

"You go out there you'll never get back out again, not without a guide at least. Now, if you'd just sign in here you can be on your way." The one not wearing the glasses pushed a clipboard toward me with her wing.

I ignored the clipboard and focused on the receptionists. "On my way where? I don't even know where I am."

"Type!" She waved her wing in the air. "This silly chit doesn't know where she is!"

The one called Type glanced up from her keyboard to give me a flat stare over the spectacles on her beak. Not finding me worth her effort, she turned back to the screen where it appeared she was watching an episode of Game of Thrones.

They had Internet? Go figure.

"As you can see..." The other head gestured toward the computer screen. "We don't have time for you. So, if you would just sign in right here we can all get on with our lives." She nudged the clipboard back toward me.

"But I don't want to sign in! I want to go home."

"Well, then, you shouldn't have come here." She flapped her wing back toward the door I came through. "Go back out the way you came."

"It's locked. I can't get out," I growled, digging my nails into the edge of the circular desk.

"Locked? Of course it's locked!" Type glanced away from the screen for a moment before turning back. "Can't be letting anybody come in and out as they please."

"What she said." The other head nodded in agreement. "If you want out, use your key."

"Key?" I patted myself even though I knew I didn't have a key or pockets for that matter. "I don't have a key."

"Well, then, you will just have to sign in, and we can issue you a temporary key." She pushed the clipboard toward me once again.

I growled and yanked the clipboard from her grasp. Looking down at the clipboard, I poised the pen in my hand as I read the sheet. It was your basic sign-in form – asking for name, date, and place. There was only one entry on the sheet of paper, written in sloppy cursive. It read: Mop and Trip with today's date and the human realm listed under place.

I almost wrote down my information and the human realm like the previous signers, but stopped. I wanted to go home, but the other doors bugged me. Where did they go?

"How am I supposed to fill this out if I don't know where I am?"

"Gripe, just tell the girl where she is already. I want to finish this season before lunch," Type piped in without tearing her eyes away from the screen.

The head named Gripe huffed. "This." She gestured around the room. "Is the Between."

My eyes followed her wing as it circled the air. "Between? Between what?"

"Everything of course." Gripe rolled her eyes. "So, where will it be?" She held up the pen and clipboard once more, an impatient look in her eyes.

I sighed and reached out for the pen, but then I heard whispers coming from the other side of the desk. Those were the ones I had heard from inside the hole! I craned my neck around the large bird and saw the curve of the rabbit's long white ears.

I stepped away from the desk and pointed toward the rabbit. "Um, I'm with him."

Gripe sniffed, putting her nose in the air and turned back to watch the screen with her other head.

I made my way over to the door on the other side of the desk. In front of the second door I had tried, stood the white-eared rabbit and a brown little man. They were arguing. As I came into view, their voices became more urgent.

"Ye idiot! She followed ye here!"

"Trip is sorry! Trip was just ever so hungry and Lady's carrots are ever so good."

No higher than my waist, the white rabbit wasn't really a rabbit at all. It had the face of a rabbit, but its white ears hung all the way to the ground. Instead of a little cottontail, it had a long, shorthaired tail with a tuft of hair at the end.

The other one was a little brown man with a pointed red hat and matching overalls. His large nose and ears seemed out of place on his small face. The beard along his chin was short and as dark as his onyx-colored eyes, which glared up at me as I appraised him.

"Please don't eat Trip!" I jumped in place as the rabbit-like creature latched onto my knees. "Trip didn't mean any harm! Trip just loves Lady's carrots so much! Way better than other humans! Blech!" He spat on the ground. "They feel like worms and death in Trip's mouth."

I tilted my head to the side at the rabbit's pleas. This was the rabbit I was chasing? No wonder he could get through all my traps. Any normal rabbit wouldn't have sharp fangs and opposable thumbs. Then again, wherever I was, wasn't on the spectrum of normal.

"What's it gonna be, Lady?" The brown little man grunted, crossing his arms over his chest. "Are ye gonna eat him or not?"

I wrinkled my nose at the thought of eating something that could talk. I had nothing against eating meat, I loved meat, but I never wanted to meet my food before I ate it. At least not any that could beg for their lives.

"Uh, I guess I'm not." The words came out slow and unsure.

"Oh, thank you, beautiful Lady, merciful Lady!" Trip, as he called himself, hugged my legs tight. "Lady won't regret it, Lady won't. Trip swears!"

"Calm down. That's great and everything, but what about my garden? And stop calling me Lady, my name is Kat." I pried him off of my leg, holding him up by his ears. Shit he's heavy. "How are you going to pay me back for all those carrots you stole?"

Trip lifted up his hands to show his empty palms. "Trip does not have anything to pay Lady with, Trip doesn't."

I shook my head at him. "I don't want your money."

I was about to say I just wanted to go home but stopped. Come home. The voices had stopped the moment I had gone into the rabbit hole. Could this be what it wanted?

I mustered the little bit of courage I had and pointed a finger at the door next to us. "Tell me about the doors and why is there a hole in the woods?"

Trip's eyes became wide, and he struggled to get out of my grasp. "Trip can't tell Lady that! No, Trip can't!"

I fought to keep a hold of the little white devil, but he slipped from my hands and scurried over to the brown pint-sized man.

"Mop tell, Lady! Mop tell!"

The brown man, known as Mop, stood in front of Trip blocking my path and glared once more. "Ye can't be askin' him that. We ain't even supposed to be talkin' to the likes of ye."

I matched his glare with one of my own and headed for the door. If they weren't going to tell me, I would just have to figure it out myself. Besides, I was a smart girl, and there was nothing I hadn't read – or Hollywood hadn't already desensitized me to – that I couldn't handle.

"No, Lady!" Trip chased after me, pressing his back to the wood of the door to block my path. "Lady mustn't go in!"

"And why not?" I threw my hands up in the air with a growl. "You took my carrots, you led me here, and now I want to know what is in there." I turned the door handle, finding it already unlocked when it wasn't before. I tried to pull it open, but Trip's weight against the door had been added to by Mop.

"Ye will get ye payment, but ye can't go in. Can't ye read the sign?" He pointed a chubby brown finger at a sign I swore hadn't been there before.

Crap kept popping up out of nowhere. I glared up at the sign. The sign read, 'No Humans Allowed' in big, black, curly letters. Well, weren't they racist, or was it humanist?

"Well then," I huffed, tapping my foot. "How do you expect to pay me back?"

"Trip here be a great guard, aren't ye, Trip?" Trip nodded his head in vigor, his tail wagging in the air. "He'll protect ye garden from other rodents and the like in return for the occasional..." The little man eyed Trip in warning. "...carrot."

I stared up at the floating sign, thinking about his proposal. I guess it sounded all right, but it didn't satisfy my curiosity to know more about the doors. I hadn't risked my hand and sanity to come all this way to leave with nothing.

"All right, you win." Trip and Mop relaxed against the door. "So, how do I get back to my world?"

Trip moved away from the door and hopped toward the other side of the Between. I moved to follow Trip across the room but stopped when Mop didn't move from his spot against the door. His eyes narrowed at me, suspicion on his face.

"Are you coming?"

He stood there debating if he could trust me, his brow furrowing further. After a moment or two, he must have come to a decision, because he moved away from the door and toward where Trip waited.

"Ya, I'm comin'."

I let Mop move ahead of me as we made our way past the reception desk. Both bird heads moved away from the computer monitor to watch me with a knowing leer. I tried not to flinch at their gaze and focus on my plan. When Mop was far enough away, I spun around and darted back to the door.

"What are ye doing?" Mop yelled out. "Stop!"

"No, Lady, no!"

My hand grasped the knob, but I hesitated at the birds' dark laughter coming from behind me. Whatever their deal was I needed to know what was in here, and I wasn't going to let fear stop me. I yanked the door open and braced myself for whatever was to come next.

C H A P T E R

IN & OUT AGAIN

THE GROUND SMELLED of lavender. It was calm and peaceful. It made a girl want to lie there forever, and I would have had it not been for the biting cold of the ground pressed against my face. It felt like stone, but stones don't usually have such a pleasant scent to them. Or did they? I normally didn't make a habit of smelling the ground. After all, people might have thought I was crazy.

I shoved my hair out of my face as my eyes fluttered open. Great, I'd lost my hair tie. My hair was going to be all over the place. I should just cut it and get it over with.

I moved into a kneeling position, searching the ground for my missing hair tie. While the stone may have smelled nice, the ugly grayish brown color wasn't doing it any favors. I winced where the edges of the stones bit into my hands as I moved to sit up.

I rubbed my eyes and stretched my back to get the dull ache from my bumpy landing out. Traveling by rabbit hole was not recommended, nor a particularly sane choice of travel. Not that going through a door without looking to see what was on the other side first was advisable.

My eyes stung as they adjusted from the blinding white of the Between to the gray of the surrounding stone walls. Above me was a blue sky with birds chirping as they flew by; it was slightly more cheery than I expected. I glanced back to where I had come from. A leafless oak tree stood in the middle of the little area and smack dab in the middle of the trunk was a hole.

I pushed aside the chance of me getting a rational explanation as to how I had come through a door and ended up outside a hole. Besides, I cared more about how my big butt had fit through it in the first place. Not that it should have surprised me since I had already been sucked through a hole and out a door once before, but the academic in me fought to find some kind of non-magical solution.

Flapping wings drew my eyes to an upper branch of the small tree as a spotted barn owl landed on its surface. It hooted a curious call.

Its unusual ice blue eyes followed my every move. Ignoring the owl, my eyes locked onto my hair tie floating in a small pond below the tree. I crawled across the stone to kneel before the pond.

The water was clear enough for me to see small fish swimming around but deep enough that I was wary of what lurked beneath. How deep did the pond go? It wasn't very big, more of a decorative pond in someone's backyard than an actual pond. It was probably no longer than I was.

As I reached toward the surface of the water to nab my hair tie, a murky white figure began to move toward me. When it got close enough to the surface to see, I tried to move back. Deathly pale skin was stretched across the bones of a bodiless face. The sockets where its eyes should have been were empty and appeared as if someone had painted over them with black paint. Its mouth opened wide to reveal razor-sharp teeth. I struggled to tear my hand back to my side, but I was locked in place by the eyeless gaze of the creature coming at me.

My heart raced as it bobbed closer and closer to the surface, my hand just barely touched the water's edge. I turned my eyes away from the water to the owl perched on the tree that was watching with mild fascination.

"Help me!" I pleaded. I turned back to the pond when he did nothing but cock his head to the side.

I grabbed my wrist with my other hand and tugged as hard as I could, the skin on my wrist pinched beneath my other hand. A scream built up in me as the sharp teeth came closer and closer to the surface. I closed my eyes and turned my head just as it was about to chomp down. I was yanked away from the pool, my hand free of its grasp.

"What the hell are ye doin'?"

I rubbed my wrist as Mop yelled at me; my eyes darted back to the pond where the white head had disappeared back to the bottom. I cringed to think what could have happened if Mop hadn't gotten there in time. I'd have one less hand and probably a less-than-flattering nickname – One-handed Kat or Katherine the Nub. I definitely would have looked into getting a hook of some kind, maybe something in platinum.

"Lady! Are ye listenin' to me?"

"Huh? Sorry." I gave a sheepish grin. "What did you say?"

Mop placed his hands on his hips and glared. "I said are all ye kind as dumb as ye, or are ye just the exception?"

"Hey!"

I was offended he would even lop me in with the other humans. I may not be the smartest of the bunch, but I was better off than some. I wouldn't have been able to trick the little brown man into letting me in otherwise.

"I was smart enough to get in here."

Mop snorted. "Only to have ye hand bit off in the first five minutes. Didn't ye mother ever teach ye not to be lookin' for trouble?"

The thought of my mother teaching me anything was laughable. When I was seven I wanted to learn how to ride a bike. She had flat out refused and had given me an hour-long lecture on how bicycles were not for ladies of our stature and asked why I couldn't take up something more suitable, like knitting. In the end, I had to beg a neighbor's dad to teach me on a secondhand bike I had gotten from a pawnshop with my own allowance.

I opened my mouth to answer when the unhelpful owl decided to make his presence known. Mop's eyes snapped to the feathered creature and he frowned harder. Glad to know I'm not the only one who didn't like the owl.

Turning back to me, Mop wagged a finger in my face. "Why couldn't ye just go home? Now, ye are gonna get us all in trouble."

"Mop doesn't think he knows, does Mop?" Trip's face appeared inside the hole in the tree, his brow etched with worry. Had he been in there all this time?

"Of course, he does! It be his kingdom." He marched up to me, one of his stubby fingers pointing at me. "We're all doomed if we donna get ye back to yer world before he comes."

Trip hopped out of the tree and landed next to us. His furry body followed suit and, in a spout of irony, tripped on his own long floppy ears. His windy tail hung in the air, limp and dejected.

I felt bad for him, I really did. After all, it was my fault we were here to begin with. But if he could have just restrained himself from getting into my garden, I would never have followed him to the cave and ended up in the damn hole.

"Why can't I just go back out the way I came?" I pointed to the hole in the tree. Mop and Trip looked at me as if I had grown a second head.

"Ye can't go back that way. It only goes one way." Mop's stubby legs teetered across the cobblestone. "The only way ye gettin' out be through the orchard." My eyes followed his pudgy finger, which was pointing to an opening in the wall that surrounded us.

"Well, then, let's go." My foot moved in the direction Mop pointed, but Trip was once again blocking my path.

"No! No, Lady!" Trip shook his head and held up his hands. "Lady doesn't want to go in there! Lady would get eaten for sure, Lady would!"

I put my hands on my hips and made an unladylike growl. I was getting tired of being told what I should and shouldn't do. "If I can't go back, then the only way to go is forward, unless you want me to stay in this spot forever?"

Mr. Blue Eyes, who had been watching our exchange, hooted as if to agree with me. The sound startled Trip, his frightened eyes darted between the owl and me. Why was he scared of a little owl?

"You're not very brave, are you?" I shook my head in disbelief. "It's a wonder you were able to steal any of my carrots at all."

Trip tugged his ears over his face and hunched down into himself. "Trip is sorry, Lady. Trip doesn't want to see Lady hurt, Trip doesn't."

His long tail seemed to be the most expressive part of his body, because it drooped down in his despair. His childlike persona had me almost regretting putting him in this situation.

Almost.

Mop shoved Trip aside and grabbed my hand, pulling me toward the entrance. "I know how ye feel, Trip. But we gotta get her outta here. Humans be forbidden, lest ye forgot. Ye don't want him to be findin' her, do ye?"

Trip stopped tugging on his ears, his eyes wide. "No! Trip no want that!" He hopped across the cobblestone and grabbed my other hand, helping Mop to lead me into the stone corridor.

I let myself be dragged along the path, and my eyes drank in the surroundings. There weren't any turns in front of us, only a long walkway surrounded by stone walls on both sides. I couldn't tell how far it went, though it seemed endless, and the foliage covering the walls only added to the effect. All along the walls were long, windy vines tipped with pretty little multicolored flowers.

"Where exactly are we?"

"Now ye want to know?" Mop grunted like it should have been my first question. I was a little busy finding my hair tie, which of course was still in the pond.

And what was up this little goblin's butt? Had I killed his grandma or something? Insulted his heritage? I couldn't do a single thing right in his beady little eyes.

"Ye have the gracious honor of being in the UnSeelie Court. Not that it means much to ye." He snorted at me over his shoulder. I was getting the distinct impression he didn't like me much.

Still holding Trip's hand, I stopped beside a small bundle of flowers, its hue a mixture of purples and reds I'd never seen before. I leaned into smell them when the flowers parted to reveal a bulging yellow eyeball.

"What the hell?" I jumped back with a screech. Mop and Trip were at my side in an instant.

"What ye yellin' for? It's just a beetle." The grumpy troll chuckled at me before turning away.

I glared at him before looking back at the so-called beetle. For a moment, I thought the eye was an illusion, like those butterflies that use their wing design to ward off predators, and then the eye began to follow me as I moved side to side. I reached out to touch it, but its wings fluttered over the eye like an eyelid and took off over the wall's edge.

"Well, that's a relief." I sniffed the flowers the beetle had been resting on. "For a moment, I thought I might be in some kind of Alice in Wonderland scenario."

Mop jerked me away from the flowers and clamped his hands over my mouth. "Are ye stupid? Don't be sayin' that name!"

My eyes narrowed at the hand over my mouth, and for a moment, I was half tempted to lick him, but then the flowers started to whisper. Mop and Trip's eyes filled with alarm as the flowers twittered to each other down each side of the walls. Each of them whispered Alice's name like it was a forbidden secret.

"Trip is scared, Trip is." Trip tugged on my hand, hiding his face behind his ears.

Mop growled next to me, "Now ye done it! It couldn't get any worse I thought, but no! Ye just had and go say that blasted woman's name! Goin' to be bringin' the whole Underground down on us now. No good, nosy child saying forbidden words–"

"What'd I say? Alice?" I cut in.

"Would ye stop sayin' it! Do ye want to be losin' ye head?" He threw his hands up in the air and shook his head as if he couldn't believe I was stupid enough to say it again.

My right eyebrow twitched. This place was giving me a headache. How was I supposed to know what to do and what not to do?

"Make up your mind. Are we in Wonderland, the Underground, or the UnSeelie Court?" Pulling my hand from Trip, I crossed my arms over my chest.

"Ye humans and ye need to define everything." Mop scoffed and stepped up to a red mossy spot on the opposite side of the wall. It was the only spot void of the chattering flowers. He tickled the fuzz of the moss, causing it to spread out along the wall and form a rectangular door shape.

"We be where I say we be. I don't know nothing bout no Wonderland though, that be what the other one called it."

"Mop can't take Lady in there!" Trip's words were filled with panic.

Mop clucked his tongue. "We have no choice. We had sometime before ye started blabbin' bout forbidden nonsense and now thems flowers be talkin'. They be notifyin' him for sure."

Mop fiddled with a bag at his side for a moment, before pulling out a ring of keys. Flipping through them, he held up a dark, fuzzy, red key with sharp teeth like prongs. He stuck the key in the hole and twisted. When the lock popped, he placed his hand on the moss once more, turning what seemed to be a doorknob.

He pushed the door open for me and gestured for me to enter. "Reaper knows who else be listenin' in when he finds out. And this way be faster."

"But here is dangerous, here is," Trip's voice shook as he followed close to me. I wasn't sure if I should be afraid or not. Trip seemed like the type to be afraid of his own shadow.

My eyes focused on the dark red within the wall. After everything I'd seen so far, this was by far the weirdest place I had ever been to. It even trumped that one time I was talked into going to a heavy metal concert with my ex-boyfriend, Todd, and ended up in a mosh pit. I was black and blue for a week.

I took a step into the door. My foot squished down into the red mossy floor. I made a small disgusted noise in my throat as I focused on the hope that the fluid coming to the top wouldn't stain my white tennis shoes. Wings flapped in the distance, and the red door shut behind me. What was in front of me made me think I'd rather be back in the mosh pit.

TEETH

WHEN MY EYES adjusted to the dark contrast of the new area, I instantly wished I had kept my diarrhea-of-a-mouth shut. The moss that made up the door spread across a room that spanned half a football field. My feet made a squishing noise as I kept close to Mop, who marched across the mossy floor without a wary glance to the shadows whispering at the edges.

I kept my eyes on the shadows and lowered my voice, "Who's this *he* you guys keep talking about? And call me Kat, would you?"

"Ye shouldn't give ye name out so freely here." Mop's eyes swept the room as if to look for something unseen. "Ye never know who be listenin'. And *he* is the glorious Dark Prince of the UnSeelie Court. Ye be lucky to never meet him."

"Prince, huh? So he's in charge of everything, then?" I eyed the shadows that seemed to be moving with the corner of my eye. We were barely halfway across the room. I expected them to show themselves by now. But the creatures, whatever they were, seemed content to watch us from afar.

Trip gripped my hand tighter and kept his voice hushed, "Only of the outer realm. It's how he keeps humans out, it is. Keep humans away from us Fae."

"Fae?" I paused to question Trip. "You mean like faeries?"

"Ba!" I jumped back as Mop spit on the ground. "Faeries! Those little pests ain't got nothin' on we Fae."

"Oh? What's the difference?" I cocked my head to the side, my interest piqued.

As far as I was concerned, Mop was as much a pest as any Tinkerbelle. Though, the idea of flying made my stomach curl. It was a good thing I was short. Heights and I had a disagreement once at a theme park. At which time, we had decided it was in both of our best interests that we go our separate ways.

"What? There be a huge difference!" Mop glared at me and put his hands on his hips. "What do ye think we Fae do?"

"Oh, I don't know. Grant wishes and stuff?" I shrugged my shoulders, and then tensed as the shadows giggled. "What's so funny?"

"Lady funny, Lady is." Trip laughed along with our creepy audience, and his tail wagged behind him.

I found it curious that Mop and Trip weren't at all concerned with the slithering forms that I could barely make out on the sides. Maybe they only creeped me out?

Mop shook his head, his eyes on the ground. "Silly girl. Many of ye kind be dyin' here 'cause they be lookin' for wishes." Mop spun around and waved a finger in my face. "Ye be gettin' the same fate if ye be tryin' to get things for free."

I gulped and eyed the slithering forms once more as they snickered. They sure knew how to prey on one's fears. I was never sleeping with the lights off again.

"Ain't nothin' free here," Mop warned as we began the trek across the squishy moss again.

I tried to suppress my disgust, as each step caused a sort of flatulent sound. I was glad I had had the foresight to wear my tennis shoes and not my flip-flops. That split-second decision when I rushed out the door had saved the pedicure my mother had insisted I get for the upcoming wedding.

As we got closer to the end of the room the moss dissipated, revealing more cobblestones underneath. The edges filled with shadows also began to disperse, though no extra light was present. Finally, the adventure in weird squishy land had come to an end.

"What is this place?" I ignored Mop's huff in response to my question. "If this way is faster, why didn't we go this way to begin with?"

"Cause." Mop dug into the pocket of his trousers and pulled out what looked like a biscuit and another key. How many of those things did he have? "The other way may be slower, but it be a straight shot to the orchard and ye way outta here. But who knows whom those weeds be talkin' to. It be safer for us all if we go this way."

Before I could ask any more questions, Mop stepped up to another part of the wall that was part moss and part cobblestone. He lifted a hand and tickled a patch above his head. This time instead of a door appearing, a large mouth with sharp, moss-covered teeth and beady eyes popped out, glowering at us.

It made me think of my Aunt Lydia: fur covered and in need of a dentist in a bad way. I covered my mouth to suppress a giggle, but when it opened its mouth to snarl at us, my laughter died in my throat.

"What do you want? Can't a wall get some sleep around here?" The voice that came out of the mouth was a surprisingly smooth tone, even with its sharp teeth gleaming through its menacing growl.

"Oh, quit ye gripin'. I brought ye a biscuit, so let us in." Mop waved the biscuit in front of the mossy wall's face.

"A biscuit! I haven't had one of those in ages!"

The smile that formed on the cranky wall's face was even more terrifying than its gnashing teeth. The fact of how crazy it seemed that I was even contemplating how scary a talking wall was, was not lost on me. It wasn't the first time I wondered if I was really here or had got knocked out chasing that damn rabbit back in the cavern.

Its eager smile turned into a wary grimace as he eyed me. "But what do you want in return?"

Curiosity caused me to lean down to Trip, who was still clutching my hand in his merciless grip. "Why does he need a biscuit to let us pass?"

Trip's eyes never left the teeth in the wall. "Lady, must remember what Mop say, Lady must. Nothing is ever free. Lady must give to get." Trip's scared eyes turned serious when they locked with mine. "Be careful what Lady trades. Fae are tricky, they are."

"Tricky? You mean like Puck?" I thought back to Shakespeare's Midsummer Night's Dream. Puck thought it would be great fun to have everyone fall in love with the wrong person. There was something telling me the kind of tricks these Fae pulled would not end with someone screwing their best friend's boyfriend.

"What is *that* doing down here?" The wall said it like it left a bad taste in his mouth.

I wasn't a *that*, I wanted to say, but a sharp look from Mop made me keep my remarks to myself.

"Don't be worryin' about her. Let us through and say nothin' bout her, and ye will get the tasty biscuit." Mop waved the biscuit in a tempting motion under what could have been the wall's nose.

The wall looked skeptical at the deal. "Only one biscuit for all that, seems like a mighty high price to keep my head."

"But you don't have a head!" I blurted without thinking.

"No head!" I covered my ears at the piercing howl that shook the ground. "You are in my head!"

Taking my hands off my ears, I glanced around, muttering to myself, "Pretty empty for a head."

"What did you say?"

I put my hands out, bracing for the ground to shake once more. I don't know how it heard me. I hadn't been talking very loud, and as far as I could tell, it didn't have any ears. Not wanting to anger it further, I changed my words.

"I said, if we're in your head, then where is your body?" I waved my arms around, trying to put on my best 'I-give-a-fuck' face. Which was only half as good as my 'please-tell-me-more' face.

The menacing fangs in its mouth gleamed as it smiled at us, and then the ground started to shake. "Why it's right here!"

"Oh no!" Trip yelped as if anticipating what the wall would do next.

The red fur covering the ground began to roll around us like waves in the sea. We cried out as a wave knocked us off our feet. I put my arms up to protect my head as we were thrown about. Then, when I was beginning to feel like a rag doll, it dumped us back on to the ground at the entrance.

"Yer just lookin' for trouble, ain't ye?" Mop stood as he dusted himself off. "Why'd ye have to go insultin' him like that?"

"Him?" I groaned, easing up off the ground. This place was not kind to the body. "It has a gender?"

"I heard that!" A roar came from the other side of the room.

"Would ye stop!" Mop glared at me. "Of course he has a gender. All beings in the UnSeelie Court be alive." He gestured to the shadowy figures slithering along the edges. "Though, not all of them be conscious of it."

He picked up the biscuit he'd dropped and thrust it toward me. "Here. Ye made the mess, ye can fix it."

I took the biscuit and turned it over in my hand, frowning when nothing unusual stood out. It was an ordinary biscuit, hard as a rock, but ordinary.

"How am I supposed to get across that?" I pointed to the roaring crimson waves, still tearing across the floor.

"That's yer problem. I'm stayin' outta it." He crossed his arms and plopped down on the ground, dismissing me with a turn of his back.

I glanced down at the white ball of fur huddled at my feet. "I don't suppose you have any advice for me?"

Trip uncurled himself from the cocoon of his ears and gazed up at me with apologetic eyes. His ears and tail hung heavy at his feet. I supposed it was too much to hope that he'd be able to help me out of this mess.

My mother always said I had diarrhea of the mouth. I always ended up saying the wrong thing at the wrong time. It usually ended with embarrassment for me, or more often than not, my mother.

"Katherine, some opinions are better left unsaid." She'd lecture me whenever I made a comment about how someone's dress made them look fat, or their engagement ring was a lot smaller than I would have expected. I was usually more mindful with my thoughts, but this place was making them bounce around like a beach bunny's breasts, only a small snap away from bursting forth into the world.

"Trip is sorry, Lady, Trip is. Maybe if Lady gives the biscuit to Teeth, Teeth will be happy again." Trip shrugged his small shoulders with an encouraging smile.

"Mop. Trip. Teeth. What kind of names are those?" I snorted. No points for creativity apparently. Next thing I know I'll be running into Doc and Dopey.

"Thems not be our real names." Mop growled from over his shoulder. "Thems be what we are known for. Only a fool would give someone else their true name."

"So, you're telling me your name is Mop because you, what, mop?"

"It sounds silly when ye be puttin' it that way." Mop frowned at the ground before his eyes snapped up to me. "There ain't no shame in keepin' a clean home."

Ignoring Mop's venomous gaze, I turned to Trip. "So, what do you do then, Trip?" The white fur ball cracked the first smile I had seen since the Between. "Let me guess. You trip people?"

"Yes, yes!" Trip nodded, his tail whipping back and forth. "Trip is the best tripper in all

UnSeelie Court, Trip is." He opened his arms wide. "In all Underground."

"Underground? That's the second time you've called this place that." I peeked back at Mop, hoping he would fill in the blanks.

An exasperated sigh was all I got, but after a moment, he finally turned to me holding up a finger. "The UnSeelie Court only be one of three realms in the Underground. There also be the Seelie Court and the Shadow Realm."

"What's the difference?"

"The UnSeelie, that be us." He pointed at Trip and himself. "We are more flexible about the rules. We go for what we want and will do just 'bout anything to get it."

"And the Seelie?"

"The Seelie. Bah!" I jumped back as he spat on the ground. "They only be carin' about appearances and doin' the honorable thing. Or what they think be honorable. Rules are rules," he mimicked. "Don't be lettin' them make ye think they won't bend the rules when it suits them."

"So, they're the good Fae? Does that mean the UnSeelie Court are the bad Fae?" I surveyed my two companions. "But you don't seem bad to me?"

"There ain't no good or bad, only the intent behind it." I tensed at the molten glare Mop sent my way. "A Seelie would kill ye just as easily as an UnSeelie would if ye be gettin' in their way. They'd just try to find a reason to back up the killin' is all." His nose quirked up as he snorted. "Don't want to be sullyin' their delicate hands."

I nodded. It kind of made sense. My mother would have fit right in with the Seelie crowd. No problem. The other doors in the Between must have led to the other realms. I was glad I ended up in the UnSeelie Court. I didn't see myself lasting more than five minutes in the Seelie Court. Though, Mop and Trip seemed fine enough, it appeared like the majority of the Underground hated humans. I couldn't imagine the shadow realm would welcome me either.

"What about the Shadow Realm?"

Mop gave an impatient tap of his foot. "How 'bout this? I'll tell ye what ye want to know when ye get us out of here. I'll even give ye a hint." He pointed to the biscuit still clenched in my hand. "It's gonna take a lot more biscuits than the one I pulled out of ye garbage to calm him down.

"Garbage? But I haven't had biscuits in over a week." My brow crinkled as I examined the biscuit in my hand again and began to notice the green tinge on the edges. My lip twisted as I dropped the biscuit to the ground with a thud. I forced back the urge to vomit when little white maggots poked their heads out of the sides.

"That's disgusting, Mop! You've had that thing in your pocket this whole time?" The fact that I had even touched it for a brief moment made my skin crawl.

"Ye didn't have to go and do that!" Mop scooped up the biscuit and shoved it back into the depths of his overalls. "Ye humans be too wasteful." He gestured toward where Teeth resided on the other side of the roaring waves. "So what if it be old? It'll be another decade before he be seein' another biscuit."

The new information spun an idea in my head. I turned back to the waves of red and strained my neck to see Teeth over them. I couldn't see him, the waves didn't make as much noise as real waves, so he could probably still hear me. Probably.

"Teeth!" Silence followed for a moment before a reluctant growl replied.

"What do you want now? To insult me further? Maybe you'd like to comment on my mother next? Or is my physical appearance all that matters to you?"

I winced at his accusations. I really did know how to stick my foot in my mouth. I may not be a big people person but I was certainly fluent in bullshit.

"I apologize for my words earlier. They were ignorant and judgmental." I glared down at Mop when he snorted. "I am new to your world, and as you'd expect, not used to seeing so much..." I paused to think of an inoffensive word. "...life around me."

The red waves died down into a low roll as my words penetrated the silence in the air. Teeth didn't say anything for a few moments, and I wondered if he had once again hidden away back into the wall. A deep bellowing laugh shook the ground beneath our feet, revealing he was still there.

"I pity you, so limited by your imagination. There are so many more wondrous and terrifying things you can find out your back door."

My companions and I peeked between each other before we inched across the calm floor. When it seemed like Teeth wasn't going to throw us back again, we hastened our stride. We didn't stop moving until we were standing in front of Teeth's menacing face once again.

Teeth looked us over for a moment with a grin still on his mouth. "Oh, all right. All is forgiven!"

Mop stepped forward. "So, ye will let us pass?"

"Ha!" Teeth barked. "Not for a measly molded biscuit I won't!" His eyes rolled so they were focused on me. "What can you offer in return?"

"Um." I thought for a second and opened my mouth to reply, but Trip tugged on my hand. Leaning down to his level, my ears peeled to hear his hushed words.

"Lady should be careful, Lady should." Trip eyed the wall beside us. "Lady shouldn't offer something Lady isn't willing to give."

Contemplating his caution, I thought about what I could offer to the talking wall. What did Teeth want that I could give him? I didn't have any money. I doubted he could use it in the Underground anyway. All I had were the clothes on my back, and they weren't even my best ones. I rubbed my hands together and grimaced at the remaining residue from the old biscuit.

Of course! Biscuits. That's what Teeth wanted.

"Well? I'm waiting."

I tapped my chin, pretending to be deep in thought. "How about in exchange for our passage I will give you a hundred biscuits?"

Hopefully, he wouldn't eat them all at once. I knew if I ate that many carbs I'd be bloated for days. Not to mention the calories!

Teeth studied me as he mused over my offer. "How do I know you will bring them? It is hard enough to get into our world; how you did it this time will be up for a long debate, no doubt" He glared at Mop and Trip, who stared down at the ground. "I can't imagine you could make it in a second time."

"Trip will be guarding my gardens in exchange for carrots. He can bring them to you."

Trip squeaked next to me. I felt bad for putting Trip in the middle of it, but Mop sure as hell wasn't going to do it. So the little rabbit-like creature was going to have to be my scapegoat.

"Very well." Teeth watched Trip who was trembling at my side. Amusement glinted in his eyes at the terror he was inflicting. Then his eyes focused back on me with a malevolent glint. "But I want a blood oath on it."

"Al–", I was about to agree, when Mop burst out next to me.

"Ye maggot-eatin', mud-chompin' eggymelt!" Mop spat out an array of other insults, half of which I had never even heard of. "Ye know damn well a blood oath ain't be worth no bander suckin' biscuits."

"What's the big deal?" I frowned down at the outraged brownie. "It's just a little blood, right? Like spitting on your hand before you shake on it."

Mop's hands curled into fists as he glared daggers at Teeth. "It ain't be just a little blood. It be an oath that binds ye life force to it. If ye break it, ye forfeit ye life."

"What the fuck!" I sputtered. "That's ridiculous!"

"Now ye see why we don't be takin' them lightly." He turned his head away and waved an arm at me. "But it be up to ye. It be ye life on the line, and we can't stay in here forever."

"Can't we just go back the other way?" I gave a longing look back toward the other door. The guards had to be a better option than this. Right?

"Not if ye value ye head."

Inside I screamed. I was backed into a corner with no way out but to do what Teeth asked. I didn't want to risk my life for a bunch of biscuits, but I also didn't want to be stuck in Teeth's head for the rest of my life. With Teeth's short temper, it probably wouldn't be long at all.

I gripped my hair in my hands, the thickness of it tangling in my fingers as I growled. "Fine. What do I have to do?"

"Lady must state the terms of the oath and Lady must swear it on Lady's blood, Lady must. Then Teeth must do the same." Trip gestured for me to come in close and put a hand up to his mouth. "Lady must get words right, Lady must. Fae will try to—"

"Trick me. Yes, I know. Thanks." I tugged the bottom of my grey sweater.

Where to start? It wasn't everyday I did a blood oath. I hadn't done a pinkie swear since I was twelve, and that was when I promised Ryan Moody I wouldn't tell anyone he tried to steal my mom's clothes at my birthday party. He said he only wanted to look at them, but the fact that he recently had a sex change had me thinking otherwise.

"I'll go first then." Teeth cleared his throat. "I, Teeth of the UnSeelie Court, swear a blood oath to let the human pass—"

"And Mop and Trip." Mop interrupted.

Teeth gave an unpleasant frown. "And Mop and Trip. To pass through into the deeper parts of the UnSeelie Court in exchange for a hundred biscuits from the human realm. Now you, human." His teeth gnashed together as he waited for me to start.

"All right. I–"

"Wait a second, wait a second," I growled as Mop interrupted again. He pointed a finger at Teeth. "Ye forgot to put ye won't be tellin' anyone bout Lady being here."

"Oh?" A not so innocent grin spread across Teeth's face. "Did I? My apologies. I, Teeth also swear to not tell anyone that the human was or has ever been here. Happy?"

"Hardly." Mop huffed but gestured to me to continue.

I turned back to the intimidating wall before us and opened my mouth to say – nothing. I didn't know how to refer to myself. Usually, I would have stated my name, Katherine Marie Nottington, but as my stick-up-his-ass guide loved to remind me, I shouldn't give out my name to just anyone.

Trip and Mop called me Lady, so I supposed I could use that, but it seemed too much like a name as well. Although, Teeth referred to me as the human in his speech, would it be vague enough to wiggle my way out of the deal if the need arose?

"The human swears a blood oath to Teeth, to bring him a hundred biscuits from the human world via Trip in exchange for the human and her companions, Trip and Mop's, passage into the UnSeelie Court and for his silence in regard to the human ever being here." I held my breath as I finished my oath, hoping the wall hadn't noticed my scheme.

There was silence for a heartbeat before Mop broke it with a chuckle. "All right ye toothy bastard, open up so we can be on our way."

"Wait. That's it? Don't you need blood?" I didn't really want to open a vein but it seemed too simple for a blood oath.

Mop snorted. "Ye don't be needin' to spill blood to make a blood oath. Ye words be the magic that binds ye. Now they be marked in ye blood. Can't ye feel it?"

No. I didn't feel anything. No tingles, nothing. Not that I was going to tell them that. "Uh, sure."

"So let us out, we got places to be." Mop turned back to Teeth with an impatient scowl.

"Keep your trousers on, you filthy brownie." His beady eyes focused on me. "I'll be expecting my biscuits within a week's time after you return to the human world."

"Of course." I forced a smile on my face as I hid my shaky hands inside my sleeves. I was almost out of here. I just had to hold on for a few more minutes.

Teeth's face melded back into the wall, and in its place was a door where the key hole Mop had turned earlier had been. The moment he was gone, I could feel the tension draining out of not just me but Mop and Trip as well. I had gotten away with it. We were going to get out of the stupid wall's head and without a single payment!

"Well, don't just be standin' there. The longer we dawdle the more Fae hear of ye presence." Mop shoved past me to the door, throwing it open without caution to what lay on the other side.

I placed a cautious hand on the side of the doorframe following behind Trip, who seemed more than eager to be out of here. Who could blame him? What lay on the other side was far more colorful than the blood red of Teeth's inner workings.

Instead of the stone walls that surrounded the walkways at the beginning, large, emerald-green hedges surrounded us. The melodious sound of a flute playing could be heard somewhere off in the distance. Enraptured by the change of scenery, I didn't notice my companions still figures until a deep silky voice met my ears.

"Well, look what we have here."

CHAPTER

THE PRINCE

TRIP SQUEAKED AT the new voice and launched himself onto my body. I stumbled to keep my balance as his arms trapped mine. The fearless Mop turned into a frightened little boy. His brown eyes darted from the door back to my unseen foe. He grappled for the key on his large ring, his hands shaking.

Was the creature with such a captivating voice really so terrifying?

"Trip." I struggled against his constricting grip. "You're going to have to let me go sometime."

"Yes, rodent, you can't hide behind the human forever." The silky voice turned snide as it moved closer to me.

Trip whimpered. His panic caused my heart to race. I tried not to think about what atrocity was awaiting me. I fought harder against Trip's grip until a warm breath on my ear caused me to freeze.

"Do struggle some more, human." The voice became smooth again and my body fought between fear and delight. "Your fear does excite me so."

I shook my head to clear it of the fog his voice elicited. Thinking back to my self-defense classes, I jerked an arm free of Trip's biting grasp and jabbed an elbow at my assailant. Instead of hitting what I hoped was his face all I got was air. His dark laugh stroked something deep in my belly. He darted around to stay out of my sight as if it were all a game.

"Ye highness." Mop stopped trying to get back in the door and stepped up to my unseen opponent.

Your highness? Could this be the ruler they were talking about?

"We weren't tryin' to smuggle her in. She followed us here." Mop's voice was shaky, but he tried to put on a brave face.

The delicious laughter halted. I stumbled when Trip was ripped from my body, allowing me the freedom to use my limbs again. Trip floated in the air before me, his eyes squeezed shut as he made his way from me to where the prince stood in his dark splendor.

From the deep ebony of his chest-length hair to his equally as black knee-high boots, he radiated temptation – and oh how I was tempted. Even the ice blue of his eyes glaring at my two companions added to his appeal.

He flicked a braid that trailed down the side of his face away to show glowing symbols that were identical to the ones in the cavern. I told myself my curiosity had everything to do with the marks and nothing to do with the lusciousness of his body. My eyes followed the swirls down his face, across his earring-filled pointed ear and down into the bottomless black of his open-chested, button-up shirt. When there were no more symbols to follow my imagination ran wild, causing my face to overheat.

How far down did they go?

"Now, now. No excuses." The prince tsked, waving a long pale finger at them like a mother lecturing her children. "You know the rules. No humans." His eyes swept up and down my body, making my insides ignite further under his gaze. "No matter how appealing they may be."

"But, ye highness!" Mop choked out as if an invisible hand was tightening around his neck picking him up off the ground. "We be sendin' her back!"

Mop and Trip's feet kicked in the air as they fought to breathe. Seeing them struggling knocked me out of whatever hold the prince had on me. I marched over to his royal deliciousness and jerked on his shoulder, causing him to drop the two to the ground.

"Hey! Stop that."

"What do you think you are doing?" His icy gaze flickered between light and dark blue as he turned to me and grabbed the hand that had shoved him.

"Let go!" I returned his glare with one of my own, trying to ignore the tingling sensation where his hand touched mine.

What was with this place? I'd never felt myself become so out of control of my feelings and actions as I did since the moment I'd darted out of my house after Trip. The weird part was I was starting to like the bold new me. That part of me marveled at the way the prince's dark blue eyes contrasted with the angry, glowing burn of swirls on his face.

"Or you will do what exactly?" His voice was a low, dangerous growl.

As I stared into those mesmerizing eyes, I had the sudden urge to throw myself down at his feet and beg for mercy or death, whichever one would please him. I shook my head to rid myself of the thoughts and glared at him. He laughed at my silence and drew me closer.

"You are not in your world anymore. Sweet. Innocent. Kat." My name coming from his lips caused my insides to clench. He was threatening me, and I was acting like a damn cat in heat. What the hell was wrong with me?

Mop swore under his breath. The fact that he already knew my name was not a surprise. I had practically shouted it when I got here. The question was what would he do with it? Would he make me his slave? Make me clean his throne, or worse, his toilet?

Bleh. I would rather die, though being his love slave was an appealing thought.

I tried to jerk my hand from his pinching grasp, but he held on tight, keeping me at an uncomfortably close distance. He had me at a disadvantage, and I didn't like my odds of escaping. That quiet, insecure part of me tried to poke its wary head out. What could I do against an almighty Fae prince anyway?

The longer I gazed into his eyes, the more I felt something pressing down on me. It was like I was in a room with too little air. My lungs burned, and my head felt like it was floating, as if more and more air was being sucked out every moment I stared into his dark, penetrating eyes. Eyes that were starting to get a bit hazy.

"Ye highness!" Mop's outcry broke the hold the prince had on me. I gasped, taking a deep breath in. "Lady has made a blood oath with Teeth!"

As if remembering himself, the prince dropped my hand, and the glow of the glyphs on his face faded. I rubbed my wrist, breathing deeply as I stumbled back from him. He wasn't like the others. Certainly not like the grumpy Mop or the jovial Trip. His mere presence caused my insides to burn. I fought between fear and wanting him all at once. The other Fae I'd met definitely never sparked such a reaction. The only thing they had ever caused was a headache.

"Someone has been very naughty indeed." The dark prince's tone teased, as he seemed to float around the courtyard. "How could you let a human follow you? I would think you would know better than that?" He eyed Trip who gave a pitiful whimper. "Certainly you did, troll?"

Mop didn't even correct him, but instead he shot me a warning look when I opened my mouth to do so. Why would they let him treat them that way? Was he really so fearsome? Remembering how he made me feel just moments ago answered my question. Yes. Yes, he was.

"Allowing said, human, to be bound to one of our own," the prince continued, tapping Mop hard on the forehead and causing the brownie to wince. "And of course, it had to be on today of all days!" He bent down and grabbed Mop by the front of his overalls. "You do remember what today is, don't you, troll?"

I gritted my teeth as I forced myself not to call foul on the prince. I painfully watched as fearless Mop cowered and stuttered before the royal.

"Of course, ye highness."

"Then tell me, because I am confused as to why you thought it would be a good idea to leave the Underground on a day like today." He rubbed his temple as if dealing with us was causing his head to ache.

Turning my eyes from the ever-curious prince, I waited to see if Mop would declare it all Trip's fault. To my surprise, the brownie frowned down at the ground and mumbled an apology with no explanation. I peeked over at Trip to see if he was going to fess up, but he too only stared at the ground in quiet repentance. Well, if they weren't going to tell, who was I to snitch?

The Fae Prince's anger pulsated around him, and with it, the symbols flared back to life. The prince's eyes flashed dark blue before his fury was wiped from his face and a smile took its place. And I thought Brandi was two faced.

He strolled over to me, tapping a finger to his chin. "What to do? What to do? I could just kill you and be done with it."

"No!" We shouted in unison.

"Are you sure? It would be a mercy over taking your heads." He tilted his head to the side, causing his hair to cascade over the side of his face. I would have thought it was adorable had he not been offering to mercy kill me.

I snuck a look at my quiet companions. If it was possible, the likelihood of losing their heads caused Mop and Trip to be even more petrified than before. Mop took his hat off and wrung it between his hands while Trip gripped his ears in his paws, pulling them around him like a shield.

"But then again, I do not know what the human promised the teeth for brains, and I do not want to be stuck fulfilling it by killing you." His lips twitched as his face filled with a cruel delight. "Besides, what fun would that be? There are so many more terrifying ways to die on your way out."

He gripped my face in his hands. When my eyes locked with his, the familiar pressure threatened to take over me. I dug my nails into my hand, the pain pushing back the feeling of submission.

"If anything, one of the less welcoming Fae will get you and save me the trouble of dealing with you myself." His icy voice matched his piercing eyes.

I had had enough. I hated bullies more than the coupon lady at the supermarket. Even if he was sinfully delicious, he couldn't treat us like we were less than dirt.

I knocked his hand away from my face and snarled, "What crawled up your ass and died?"

"Lady!"

"No." I ignored Mop's horrified warning. "I want to know. You can't just let him bully you."

"Yea, he can. He can do what he likes." Mop tried to pull me away from the prince, but I wouldn't budge. I shoved down the chill crawling up my spine and waited for his answer.

The dark prince threw his head back and laughed, causing Mop and Trip to jump and quiver. He took a step closer to me, and I braced myself for whatever he had planned. He grabbed my hair in a painful grip, making me wince as he forced my face up to his.

"Tell me, dear Kat." There was no teasing in his eyes now. They were hard and promised pain. "Would you really like to find out?"

"If that's what it takes to get rid of you," I spat in his face. My gaze was fierce and unyielding as he studied me for any signs of weakness. I tried not to flinch when he tightened his hold on my hair, causing a painful twinge in my neck.

Coming to his own conclusions, none pleasant I was sure, he laughed again before shoving me away. My feet failed me and I crashed to the ground. I glared up at him, dying for something to chuck at him.

"Get out of my sight before I decide to show you." The prince, who I had yet to get a name for, turned his back on me.

"So, Trip is not going to be punished, Trip is not?" Trip's voice was hopeful but wary.

The prince snatched Trip up by his ears, causing the white creature to shriek. He yanked Mop up by the back of his trousers and brought them close to the manic grin on his face.

"Of course you are. Do you think getting her out undetected will be easy?" He gave them a little shake. "I am not going to get blamed for your mess. Reaper only knows what that mad woman is thinking nowadays."

Mop and Trip's crestfallen faces perked up. As far as punishments went that wasn't so bad. Maybe I misjudged the pointy-eared prince.

"But if you fail and the Queen finds out." The prince flashed his canines. "You will wish I had killed you."

I hadn't.

"But that's not fair!" I stomped my foot in protest.

"You know what is not fair?" The prince's cold eyes focused back on me. "Being stuck in this God-forsaken place when I should be lounging in the palace!" His eye twitched as his rage triggered the swirls on his body. He gave a harsh laugh and waved us away. "Go. Be on your way."

Mop and Trip ushered me toward one of the archways, but we paused when the prince called out again, "Oh, and one more thing. Stay out of the Seelie Court and away from that damn cat."

Before I could ask what he meant my guides shoved me out of the hedged maze and toward a dark and ominous forest. I looked behind me. The prince's shoulders slumped down, and he ran a tired hand through his hair. Maybe there was more to him than I originally thought.

AN OWL HOOTED in the distance as we made our way out of the hedges and into the eerie forest. The trees were snarled, blocking out any light from above and leaving us in a false twilight. The ground was mushy beneath my feet, but I couldn't see them because a thick fog rolled across the ground. Was there no place here that wasn't set up for a horror movie?

"Do you even know where we are going?" I picked a foot up and frowned down at the brown, muddy mess my tennis shoes had become.

Mop stopped at a tree and dug into a hiding place in the trunk. He shoved items around and threw a few out of the hole – a book, a miniature shovel, etc. Finally, he popped his head out of the hole.

"Aha!" He held up a large object almost twice his size. "Here be what we need – a lantern."

"I can see that." I put my hands on my hips and tapped my foot. "What I want to know is how we are going to get out of this place?" My shoulders tensed when laughter from beyond the trees filled the air. "What other terrifying ways was he talking about?"

Mop snorted. "Bah, don't listen to him. He just be tryin' to scare ye."

"Well it's working."

Trip and I followed behind Mop, jumping at every sound and shadow. There were far too many eyes peeping out from the fog to feel safe even with a lantern.

It reminded me of the time I got talked into going to Scary Manor, a haunted house carnival, which happened every Halloween. I almost ended up with an assault charge when a guy with a chainsaw jumped out of the bushes. It was safe to say I was never invited back again, which was fine by me since my idea of fun was curling up with a good book, a glass of wine, and surrounded by a warm quilt. There was something certifiably wrong with people that paid to be scared. I was beginning to feel like I did back at the haunted house – irritated and altogether pissed off. I did not do scared well.

"Lady is right to be afraid, Lady is." Trip gripped my hand. "His highness is unpredictable, he is. Might not kill Lady today, but might kill Lady tomorrow."

"Is that why he's so...." I trailed off not sure how to describe his split personality. I clenched my fists to keep from screaming as something moved in the bushes near me. Trip squeaked and I loosened my grip.

"Wishy-washy? Nah." Mop shook his head. "He can't be helpin' that; that be due to the magic bindin' him."

"Oh, you mean the symbols on his face?" I really wished I had some paper to copy or my phone to take a picture. The one time it wasn't permanently glued to my hand and I actually needed it.

I tilted my head a little as my companions gaped at me. "What?"

"Ye can see them?"

"You mean the swirly-glowy symbols running down his face?" I gestured to the left side of my own face. "Yeah. Can't you?"

"Well, yea. 'Course." Mop scratched his head. "We be Fae, but ye just a human. Ye shouldn't be able to see them."

"But I could see them back at the cavern too. All over the ground and walls."

"Aha!" A smile spread onto Trip's face, and his tail whipped around behind him. "Trip not lead Lady to Underground. Lady finds it on her own, Lady did." Trip hopped around me, making me dizzy from tracking him. "It not Trip's fault, it's not! His highness may let Trip and Mop go. His highness might!"

"I doubt it. He wouldn't care whose fault it be, only that we be there. So, we be gettin' the blame." Mop turned back to the path only he could see.

I frowned at Mop's pessimism. What kind of ruler would put the blame on the wrong party just so there was someone to blame? I liked the prince less and less.

"So, the symbols are binding him to this place? Who put them there?" My eyes stared out into the darkness surrounding us, ready for anything that might pounce.

"The Queen did." Mop handed me the lantern as he climbed over a fallen log.

"The Queen? You mean his mother? That's horrible!" Even my mother, for all her faults, wouldn't stoop so low. At least I hoped not.

"Not our queen. The Seelie Queen." Mop scoffed like I should have known.

"But why?" I handed the lantern back to him.

"His highness made a mistake, his highness did. His highness is being punished, he is. Just like Trip and Mop are being punished." Trip's tail drooped down, his face crestfallen and pathetic.

"What did he do?" I thought back to the despair that lingered on the striking prince's face. What had made him so sad? Was being trapped here so bad?

"How am I supposed to know? I'm just a brownie, not his royal confidant." Mop placed his hands on his hips and scowled. "If ye want to know so bad, ask him yer self."

I so didn't want to do that. The less time I spent in his royal haughtiness's presence, the better off I would be. My head was hurting from the contradicting information I was getting.

I had a cursed prince and a queen that may or may not be crazy, but not their queen, and not to forget the possibility of losing my head, which was a fate worse than death. Just a typical day in Wonderland – or Underground, whatever this place was.

Bringing my thoughts together, I remembered something else the nasty prince had said. "What day is it?"

"Thursday," Mop grunted.

I rolled my eyes at his avoidance to my question. "You know what I mean. What did he mean today of all days? What's so special about today?"

"Oh, that." The brownie mulled. "It be the anniversary of the princess's death."

"And that means?"

"The whole Underground be in a state of mourning." Mop snorted. "Like we haven't been mourning for the last century. Life goes on."

"So, it's like a national holiday?"

"No, Lady." Trip tugged on my hand. "No holiday. It's like...like..." he trailed off, his face scrunched up hard.

"Don't hurt ye self, Trip," Mop interrupted. "The whole Underground be under lockdown. We ain't supposed to be havin' fun, workin' or even leavin' the kingdom." He glared at Trip for the first time, showing his disapproval of his friend's adventures in my garden.

"Trip is sorry, Trip is." The white-furred creature's ears wilted under Mop's gaze.

Mop rolled his eyes as if he was used to hearing Trip's apologies. "Anyway, his highness only be worried 'cause the queen be blamin' us UnSeelie for her daughter's death." Mop snorted. "Like we be havin' any say in the matter."

"How'd she die?"

"Ye'd have to ask his highness that one. It not be my place to tell." The brownie paused by a tree, looking around for a moment before turning to his left.

"Why's that?" I hurried to stay close to him. I didn't want to get lost in the woods. Not that Mop and Trip counted much for protection, but they were all I had and beggars can't be choosers.

Before Mop could answer there was a loud outcry of laughter over the next brush. Not at all bothered by the insanity we were hearing, Mop lifted his shoulder in a matter-of-fact way. "She be his betrothed, of course. Or was."

"Of course," I murmured to myself.

It made sense. The prince would know how his fiancé died, but what didn't make sense was why the Seelie Queen thought it was the UnSeelie's fault? Did the prince kill her? With his temper I could see some kind of domestic abuse going on.

I didn't understand women who got themselves into those situations. If a man ever tried to hit me, he'd have a head full of lead and one less appendage for the afterlife.

I almost ran into Mop when he stopped before a collection of bushes. The laughter around us grew louder and seemed to be coming from beyond the bushes. I was afraid to ask my next question, knowing the answer was probably worse than my imagination.

"Who's that?"

"Trip's cousin, it is!" Trip hopped ahead of us with his ears and tail whipping around him. "Come, Lady! Hare will help. Yes, Hare will."

"Hare?" My brow furrowed.

It couldn't be, could it?

I had all but given up on the idea of Wonderland, especially after Mop's vicious denial. But if Hare was here, I had no doubt what would be on the other side of those bushes. Nothing good ever came from that scenario.

"Come on before Trip hurts himself." Mop waved me over to the brush.

I hesitated as another round of maniacal laughter filled the air. A sense of foreboding washed over me. What was I getting myself into?

CHAPTER

HAVE SOME TEA

THE MOMENT I pushed through the bushes the manic laughter came to a screeching halt. It was so quiet I could hear my heart beating in my chest. After a moment of intense observation, the crazed laughter began again as if I had never interrupted it.

The laughter was coming from the tea party's three occupants. Though, the rest of the woods were covered in a dense fog, it seemed to cut off right at the edge of the dimly lit dining table. There were eight chairs around the table, all mismatched and looking very much out of place in the middle of the forest.

Trip and Mop stopped next to the head of the table, where a creature that could have been Trip's twin, save for the bloodshot eyes and red-tinged fur, sat on the right hand side. I had to assume the doppelganger was Trip's cousin, Hare.

The other two occupants of the table were just as bizarre as my own companions. A child-sized bat, with wings that twinkled in the light, sat at one end of the table. He had a clawed pinky up in the air as he sipped from a cracked teacup. Curious eyes watched me as I moved around the table. I found it oddly amusing that the bat felt the need to show such decorum at a tea party full of mismatched cups and a moth-eaten, stained tablecloth. Who was he trying to impress?

The bat's neighbor had no such illusions of grandeur. Next to the bat, at the end of the table, was a mouse the size of a full-grown bulldog picking its nose. It twitched said nose at me before opening a blue door latched to the front of its body. Its heart visibly thudded as he scratched his small intestine with one of his paws. A small alarming sound came out of me when he reached between his stomach and diaphragm to pull out a cup and saucer. His little black eyes glinted as his companions and he cackled at my horror.

Letting out a shaky breath, I plopped down in a chair next to Hare. My stomach gave an unhappy grumble. I'd never been one for blood and guts. My friend's delivery room was as close to carnage as I had allowed myself, and that had been pushing it.

"So you two are cousins?" I let out a nervous laugh, trying to distract myself from what I'd seen. "What exactly are you anyway?"

Unlike Trip, whose demeanor was more child-like, Hare couldn't have been more different. There was something disturbing about the way his bloodshot eyes gazed at me, like he was wondering what my insides tasted like.

"Trip and Hare is opalaughts." Trip's tail swished back and forth behind him. I couldn't see Hare's tail to see if he was as happy as Trip was to see him, but if it was anything like his partially chewed ears, I didn't think I wanted to.

"Hop-a-lots? Because you're like rabbits?" My eyes questioned the unusually quiet Mop. He shrugged his small shoulders and slumped down further into his chair. What was his problem?

"No, no. Not hop-a-lots! Opalaughts. And Trip not like rabbit at all, Trip is not." Trip crawled into the chair across from me and grabbed a moldy looking sandwich off the table.

Seriously? Didn't they have any normal food? My stomach rolled as Trip munched on his sandwich, red goop, which vaguely resembled blood, oozed out of the sides. On second thought, even if they did, I didn't think I could eat any of it. The thought of eating alone made me want to hurl.

Holding back the bile that had built up in my throat, I choked out, "But you eat carrots like rabbits."

"Not the same." When Hare smiled, his sharpened canines peeked out of his mouth. He pushed a plate of sandwiches toward me.

I gave into the urge to lift the edge of the sandwich and immediately wished I hadn't. The red ooze coming out of Trip's sandwich was indeed blood. It was gelled around chunks of some kind of raw meat. What kind of meat? I wasn't sure I wanted to know, but my stomach decided it had had enough. I covered my mouth and dashed for the bushes. The door mouse and bat chattered behind me.

"Oh, what a shame."

"Not very tame."

I wiped my mouth with the back of my hand, pulling my hair off of my neck. Still a bit shaky, I walked back to the table and grabbed the nearest chair, which ended up being at the head of the table. Before I could even sit down, Hare jumped up on the table, his grungy fur standing on end as he hissed at me.

"No! Not there."

"Hatter's chair!" The door mouse growled, gripping the edge of the table.

The bat didn't seem very interested but said his part anyway, "It's not really fair."

"Okay." I drew out the word, holding my hands up in defense. "I'll just go sit back over there." All the rhyming was making my head hurt. Once I was seated again, Hare nudged a cracked, pink teacup and saucer toward me.

"Here, have some tea."

I held the cup between my fingers and sniffed its contents. It smelled like normal tea, but then again, nothing here was normal. I brought the cup to my lips but paused when the other two didn't pipe in. Their eyes were focused on the cup in my hand as if waiting for something. I sat the cup back down on its saucer, suspicion rearing its ugly head.

The door mouse took a sip of his own tea and gestured to mine. "It's really lovely tea!"

"So sleepy you will be." The bat yawned beside me.

There it was. The little cretins were trying to roofie me! I shoved the cup as far from me as possible while trying to keep my anger under control. Keep calm. Don't antagonize the animals, Kat.

"No, thank you," I said through clenched teeth.

"No, no. You must have some tea!" Hare pushed the cup toward me again, his eyes demanding me to do as he said.

"It'd be rude, you see!"

"Eaten you will be!"

Mouse and Hare glared at the bat. Who yawned and ate a sandwich from one of the plates, unaware of his companions' ire.

"Stop it, ye rhymin' buffoons." Mop finally jumped in, shoving Hare away. "She don't want no stinkin' tea. She just needs the key. Blast it! Now I be doin' it!"

"What key?" Hare went back to sipping his tea as if they hadn't just tried to poison me.

"Not that key?" Dubious eyes glanced at one another around the table.

"Where could it be?" The bat barked out laughing, causing the other two to join him until the entire clearing was filled with that uncanny fanatic laughter.

There was no question they were all mad. No way did I trust their word on anything. Unfortunately, I was out of my element and didn't have much choice but to follow Mop and Trip's lead. If Mop said I needed a key, and then I was going to get that key.

I grabbed Hare by the ears, startling the opalaught into silence. Giving him my best scowl, I brought him up to eye level. This was my 'I wasn't going to deal with anymore of his bullshit' glare that I liked to use on the preteens at work when they started to get too obnoxious. It worked like a charm. I just hoped it worked as well on Fae as it did thirteen-year-old teenagers.

"We need that key." I gnashed my teeth at him.

"We don't have the key." Hare glared back at me, not at all intimidated. Maybe my scowl needed some work.

"Key's not here, you see."

"I know," I interjected before the bat could jump in with his part. "You said all that. If it's not here, then where is it?"

Hare exchanged a look with his tablemates as confusion filled their faces. "No key since she."

"Yes, she had the key!" Mouse waved his chipped cup in an exaggerated manner.

"Alice! Alice! She be!"

"There's that damn name again. Do ye wanna lose ye heads too?" Mop's warning had the opposite effect on the demented Fae around us.

"Head! Head! Alice lost her head!" Hare threw his body so he swung back and forth in my hand, making my arm hurt enough to drop him.

"Who needs a head?" Mouse cackled.

"Maybe he'll take yours instead!"

"What do we do now?" I grabbed my hair in my hands, yanking on it. "We can't just stay here."

The forest wasn't particularly homey, and I couldn't imagine staying here with these loons.

It was worse than my sister's sorority house. I would rather roofie myself.

"Now hold ye horses. We just need to be findin' her to get the key." Mop plopped down in a chair with a thump.

"Her? But I thought she lost her head? How is a dead girl going to help?" I had a horrid thought. "We aren't going to rob her grave, are we?"

"Don't be stupid. No one said she was dead." Mop sniffed.

"Where I come from you can't be alive without a head," I pointed out to them, the very thought of a headless Alice gave me the creeps.

Trip giggled in his seat. "Lady forgets where Lady is. Lady is only human in Underground, Lady is."

"Only human!" Hare giggled, his companions following along.

"We like human!"

"Taste nice with cumin."

"Is ye stomach the only thing ye can think 'bout?" Mop paused when a hoot broke through the trees and Mr. Blue Eyes landed on a branch near us. "He already knows she be here. We need to get her outta here before the queen be findin' out too."

Without warning, Mop jumped up onto the table and grabbed the teapot. I could feel the air around the party thicken as Mop held the pot high above his head. Bloodshot and beady eyes alike were pinned to the kettle in Mop's hands.

"Tell me where she be or ye will get no more tea!" Mop grimaced when his words once again came out in rhyme.

A collective outcry was heard around the table as they all began talking at once. It would have been funny except for the wildness that appeared in their eyes at the thought of losing their precious tea. I thought I was addicted to caffeine.

"Hold on, hold on! Don't be talkin' all at once!" Mop held the pot in one hand and pointed at the bat. "You! Twinkle!"

Of course. Why wouldn't a bat be named Twinkle? I couldn't help but snicker at the name, earning me a glare from Twinkle.

"Yes?" If his eyes were not focusing on the pot with such intensity, I would have said he was bored.

"Where be..." Mop lowered his voice, his eyes looking back and forth for eavesdroppers. "...Alice?"

"We don't know."

I waited for the chime of the rhyming that usually followed but was disappointed when there was none. Maybe it was only a game? Were they only serious when there was something to lose?

"Fartnarkles." Mop let out an aggravated breath.

We weren't getting anywhere. I leaned on the arm of my chair, my eyes wandering around the table. Finally, they landed on the largest chair at the head of the table – Hatter's chair.

"Where's the Hatter?"

My question caused Hare's grungy ears to perk up at my question. "He knows! He knows!"

"Who? The Hatter?"

"Yes, yes!" The Hare bounced onto the table, eager eyes on the pot in Mop's grasp.

"Well, where'd he go?" Mop tightened his grip on the pot at the opalaught's presence. His dark eyes filled with panic when the other two partygoers joined him on the table. They stalked Mop, their eyes becoming fiercer the closer they came.

"To get some more tea!"

"Yes. He had to pay the fee!" Mouse licked his chops as they closed in on the brownie.

"Got lost in the foggy sea!" Twinkle exclaimed just before they pounced.

I cackled at the scuffle on the table. Small legs and arms were thrown everywhere as they tried to get a hand on the teapot. I should have stopped them, I really should have, but instead I found myself laughing at the sight.

"Get off me, ye rodent!" Mop shoved them back while trying to keep the teapot out of their reach. His desperate eyes pinned on me. "Whatcha smilin' at? Help me!"

Smiling?

I frowned as I realized I had been smiling. It wasn't amusing. I didn't find other's suffering funny. For just a brief second I found myself wondering what would happen if I let them have him. Would they eat him up? String him by his feet as they drained him of his fluids to make their precious tea?

I frowned harder, shaking my head. Those weren't my thoughts. What was wrong with me?

"Lady." Trip pulled on the sleeve of my sweatshirt. "Lady needs Mop to find the Hatter, Lady does."

Uncrossing my legs, I sighed. Though I was weirdly enjoying their fighting over the mysterious tea, I still needed the grumpy little man. I reached a hand into the pile that had become their bodies and grabbed a hold of the first red clothes I could see.

I pulled Mop out of the pile of hissing creatures and set him down on the ground. Mop swept up his hat that had fallen off in the fray and tugged it back onto his head. The rest of the pile never noticed his absence. They were too busy playing a game of tug of war over the teapot. It seemed like the door mouse was going to win before Hare snatched it away and hopped back to his seat.

"My tea!"

"Almost my tea!" The door mouse sulked back to his own chair; his rhyme less enthused than it was before.

"Curses on thee!" Twinkle glared at Hare, who sat in a triumphant glow, stroking the pot with a paw.

It wasn't hard to figure out that the teapot decided who was in charge of everything, including the conversation. I imagined that was why they were so keen on getting it. Whose sick idea was that? To be forced to talk only when the leader talked and only about what he wanted to talk about? Hare had obviously been in control for a while, and it was probably getting old. If I were them, I would just leave, but then again maybe they couldn't?

"What now?" I turned to Mop, who was cursing up a storm next to me.

"That!" Mop gestured out into the fog.

It seemed to have gotten worse while we had our little visit. It was so dense I couldn't make out more than a few feet in front of me and that was with a lantern. Getting lost out there would be a nightmare. Who knew what kind of baddies hid in its cover?

"It'll take forever to search this mess for Hatter." I followed Mop's gaze as it darted toward the owl that had been tailing us from the beginning. What was with that owl? "I doubt we be havin' that much time left."

"So, what do we do?" I held my hands up to the brownie in question.

"Hare knows!" Trip jumped in. "Hare knows where Hatter goes for tea, Hare does."

We all turned to look at Hare. He didn't even glance up from the teacup with which he was having a hushed conversation. Maybe it wasn't just the tea making them all mad.

"They want to know where he's at," Hare spoke into his cup.

"Where's he at?" The door mouse, which had been fiddling with his doorknob, looked to Hare with interest.

"Yes. Where is he at?" Tinkle quirked a nonexistent brow at Hare.

"Would ye just tell us?" Mop grabbed the cup from Hare's hand. Slamming it down on the table, its essence spilled onto the cloth. I had a brief moment where I thought 'Oh what a shame' before I shoved it down. This place was really messing with my head.

Hare's eyes were hard as he hissed, "He's with the Smiling Cat."

"Oh, that's where he's at!" The door mouse fiddled with his handle once more as if he'd known all along.

"He's crazier than a bat!" Twinkle giggled at his joke.

"Great, just great!" Mop threw his hands up in the air. "Just what we need, someone else to be wastin' our time."

"They aren't talking about the Cheshire Cat are they?" I had a sudden image of a fat striped cat with a grin the size of his face.

"Come on, let's go." Mop ignored my question and grabbed the discarded lantern, following an unseen path deeper into the forest.

"But, Mop!" Trip clamored after the brownie. "His highness said not–"

"I know what he said. But it ain't like we got a choice, now do we?"

"Trip guess not, Trip does."

Someone had better start answering my questions soon or I was going to get pissed. I wasn't used to having so many questions with none of the answers. I exchanged a searching look with Trip before we chased after the grumbling brownie.

It seemed all I was doing lately was running, but at that moment, I would do almost anything to get away from the tea party. I wasn't sure what was wrong with me, but staying there was not going to help me become any saner. I kept that thought in mind as we left the party's occupants behind, their annoying rhyming following in our wake.

"Ungrateful brats!"

"Useless gnats!"

"Hey, where's my hat?"

CHAPTER

CHESHIRE S. CAT

"NO GOOD, PAIN in the arse, feline! Don't know why it had to be him!" Mop grumbled as he stomped his feet with every step he took. "Worse than a dingle berry bat."

I strolled along behind the angry brownie, becoming more amused by the minute at the creative insults with which he was coming up with. I had yet to meet the Smiling Cat, but I was already looking forward to it. If Teeth didn't cause Mop to fret, how bad could the Cheshire Cat really be?

"Why do you hate the Cheshire Cat so much? He's just a cat who speaks in riddles, right?" At least that was what I remembered from the book.

My eyes darted to the foggy trees when something growled. I jumped and screamed when something slimy brushed my leg in the fog. I hugged myself as the dark laughed at me. Damn it. I hated sounding like one of those defenseless girls that needed to be saved all the time. If only I had a weapon, then we'd see who was laughing.

"I could do with a good old-fashioned riddle right now," I muttered to myself.

"Smiling Cat is not all bad, Smiling Cat's not." Trip gripped the edge of my sweatshirt. "But Mop hates Smiling Cat something fierce!"

"Why's that?" I turned to Trip, trying to distract myself from the creepy eyes in the forest shadows.

Trip opened his mouth to speak, but Mop beat him to it.

"I'll tell ye why!" The lantern in his hand swung wild in the air. "That damn cat only thinks of himself and what he can get outta it."

"But isn't that the way all Fae are?" I gestured to the two of them. "You guys are only helping me because his royal douchiness would kill you otherwise, right?"

"Lady must not talk of his highness in such a way, Lady must not!" Trip's wide eyes searched the trees. "He will take Lady's head, he will!"

"It's not like he is going to hear me, you know." I patted Trip's head like you would to reassure a child who said something silly.

"Lady never knows, Lady doesn't," the opalaught whispered ominously.

"Anyway, the Cheshire Cat can't be any worse than your sorry excuse for a prince." Our feathery shadow gave an irritated twitter as if it were him I had been insulting.

Mop's eyes stared down at the ground, a frown between his brows. "Nah, but he be a close second." His gaze snapped to mine. "And ye're right. We were just helpin' ye to save ourselves, but that was before."

"And now?"

"Ye're more than just a stinkin' human now." His large lips curled into the first hint of a smile I had seen since my adventure began.

"Gee, thanks." I rolled my eyes at the backward compliment. I rated higher than a flea. Great.

"Trip liked Lady before, Trip did!" The opalaught beamed up at me as his tail wagged in the air. "Lady has yummy carrots, though Lady makes them very hard to get to. That fence hurt Trip's teeth, it did."

"But, Trip, you just said you only liked me for my carrots," I pointed out. "Besides, if I don't get out of here, there won't be any more carrots for you to eat."

Trip opened his mouth to protest but then quickly closed it. His tail drooped down to the ground as he processed my logic. It was a good thing I didn't tell him that it was him I had been trying to keep out. I didn't think his little heart would be able to handle it.

"Lady is right, Lady is. Trip is sorry."

I patted the fur between his ears. "It's okay. Humans are the same way." I bent down to his level and crooked a finger at him. "I'll tell you a secret, though."

Trip's ears perked up, and his nose twitched in anticipation. Mop huffed, tapping his foot in apparent impatience. I glared at him and turned back to Trip. Mop would just have to keep his trousers on.

I tapped a finger on the tip of Trip's pink nose. "I like Trip too."

"Bah! We don't have time for this. Besides, ye don't know nothin'." Mop picked up the lantern and continued on his way. "Ye think humans are self-servin', but ye haven't met this cat. He's manipulative, cunnin', and two-faced. He always has another agenda." He ticked each trait off on his hand. "In short, he can't be trusted."

"Plus, Smiling Cat cheats at cards, Smiling Cat does." Trip gave a solemn nod.

"Really?" I giggled at the seriousness they were giving the accusation. "That's why you don't like him? Isn't that a little petty?"

"Not just 'cos he cheats!" Mop huffed. "When he does lose, he finds every excuse not to be keepin' his part of the deal!"

"Sounds like my sister," I grumbled to myself. "Why doesn't your prince want us to see him? Did he play cards with him too?

"No. No." Trip shook his head. "His highness would never play cards with the Smiling Cat, his highness wouldn't."

"Why not? Too good for him?" I snorted. I could see the dark-haired prince thinking just that. He was someone who couldn't be bothered to spend time with the commoners; it might ruin his dark and sexy image.

"He be royalty," Mop stated as if the prince's station was a logical answer.

"So? Doesn't he give any thought to his fellow man–uh, Fae? A good ruler knows his people. He doesn't just lounge around shouting orders and expect to be obeyed." I placed my hands on my hips, trying to give off an air of confidence.

Mop and Trip barked out laughing. Trip grabbed his ears in his hands and rocked back and forth, almost to the point of balling up into himself. Mop slapped his thigh, his chuckles causing the lantern to shake in his hand.

Frowning, I dropped my arms. "What's so funny?"

The brownie wiped a tear from his eye. "Ye are. If anyone be shouting orders at anyone, it'd be the Queen to him. I highly doubt he be havin' the time to lounge 'round, as ye call it, in over a century."

"No. No lounging for his highness, no." Trip gave a small, sad shake of his head.

"Okay." The word came out slow and unsure. I wasn't really following their explanation. The prince was a prince to be feared, but he also was a prince who didn't have any power? It didn't make sense.

"And as far as Chess, well not everyone agrees with his reputation so to speak." Mop gave an awkward chuckle.

"Reputation?" I quirked a brow, my interest increasing exponentially.

"Just wait. Ye'll see what I mean." Mop waved me off, pushing a tree branch out of his way to reveal another clearing.

The clearing itself was untouched by the fog, which seemed to fill the rest of the forest. It cut off just at the tree line, creating a perfectly circular outline of milky white. I wished I had that kind of lawn control.

While the tea party had a sort of ominous lighting, in this clearing it was like the clouds had opened up just enough to illuminate the area. In the middle of the clearing, sparkling in the sunlight, was a large willow tree. Its long, fuchsia vines were covered in bright violet leaves. They hung all along each side and reached down to brush the ground.

Mop stopped at the wall of vines as if waiting for something. The vines rippled and whispered, even though there was no wind to move them, and then the vines pulled back, opening like a curtain. A lone vine whipped inward as if to welcome us inside.

Mr. Blue Eyes didn't follow us into the depths of the tree. He landed on a tree branch outside the clearing, hooting and ruffling his feathers in an agitated manner. I had a feeling he didn't approve of our destination. It made me doubt that the cat was the kind of help we wanted.

My eyes wandered about the tree as I tried to take everything in. I felt like I just stepped out of a demented kid's nightmare and into a sugary fairyland. There was no longer a squishy floor, or gnashing teeth, or a table full of tea-addicted animals. Once inside the willow branches, I discovered exactly what I always imagined Wonderland to be.

Luminescent, emerald green grass carpeted the ground in place of the fog-covered dirt. Flowers were scattered across the grass in every hue and color. A path of grass lined by bright pink mushrooms trailed up from the willow vines to the base of the tree where a lone figure was splayed out on a high-backed chair. He was enwrapped in the fuchsia-colored vines, which appeared to be more of a throne, especially with the way its owner lounged upon it.

One eggplant-painted leg, encased in a matching knee-high boot, was thrown over the side while the other stretched out along the ground. The tightness of his pants caused a slight heat to rise to my cheeks. There was no mistaking what gender their owner was. I tried my best not to stare, but the multitude of extravagant leather and fur belts wrapped around his waist made it impossible to cast my attention elsewhere.

"As much as I enjoy your ogling of my goods. And I do enjoy a good ogle." Though, he was still a few feet away, when the figure purred I felt it sliding up my spine. "What is it that you humans say? Oh yes." Fighting the need to shiver, I watched as a clawed hand, which was holding a leather riding crop, pointed up to his face. "My eyes are up here."

I followed the riding crop up along the expansion of his well-defined abs, and over his muscular vest-covered chest, and locked onto big, crystal green orbs, circled by long pale lashes. A straight nose led the way down to a fang-tipped smile. I had the sudden urge to say 'Oh my!' but swallowed it as quickly as it came up.

"There's a pet." Pale pink and purple striped cat-like ears twitched on top of a head of long, pale pink hair that had been braided over one shoulder and hung down to his waist.

Mop snorted next to me as he glared at our host, who unwrapped himself from his throne. His slender form glided toward us, one foot in front of the other like a large feline stalking his prey. The furry pink and purple striped belt unwound from his waist and flicked in the air behind him, but his eyes never left mine.

This beautiful creature couldn't be the Cheshire Cat? He looked like he belonged in a rock band as opposed to the middle of a Fae forest. I gulped as I realized the tingling in my spine was still there. I was in trouble.

"Well, isn't this a lively bunch?" His eyes crinkled at the corners as he took in our raga band group.

Mop, who had an irritated frown, crossed his arms and glowered at the Fae. Meanwhile, Trip just stood there with a content grin on his face as he played with his tail. As for me, I was fighting the need to melt into a pile of goop on the floor.

Stepping toward me, he wrapped his tail around my waist and drew me into him. I held my hands up to ward him off and ended up touching the hard surface of his bare chest. My fingers had a mind of their own, and before I could stop myself, they began to trace the faint scars that marred his skin. A purr rumbled through his chest and into my hands. I jerked back and my already red face became as hot as a tamale.

Dropping my hands seemed like a bad idea, because I would've been touching him more intimately than I would've liked. I decided to wrap my arms around myself in a hug in hopes that it would somehow protect me.

The laugh from my captor reverberated out of him and vibrated down into the tail wrapped around my waist. Similar to the prince, his laugh made my toes curl and parts of me feel hot with need. What was it about the Fae men that affected me so? Why did they all look like they came out of Wet Dreams 'R' Us, while the rest of the UnSeelie Court's occupants were deranged animals?

"Aren't you a peach?" He purred in my ear and pressed the length of the riding crop against my lower back, drawing me against him. His nose trailed into my hair as he inhaled my scent. "Do you taste just as good as you look?"

My breath caught in my throat as the tip of his nose slid across the side of my neck. I didn't know what was going on, but I felt like I was losing IQ points with every new male Fae I met.

I wasn't some blushing virgin. I had boyfriends in the past. Hell! I'd even had friends with benefits, but for some reason, I couldn't explain why my insides quivered with every touch of his clawed hands. I even reacted weirdly when the prince gripped my arm. It hurt, but in a good way. Not that I would have admitted it out loud.

"Knock it off, ye lech! She ain't here for that!" Mop's grouchy voice broke through whatever spell the cat had me under.

I shook my head to clear it and jolted back from the body still pressed up against mine. Space was good. Lots of space. The toothy grin I received as I moved away only solidified my desire to not let him touch me again.

"So, you're the Cheshire Cat?" I cleared my throat and tried to pretend he didn't affect me. I forced my eyes up to his face when they tried to wander back down to the bare skin of his chest. Eye contact. Eye contact was good.

"Cheshire S. Cat, but you, my lovely sweet," he bowed to me, grabbing my hand before I could object, "...may call me Chess." His mouth snaked across the back of my hand, the tip of his tongue tasting the skin there.

His tongue was slightly rougher than a human's, kind of like a cat's. A vision of what else he could do with his tongue popped into my mind before I squashed it. I was so not going there.

"Great." I snatched my hand back, rubbing it on my shorts as if it would remove the tingling his mouth left there.

Chess made a satisfied purr deep in his throat, and the pink tip of his tongue danced across his lips. "You do taste as good as you look." His crystal eyes trailed down my bare legs, making me fidget in place.

The feral look in his eyes could've been food or sex. It was hard to tell the difference, which I guess was true for most men. Apparently, the Fae weren't that different from humans in that aspect.

I watched his clawed hand stroke his chest in a sensual manner and gulped. Sex, definitely sex.

I really didn't see what was so appealing about me. I was short. I didn't have nice long legs, and I was wearing my least attractive pajamas. My breasts were all right sized. I didn't have a flat butt, but I also wasn't winning any awards for it. My eyes were too narrow and my nose too pointed. I had freckles on every inch of my face. The only time I used makeup was to cover them up in the summer months when the sun made them stand out even more. I was average on a large scale. The only thing I had going for me was my thick copper hair. It was not quite straight nor was it curled, leaving it impossible to fashion in any way that was presentable. For some reason, it drew more attention than I liked, even with my mediocre features.

Was it just the fact that I was human that made them interested, or were all Fae men perverts? I was betting on perverts.

"Don't mind the cat. He be all bark and no bite." Mop frowned harder, if that was possible, at the leering feline.

"Now that's not true. I've been known to bite in some situations." He smirked at me before he turned back to Mop. "And I'm hurt that you would think so little of me." Chess closed his eyes and gripped his chest with a hand in a dramatic pose.

"No, ye ain't. Stop ye foolin'. We ain't got time for none of ye games."

"But all of life's a game." Chess tried to pick up my hand again, but I stepped back. Not to be deterred, he grabbed a strand of my hair and wrapped it around his finger as he grinned. "Only some of us are lucky enough to know whose playing. Would you like to play with me, my little kitty Kat?" He gave my hair a little tug, causing me to 'eep' at the sharp sting.

"Uh." This guy just didn't give up! I could see why the prince didn't like him. If I didn't watch it, he'd have me out of my shorts before I knew it.

"Yea, yea." Mop thankfully interjected, placing himself between me and the flirtatious cat. "Like I said, we ain't got no time, not with it being what day it is."

"Oh?" Chess' coy grin dipped down in a thoughtful frown, and his ears twitched on his head. "I'd imagine not. I'm surprised you have gotten this far with your delectable guest smelling the way she does. I can imagine he is not too happy about that." For the first time since we arrived, he turned his gaze from me to somewhere beyond the willow tree's curtain of vines as if he could see something we couldn't.

"In fact, let us take this little party into my humble abode." He turned on his heel toward his throne. "You never know who could be listening." He gave me a cheeky grin before walking right through the trunk of the tree.

Gone!

Just like that!

There was no door or poof of smoke. I didn't know why I was surprised. Mop and Trip certainly didn't seem impressed. In fact, they followed suit, disappearing into the tree to whatever lie beyond its bark.

The last couple of times I had gone through a portal without knowing what was on the other side, I'd ended up worse off than I was before. I was tired of leaps of faith and even more so of not knowing what the hell was going on. I was usually the one with all the answers.

I was the one people turned to for help, not the other way around. I didn't like feeling helpless and out of control. It was possible that the slight change in my personality had to do with my unease, but I had a suspicion it was a lot more than that. If only I knew what.

Chess' head popped out of the side of the tree, startling me out of my thoughts. "Don't do that!"

I glared at the head that seemed to be floating in the air. Was that where the story got started? Had Alice stood in this very place, too young to understand what she was seeing? And if she was still in Wonderland, how did Lewis Carrol even hear her story?

"Are you coming, pet?" He held out a clawed hand at my hesitancy. "Do not be afraid. Come on inside."

"Said the spider to the fly," I muttered to no one in particular before I placed my hand in his and was tugged inside.

CHAPTER

CHANGES & SHADOWS

"WHAT'S WRONG WITH what I'm wearing?" I opened my arms and twisted around to see what was so distasteful.

While I wasn't wearing my most flattering pajamas, I could've still gone to Walmart and been more fashionable than the majority of its customers. I would've been more outraged if I had thought Chess was ogling my bits as he liked to call them, but his eyes were all business as they scrutinized my clothes.

"While your legs are quite delicious to look at, not all parts of the Underground are as warm as this forest." He picked at the sleeve of my sweatshirt and grimaced. "And your ensemble does leave something to be desired."

"Well excuse me if I didn't have time to primp myself before I chased after what I thought was a rabbit!" I huffed and crossed my arms over my chest.

"You are a little spit fire, aren't you?" Chess chuckled as he moved into his expansive walk-in closet. From where I stood in the middle of his bedroom, the wardrobe was easily triple the size of my own closet and had rows upon rows of clothes and shoes piled throughout.

I couldn't imagine having so many clothes – slacks for work, jeans or sweats for home. What else did a girl need?

The way most people felt about going to the dentist was how I felt about trying on clothes; it was a necessary evil and should only be done when there was no other option. I could've counted the number of times I'd gone shopping in the last year on one hand, and I still would've had five left.

While I waited for the cat to find my new ensemble, I took in the massive expansion that was his room. Next to the closet, a long purple chaise sat to one side near a three-way mirror. In front of the mirror was a small, round dais that you would see in a bridal store. The thought of Chess standing in front of the mirror turning this way and that as he admired himself caused a giggle to slip out of my mouth.

"Did you say something?" Chess called out from the closet.

"Uh–" I coughed, covering up my giggles. "No, nothing. Just admiring your room."

"Oh?" His voice held a hint of humor at my obvious lie before his voice turned teasing. "Do make yourself comfortable. The bed is especially soft and the sheets feel delightful against your skin."

My eyes trailed over to the bed he was describing. A large, four-poster bed that was covered in silk sheets and a fur-lined duvet looked like it promised everything he said and more. A mental image of Chess wrapped in nothing but those sheets caused my face to heat up. I shook my head to dispel the image and chastised myself for letting the perverted Fae rub off on me.

The inside of his bedroom was just like the rest of the willow. It screamed Chess in a very severe way. Fur carpet covered the floors and all of the furniture in a nauseating combination of neon pink and purple. It was like a unicorn had thrown up all over the place. I wouldn't wish this décor on my worst enemy.

When we first arrived, Mop tried to explain our ordeal to Chess. He had listened to our plea with all the attention a cat could give, so none at all. This, to my amusement, had aggravated the brownie to no end.

"Don't act like ye don't know. Hare said Hatter was here." He stomped his little foot in the plush carpet, the soft flooring not helping him emphasize his anger.

"How can someone as lovely as you be dressed like such a peasant?" Chess ignored Mop's little fit. I watched the brownie's face turn purple with rage. "You should be wrapped in silks and lace. Not..." He picked at my sweatshirt again. "...whatever this is."

My attention was torn between keeping the cat's groping hands off me and waiting to see if Mop exploded. He opened his mouth to give Chess what I was sure was a piece of his mind when Chess grabbed my hand and dragged me into his bedroom, leaving a slack-jawed brownie in our wake.

After what seemed like forever, Chess stepped back out of his wardrobe. "Why do you even have so many clothes? Do you get many visitors?"

"One should always look one's best." Chess flipped his braid over his shoulder as he handed me a pair of golden leather pants and a matching sheer top. He arched a perfectly curved brow at me. "Even when no one is around."

I eyed the clothing he held out to me. "I thought warmth was the goal here?"

I picked up the edge of the golden sheer top and rubbed it between my fingers. There was hardly anything to it. It was more of a vest than a shirt with strings that tied in the middle.

Chess gave a devious grin. "Your legs will be warm."

I rolled my eyes at him. "How do I know this isn't a ploy for you to get me undressed?"

His fiendish grin grew darker, and his eyes filled with heat as he wrapped his tail around my waist. His scent drifted to my nose as he brought my body up against his. It was a heady combination of sweet lilac and male musk. Once again my body had a mind of its own, and a low desire began to form in the pit of my stomach.

Damn it. Get a hold of yourself, Katherine!

"If I wanted you out of your clothing I wouldn't need an excuse." Chess' low voice purred against my skin, causing my hairs to stand on end. "Or perhaps you need one to make yourself feel better?"

"No. I, uh–" I coughed, clearing my throat. I put my hands on his shoulders and gave a little push. "You think very highly of yourself, don't you?"

"If I didn't, who else would? Now be a good little girl and put those on." He gave me a little shove toward a door on the other side of the bedroom. "You can use my bathroom. Feel free to shower as well, but I'd hurry it up. I doubt your protectors will let me have you alone for much longer."

Mop had poked his head in the bedroom after he had recovered from being ignored and made a huge fuss about not trusting the cat to be alone with me. He was afraid Chess would find some way to trick me in to doing something I didn't want to do, and he would have none of it.

He had actually said, "Ye yellow-bellied feline better keep ye paws and all the rest of ye off of our human! I won't be havin' the likes of ye taintin' her."

He had said a few other choice insults that would make my grandmother blush, but that was the gist of it. I'd thought he was being silly at the time, but now that I was alone with the cat it wasn't him I didn't trust, it was me. I didn't think my libido could handle one more spike to it without me ending up a complete slut by the end of it.

"I didn't think you'd have modern amenities." I brushed his ever-caressing tail away and headed to the bathroom, my golden duds in hand. A shower sounded delightful, but I didn't trust the lecherous cat not to come in while I was in such a vulnerable state.

"Why would you think that?" Chess sat down on a violet chaise practically melting into it while his eyes watched my every move.

Ignoring his eyes drilling into my back, I closed the door behind me. I dropped the clothes to the floor and darted for the sink. Splashing my face with water, I swished some around in my mouth, hoping to get rid of the lingering acrid taste from the tea party. God I hoped my breath didn't smell.

"Taking a bath? Want me to come wash your back?" Chess' voice called out from the door, his voice muffled, but no less alluring with the door between us.

"No!" I shouted more than I meant to and dashed back to the door, locking it quickly. I picked up the leather pants, my nose wrinkling before I dropped my shorts to the ground. "You're a cat, right?"

"Of sorts."

"Don't you, you know–" I tried to think of a less sexual word than the one I was thinking as I struggled into the tight pants.

"Don't I what?" I could hear the smile in his voice as if he could see my mental struggle.

I sighed in defeat as I buttoned the pants. I really should stop saying whatever pops into my mind. "Lick yourself?"

A chuckle came from behind the door so close that I spun around to make sure he hadn't entered the room. "Normally I bathe in the bath tub. I do enjoy a good soak."

My eyes wandered to the claw foot tub. It was big enough to fit three people and then some. I loved a good hot bath, but there wasn't enough money in the world to get me in that tub with Chess waiting on the other side of the door. If there was one thing he had done consistently it was try to get into my pants, or rather, me out of them, which he had apparently done. I tied the tie of my overly revealing top and opened the door.

"I could make an exception for...." Chess' voice trailed off as his eyes devoured my appearance.

The pants were snug and low on my hips where the vest floated against my skin. I was glad I had worn my nice matching black underwear tonight instead of my usual worn out white bra. I felt exposed, but the look on Chess' face was enough to make anyone feel like the most desirable person in the world.

After a long moment of Chess' leering, I cleared my throat. "Chess. You're staring."

Snapping his mouth shut, the fanged grin I was coming to anticipate slid back onto his face. He circled me like a vulture. I had to bat away his tail that kept trying to stroke the open skin where the shirt met the top of the pants. Each caress of his tail made me feel more and more vulnerable. He stopped in front of me, glaring down at the tennis shoes I had shoved back on my feet.

I frowned. They did seem a little out of place.

"Hmm. Almost perfect." He tapped a long claw on his chin before smiling. "I have just the thing!"

I eased down onto the chaise; the leather pants made bending pretty impossible. It was my turn to stare as Chess dug through his closet with his butt sticking up in the air. I watched his tail wag back and forth. How did he put his clothes on when there wasn't a hole in the back of his pants? Just when I was starting to think that Chess was drawing out his search so I could stare at his butt, Mop burst into the room.

"Time's up, Cat! Where's Hatter?" He tapped his brown, bare foot on the plush carpet.

Chess popped up out of the closet holding a pair of golden brown knee-high boots in his hands. "Hatter's not here."

"How do you expect me to walk in those?" I stared in disbelief at the four-inch heel.

I'd never worn anything higher than a small wedge. I was short, but I didn't have a complex about it. Flats had always been my shoe of choice.

"Then where?" Mop growled, ignoring my complaints.

"Who knows?" The feline gave a graceful shrug of his shoulders before picking up one of my legs. He slipped one of the boots up my calf, his hands caressing me far more than necessary. I glanced down at him to see his eyes peeking up at me beneath pale lashes as he laced up the corset along the side of the boot, making the act more intimate than it was.

His voice became low and silky , as he whispered, "Certainly not me."

"Then why ye wastin' our time?" Mop's angry voice broke the sensual atmosphere Chess was causing, and I jerked away from the smirking feline.

"Trip knows. Oh, oh Trip knows!" The white opalaught jumped up and down, pointing at my new outfit. "Seelie Court!"

"What?" Mop grunted.

"Hatter's in the Seelie Court, Hatter is!" Trip stood next to me, pulling on the edge of my sheer vest. "See, Lady dressed like a Seelie Fae!"

Mop stopped his grumbling and took in my clothes for the first time. I'd thought Chess was dressing me up for his own pleasure. It never crossed my mind that there could be a more logical reason behind his clothing choices.

"Why didn't ye say so in the first place?" Mop shook his finger at the feline who was still kneeling at my feet.

"The shadows came and Hatter left." He examined his nails, showing utter disinterest in Mop's question.

I glanced between the Fae around me. "Shadows? What shadows?"

"Hatter hides where the shadows won't dwell." I frowned at Chess' sudden flip from persistent flirt to cryptic messenger. "The shadows are the rejected Fae, well some of them. They don't fit into the Seelie or UnSeelie Court. They live in the Shadow Realm."

"The nightmare realm," Trip whispered. His eyes were cautious as if saying the words would bring the shadows down upon him.

Mop never finished explaining about the different worlds. I knew the Underground consisted of three different realms; there was the UnSeelie Court, where we were, the Seelie Court, and now the Shadow Realm. From what I had experienced of this Court, I couldn't imagine what horrors awaited in the Shadow Realm.

"So, what are they doing here?" I asked, tugging the other boot out of Chess' hands so I could work on putting it on.

"They want what we have." Chess slid onto the chaise next to me. His fingers found my blonde strand of hair, which he twisted between his fingers. Whenever his fingertips accidently touched my shoulder a tinge of heat spread along my skin. I tried to fight my body's reaction, but it was a lost cause.

"And what's that?" I swallowed a hard lump in my throat and moved away from Chess' distracting presence.

"Dreams," Mop chimed in. "We Fae be relying on the dreams of humans. It be what keeps this place..." He gestured around us. "...alive. The Shadow Realm be cut off from the humans and, in turn, the power they bring."

"But humans are forbidden here, right?"

Before any of them could answer a shrill cry sounded from somewhere above, causing us all to jump.

"What's that?"

I sounded like a broken record. Not that I had a choice. With no knowledge of the Fae world, I had to literally rip the answers from my reluctant companions. The whole mysterious world, and its rules, were really starting to piss me off.

I jumped again at the pounding on what sounded like the outside of the willow.

Chess stood up, holding a hand out to me. "Time to go, Lady."

"The shadows come, they come!" Trip clenched onto my pant leg, his ears dropping to the floor.

"The shadows?" My eyes stared up at the ceiling and my curiosity piqued.

"They probably smelled ye in the woods and followed us here." Mop turned to Chess. "We need to use yer mirror, Cat."

Chess ushered us into the closet and closed the door tight behind us. He moved toward the back of the wardrobe, where a full-length mirror with a gilded frame stood. He scratched a claw across the surface of the frame, which activated the symbols that were barely visible to the naked eye. They gave off a faint glow, and then became bright enough that we had to shield our eyes for a moment before they went out completely. In their wake, the surface of the mirror rippled inside the metal.

"In you go." Chess stepped back from the mirror and gestured us in.

As usual, Mop and Trip didn't question the liquid portal and hurried through when another loud bang sounded. They seemed to be getting more violent with every minute. Would the tree be able to withstand such abuse?

Before I could step through the rippling glass, Chess grabbed me about the waist and pulled me flush against him. I opened my mouth to protest, even though it was hardly the time for flirting, but my words were swallowed when his mouth met mine. It wasn't a gentle kiss. It was as if he were trying to eat me whole. His hands were splayed along my back and arms, and my skin heated from every inch he touched.

His tongue was rough, causing my mouth to tingle as he searched out my own. He drew it into his mouth, sucking on it hard enough for me to jerk back and nick it on one of his sharpened canines. The blood from the wound seemed to spark something in him. A low rumble came from his throat. He pressed a hand to the back of my head to keep me from pulling away as his mouth worked on the wound.

The feeling of his mouth on mine made me lightheaded in the best of ways. In an effort to stay afloat, my hands gripped on to his vest and pulled him closer. I admit I was more than a little disappointed when my movement caused him to pull away.

My chest heaved as I tried to regain my breathing. He leaned his forehead against mine, his own breath coming out in pants. At least, I wasn't the only one affected.

"What was that for?"

A cracking sound broke our little moment, and Chess took a step back. The billowing fog from the forest leaked in under the wardrobe door. All thoughts of Chess' kiss fled my mind as terror began to overwhelm me. I didn't want to know what lie behind that door.

"You need to go now, Kat." He ushered me to the mirror before turning back to the door.

"Wait!" I tugged on his arm. "What about you?"

"Who? Me?" Chess gave a coy smile that didn't reach his heated eyes. "I'm just a cat."

"Are you mad? Come with us!" My voice became desperate as the door banged open. And then there was silence.

The light from the bedroom was gone, and there was only darkness. It was the kind of blackness you were afraid to look into for fear of someone looking back. I knew in the pit of my stomach bad things would happen if that darkness found me.

Chess turned to me once again and brushed his lips against the shell of my ear. My eyes were focused so much on the approaching blackness that I almost didn't hear what he said. I frowned, and my brow furrowed at his words, but before I could question him, he shoved me through the mirror's surface.

CHAPTER

THE LOOKING GLASS

"WHY DO YOU taste so old?" Chess' confusing words echoed through my head as I pounded on the glass of the mirror.

It didn't surprise me that Chess could tell how old I was based on taste alone. It was obvious that I was becoming desensitized to the strangeness of the Underground. I didn't even question it. Why wouldn't he be able to differentiate by taste alone? It only made sense. He was a cat. Well, a cat-Fae, but still.

The part I couldn't discern was why he said I tasted old? I was only twenty-two, which was not even close to old in human years, let alone Fae years. The majority of the Fae were probably three times my age. Surely he was older than me?

"Yer not gonna get back that way."

I paused in my assault and scowled at Mop. "We can't just leave him there."

"Pfft. The cat will be fine." The brownie waved me off. "Ye, on the other hand, need to be keepin' a low profile. That get up won't fool many Fae. Just keep yer head down and follow me. I know where Hatter be."

I kicked the frame of the mirror one last time, my eyes full of longing and regret. Chess wasn't anything like Mop described, or any descriptions of him in the human world for that matter. While there was a certain dangerous charm about him, he was more of a harmless flirt than anything. He certainly didn't have any of the malicious intent Mop kept implying. And I would rather be back there with him than where we were now.

The moment I'd stepped out of the mirror, I'd wanted to jump back in. The room was dimly lit with black shiny, almost reflective floors. Mirrors lined all the walls. But unlike Chess' mirror, which reflected my companions and me, these mirrors didn't reflect anything. Well, not completely. I could see the other mirrors and the floor, but it was as if we didn't exist.

I hadn't turned into a vampire, had I? No one had bitten me, that I knew of, and I doubted that small nick from Chess would count. I trailed my tongue along the edges of my teeth feeling for any sharp edges. No fangs. Heartbeat? A little fast, but still there. I didn't have any overwhelming urges to drink blood, not that I could after the tea party incident.

"What ye doin', ye daft girl?" Mop frowned at me from the exit, which was the one spot in the room not covered in mirrors.

How did he get over there?

"I'm checking to see if I'm a vampire."

"Lady, not dead. Not yet, Lady not." Trip sniffed around me. "Trip can still smell Lady's pretty shampoo, Trip can."

"Uh, thanks, Trip." Awkward. "Why don't I have a reflection then?" I turned this way and that in the mirror, but saw no change.

Mop huffed at having to explain it to me again. He moved back to where I was before the mirrors. "That be 'cos they ain't meant for reflectin'."

"What do you mean? Why are they here if they don't show anything?" I stared into the mirror where my reflection should have been. It was freaking me out to have no reflection.

"I didn't say they didn't. They don't reflect the present." Mop tapped on the glass of one of the mirrors and it rippled beneath his hand.

The mirror cleared to show Mop and Trip arguing at the door in the Between. Though there was no sound, I knew the moment they noticed me coming over to them. Trip's eyes widened and his tail shook as Mop's face closed down and filled with irritation. I stepped closer to get a better look, but before I could see what happened next, Mop removed his hand and the mirror cleared to show the empty room.

"Ye get it?" Mop turned away from the mirror and glanced up at me.

"So, it shows the past? Any past?" I asked more to myself than to the brownie.

I eyed the mirror for a moment as the possibilities turned endlessly in my head. I could see anything. All of the mysteries of the universe were bared before me. Just the thought of what I could do with that information had my hands moving on their own.

My hand stretched out to touch the mirror, I almost touched the surface before Mop's voice piped in, "I wouldn't be doin' that if I be ye."

"Why not?" I frowned down at him. "You did."

"That's 'cos I be Fae and know how to use it. Ye human, lest ye forget." He shook his head. "Besides, this be Fae magic and Seelie at that, ye might not see what ye want. Ye never know how it will react to ye. Best be movin' along." Mop and Trip headed for the door once again.

I frowned and dropped my hand to my side, but I didn't move away from the mirror. So many remarkable findings and always the answer was no.

No, Katherine, you're a silly human. You're not allowed. You can't do that. It's not proper. Be normal like your sister. Well, I was fed up with proper, and I was fed up with rules.

I put my hand on the cold surface of the glass and then pulled it back. What did I want to see? There was so much I didn't know, so many questions that still weren't answered. Chess was a mystery all in his own glorious self, a riddle I was dying to uncover, but there were so many more questions I had that were more important than my traitorous libido. Like, why weren't humans allowed in the Underground anymore? What happened to the Seelie Princess to cause such a strain between the two courts? And why did every question and answer end up with the dark prince involved in some way?

The surface beneath it began to ripple after that last thought, and my eyes watched the surface in a mixture of fear and curiosity. I hadn't even been touching it when I thought about the prince, so why was it activating on its own? My thoughts of the UnSeelie Prince must have been enough, because the mirror in front of me disappeared, and in its place was a room.

It was a bedroom to be exact. But it wasn't my bedroom or any bedroom I'd ever seen before. The bed was moderately sized with a pale, yellow duvet. There was a small table with a set of wooden chairs set to one side. On the table was an unused tea set and a few writing utensils as well as some random everyday items. The room was different from my own back home, which was littered with the laundry from that week and unpacked boxes.

The room was nice enough for me to know it was owned by someone important, but small enough to get to everything within a few feet. While it was neat and tidy, it seemed to lack the feeling of a home – like a stage waiting for its actors to arrive. I placed my hand up to the mirror to get a closer look but instead of feeling the glass beneath my hand it sank through the surface, which caused me to tumble head first into the room.

I landed face first on cushy, golden carpet. The ends of it tickled my nose, making me sneeze. I inched up onto my knees and gazed back toward the mirror. Instead of seeing my face reflecting back at me I saw the room of mirrors. Mop and Trip came back and were silently yelling at me as they beat on the glass.

Apparently this was an invitation-only trip.

I moved back to the glass and held a hesitant hand up to it. The surface rippled and swirled under my hand as it pressed through the fluid glass. At least, I knew I could go back.

Instead of going back the way I came, I moved away from my panicked companions, irritated in Mop's case, and turned back to the room. Where was I?

I fiddled with a few of the perfumes and combs on the vanity next to the mirror, looking for any clue of where I was. Not finding any, I moved over to the table where the tea and writing pad sat. The teapot was cold, and when I lifted the top there was nothing in it. The teacups sat upright as if waiting to be used while the writing pad sat next to one of the place sets. The pad had something written on it.

Picking it up, I squinted at the words that were written in small, tight cursive. This was one of those moments where I wished I had reading glasses. Who could even read this? If the formatting was anything to go by, it was some kind of letter, but all I could make out was flowers and white. The rest was too illegible for me to decipher. I tossed the pad back on the table.

Well, this was boring and uneventful.

I turned from the table and back to the mirror where Trip and Mop waited, but before I could put my hand through the surface, the door opened.

Shit.

"I could only sneak away for a moment," A deep voice rumbled. Footsteps hurried over to me before warm muscular arms wrapped around my shoulders, drawing me back against them.

My body tensed at the contact that came with that voice. I didn't need to have a working mirror to know who entered the room, and I was too terrified of being caught to turn around to face him. My silence and reluctant stance didn't seem to bother the UnSeelie Prince as he continued to caress my shoulders.

"Our mothers are going to be at it for a while. They started talking about troll population control, and you know how that gets them going." He pushed my hair to the side and rubbed his face into my neck.

Mothers? What was he talking about?

My eyes searched for Mop and Trip in the mirror. They weren't banging on the glass anymore or yelling at me. In fact, the look of terror on their face solidified how much deep shit I was in.

"Meaning we finally have a few hours to ourselves." The pounding of my heart thudded in my ears as the prince pressed his front firmly against my back, which showed me how happy he was at that prospect.

Fuck. What was I supposed to do? While part of me was getting a little turned on from the feel of the beautiful prince pressed against my butt, the other part was screaming for me to take my chances and jump back into the mirror.

Apparently, I was quiet too long, because he stopped his nuzzling and turned me around in his arms. "Are you all right?"

The dark-headed prince before me wasn't the same prince I had met outside of Teeth's head. I mean, it was the same person, but he seemed younger. Less bitter. The swirling glyphs that decorated the left side of his face were noticeably missing. His hair was unbraided and draped freely past his shoulders, brushing the hard plains of his chest through his blood-red, silk shirt. Long dangling earrings hung from his ears and ruby-colored gems swung back and forth as he moved.

He already caused a profound effect on my insides before, and without the ice blue eyes and the markings, he was the definition of an exotic faerie prince. If that wasn't bad enough, the heated gaze he was giving me seemed to penetrate out of his gorgeously chiseled face and straight into my girly parts.

Ignoring my traitorous body, my mind tried to fit all the pieces together. The dark eyes, the lack of markings, and the tempting long hair caused something to click inside of me.

This was the past. His past. I was seeing him before he became His Royal Stick Up His Ass. Before his punishment. Before –

"Lynne?"

–She died.

I didn't know who Lynne was, but if I had to guess, I'd say it was his ex-fiancé. But why did he think I was her? I frowned down at myself, searching for any indication that I changed into a faerie princess.

Nope. I was still me. Deciding to play along with the scenario, I glanced up at the expectant prince, my voice unsure, "Yes?"

"I asked if you were all right." He tucked a strand of my hair behind my ears, his eyes soft and full of concern.

My heart fluttered a bit, causing me to stutter. "I'm fine. What were you saying about Mother?"

The prince cupped my face in his hand, stroking my cheek as he watched my face for any sign of a lie. When he didn't find anything, he relaxed against me, pulling me closer to him still. I gulped when the side of my face touched his bare chest. The sound of his heartbeat pounded in my ears, its pace as rapid as my own.

"I know you're worried about the disappearances, but you really shouldn't work yourself up so." He pressed his forehead against mine. "You're going to give yourself wrinkles."

"Would you care?" The words came out of my mouth before they ever made it to my mind, but I found part of me really wanted to know.

"What kind of question is that?" He leaned away from me, confusion on his face. "Of course, I wouldn't. You'll always be beautiful to me. I love you, Lynne."

My eyes became as round as a beach ball when his mouth captured mine. I tried not to tense up as he tangled a hand in my hair, deepening the kiss with a sweep of his tongue. I felt like I was betraying Chess in some way by letting him kiss me, but I didn't know what else to do.

His kiss was so different from the aggressive way the feline had taken control of my mouth. Instead of trying to devour me all at once, he seemed to be trying to savor each stroke of his tongue, each press of his lips, and each moan that sounded.

Moan? My eyes snapped open, having closed without my knowledge. This wasn't right. I shouldn't be kissing him. I felt like an intruder. I wasn't his princess, and this was a private moment for him. One I was never meant to see. One I shouldn't even be in.

I tried to pull away from the kiss by taking a step back, but he only followed my movement and even encouraged it until he had me pressed against the vanity. The answer to if he was actually seeing me or someone else was answered when his hand found my skin beneath my sheer top. It stroked along my skin and inched up to cup my breast.

My face heated up as I realized what we must look like to Mop and Trip. I could barely see the mirror out of the corner of my eye, but from what I could see, they weren't there anymore. In fact, the mirror wasn't showing the other room at all. It was reflecting back the bedroom with me pressed up against the vanity, a Fae Prince attached to my face.

I placed my hands onto the prince's chest and pushed, disengaging our mouths. A small part of me pouted at ending the kiss, but it was completely overridden by the panic I felt at being trapped. I struggled against the arms around me; ignoring the confused and hurt look on the prince's face as I put my hands on the mirror.

Solid. The glass was solid. I pounded on the glass; the sound of the prince questioning my actions was drowned out by the whirlwind of thoughts flying through my brain.

Why did the mirror bring me here? What was I supposed to learn from being here? I wanted to know what was going on, but I didn't want to live it, especially since I knew how this story played out. Suicide was so not me. I liked myself far too much to deprive the world of my witty sarcasm and intellect.

"Let me out!" I shoved against the glass, trying to force my way back through, all the while shoving at the hands trying to pull me away from the mirror.

"Lynne? What are you doing? You can't get out that way." The Fae prince tried once again to pull me away from the mirror. Concern etched his face, but I didn't care. I just wanted out.

"Don't touch me!" I shoved against him, my voice becoming hysterical.

At my words, his face shut down. He took a step back, his eyes going dark and frightened. I cringed against the mirror. What now?

"Fine." He whipped around, his earrings swinging in the air as he marched back to the door. "You know where to find me when you figure out what you want."

I winced as the door slammed shut on more than just our conversation. Forgetting the possibility that I could have disrupted their timeline by my little scene, I turned back to the mirror. Pressing my face to the cool glass, my eyes filled with tears of frustration.

I just wanted to go home. Back to my stupid job at the library. Back to my overbearing mother and perfect sister. Hell, I would settle for Brandi at this point. I would do anything to get out of this place.

Placing my hand on the mirror, I pleaded to whatever Fae magic was at work. "Please let me through. I don't belong here. Please. Please."

I repeated it over and over again, hoping the mirror would give in to my pleas. After a few minutes, when nothing happened, my distress turned to anger. A building rage I didn't know I had pushed at the surface of my skin.

Getting up from my sprawled-out position, I placed both of my hands on the mirror and snarled, "If you don't send me back right now, I'm going to find you in this time and shatter you. You hear me! I will smash you into tiny little pieces and scatter them all over the Underground, so they will never be able to put you back together, and then just for good measure, I'll shatter all of your brothers and sisters too."

The mirror did nothing for a moment, but when I moved backward to make good on my word, the surface rippled and I fell through the mirror. This time landing hands first on the hard black floor with Mop and Trip on either side of me.

"Lady! Lady is back, Lady is." Trip hopped around beside me, making me feel more tired than I already felt.

"Finally." Mop grouched. "Thought I might have to come in after ye." He shook a finger at me as I moved each aching limb into a standing position. "I told ye to leave it alone. I told ye and ye did it anyway. I swear ye have a death wish, ye do."

"Yea, yea. I know. I should have listened. I won't do it again." I rolled my eyes but gave a wary glance back to the mirror and the man I had left in the past.

My lips still tingled where we had kissed. I didn't know how I was going to face him again without thinking about what happened. Would he remember? Did I break something here?

"Don't sass me, girl." Mop glared. He grabbed my hand and pulled me out of the room and into a golden hallway. "While ye were playin' around we found Hatter, so let's get him and get out of here before that damn cat be lookin' for us."

At the mention of Chess, I felt even worse about my little make out session with the prince. "You're wrong, you know." I followed Mop down the corridor. Trip hopped along beside me. "Chess isn't as bad as you made him out to be."

Mop snorted. "A little pheromones and he's got ye wrapped round his finger."

"Pheromones?"

"Yeah, some Fae give off a pheromone that bends humans to their will, makin' them more pliable. I'm not surprised ye didn't notice." Mop harrumphed.

That was actually kind of a relief. Not that I could be controlled by some Fae mojo, but that I wasn't just being slutty, though being controlled wasn't a pleasant thought either.

"What about the prince? Does he have these pheromones?" I was pretty sure I knew the answer, the pressure that pressed down on me when he had me locked in his gaze had to be some kind of magical influence, but I had to be sure.

"Of course, he does. The stronger ye be the stronger the pheromones are. I'm surprised ye could even put two words together with him, let alone talkin' back the way ye did."

We approached a large set of double doors that were darker than the golden walls by only a fraction. Muffled music from the party could be heard from behind them. Who would have a party at this time of day? It was late in the human world, but here? It couldn't have been more than ten in the morning. Not that I had a watch to go by.

"Anyway, ye need to be watching yer self. Cheshire is a liar. He can't help himself. He'll do whatever it takes to get what he wants. Ye be wise to not trust him with ye heart or any other part of ye." Mop nodded his head at me as if I would naturally agree with him.

He reminded me of my dad when he tried to warn me off boys. Sometimes I wish I'd listened to him and stayed away from the whole lot of them. I'd go on random dating boycotts, but it never lasted. I would see a pretty one and think 'I bet he could reach that pot on the top shelf!' It was survival, I swear.

"You're just pissy because he bested you at cards." I scowled at Mop.

Mop pulled open one of the large doors and peeked his head in. After a moment, he pulled his head back and growled in a low voice, "It wasn't just a card game. I lost half me jewels to that game! I would have finally won too if that damn cat hadn't pulled a flush out of thin air!"

"Is that so?" I smirked, raising my brow at his childish rant.

"Don't be lookin' at me like that, ye weren't there." The brownie snapped at me, trying to keep his voice down.

"Trip was! Trip was!" The white opalaught waved his paws in the air.

"Well?" I looked to Trip, a smile on my face. "Did Chess cheat?"

"Trip's not sure. Trip will think, Trip will." Trip's tail straightened out severely as he tried to remember.

I watched the opalaught as he scrunched his eyes closed. The fur on his body shook with the effort he was putting into it. My curiosity wasn't worth his discomfort.

"That's all right. I'm sure it will come to you. There are more important issues to worry about right now." I gave Trip an encouraging smile and changed the subject. "So, what's the plan?" I peeked over Mop to see into the ballroom.

The ballroom was pretty much what I expected. Large columns circled the room holding up the high ceilings. The décor was an array of gold with hints of white here and there to accent it. Even the planters had gilded flowers and leaves. And the guests were no exception to the gold theme.

Beautiful men and women, dressed in various shades of gold and white, circled the room. Some of them danced to a weird floating kind of music while others socialized or ate from the refreshments being passed around. The dais at the top of the room with three golden thrones was the only thing that kept me from thinking it wasn't some kind of costume party.

On top of two of those thrones sat a man and woman. Neither wore a crown, but they didn't need one. Their regal presence stated clearing who ruled the room's occupants. The queen was just as beautiful as the rest of the guests, if not more so, but unlike them, she did not laugh or smile. She simply watched the crowd with cool, calculating eyes.

The White Queen.

Her white dress fit her like a glove, pressing her breasts above the bodice and her small waist. The gown swept over her legs and down to the ground, where it was trimmed with golden lace. Her hair was pulled up into a braided crown and was set with small gems that sparkled in the light. Her face held no makeup, save for the golden-colored paint on her bow-shaped lips. Those lips were set in a stern, straight line, and I could hardly imagine she had ever smiled before.

Wasn't she supposed to be the nice one? I had expected an overwhelming presence, but the hardness on her face was not what I had thought the White Queen would be like.

Her king, on the other hand, seemed to be the friendlier of the two. His own pale blonde hair curled at the edges as it swept the top of his matching white shirt. He was the perfect opposite of his mate.

The king craned his head from where he sat to chat with an attractive male who had long silvery hair that was pulled back into a severe knot at the nape of his neck. A tall top hat sat on his head and, unlike the rest of the room, he wore a golden patch-covered suit with a tail coat. He had a small, amused smile on his face as he mumbled to the king. Every once in a while his eyes would cast a wary glance over to the queen.

"There's Hatter!" Mop pointed at the man on the dais. "Now to get him."

"You have a plan?" I looked from the Fae to Mop. Were any of the stories of the Wonderland occupants true? This Hatter was far too young to be the one of the classic fairytale.

"Smiling Cat dressed Lady up real nice, Smiling Cat did." Trip tugged on his ears, looking me up and down.

"What he said." Mop pointed at Trip with his thumb.

What was their point? I was wearing the same clothes as the Fae in the ballroom, yes, but that didn't make me look anything like them. Only an idiot would think I belonged. I shook my head at them, backing away from the door.

"No. No way." I waved my hands in front of me. "I can't go in there!"

"And why not? Ye look just like them. We'd stick out like a troll doing the samba." Mop gestured to Trip and himself.

He had a point. Between the three of us, I was the only one who looked the part. Compared to the Fae in the ballroom, I wasn't a hundred percent sure I would even pass as one of them. If it had been the prince, or even Chess, it would have been all right. They were attractive enough to make the cut, but I wasn't even pretty enough to be in the running.

"Why do you look so different from the other Fae? They all look like they came out of a fashion catalog while you and Trip are....uh...not." I couldn't think of a nice word that wouldn't offend my companions, but who could compare to such beauty in the other room?

"Just say it." Mop shot daggers at me. "Ugly."

"Well, yea." An awkward frown filled my face as I surveyed the ballroom door. "But it's like comparing a novel to a book of poetry. A novel might be a glorious piece of art in whole, but a few lines of poetry can touch you so much deeper and stay with you longer than any novel could."

"Pretty words for someone who ain't ever been called ugly." Mop crossed his arms over his chest.

He was right. I'd never been called ugly before, but it had been implied.

I once had a boy from school take one look at my family picture and then look and me and ask, "What happened to you?" As if I had been slapped with an ugly stick. But I was used to it. I was always being compared to my younger sister in looks and personality.

She was tall and leggy with high cheekbones and fashionable clothes. I had never been into that kind of thing. I'd rather spend my days surrounded by books than all the expensive clothing in the world.

That was probably why I was a librarian and she was soon to be a rich man's trophy wife. If only people didn't judge everyone by their cover and got to know them as a person first, then maybe they would know what a raging bitch my sister really was.

"Seelie are High Fae, Seelie are," Trip offered. I could always count on him to tell me what was what. "Trip is Lower Fae, Trip is."

"What about Chess and the prince? Are they High Fae? Are your looks the only thing that distinguish what level of Fae you are?" It didn't seem fair. They couldn't help what they looked like and to call them lower beings because they weren't the same was just superficial.

"Of course not! The Seelie Queen may be shallow, but she doesn't decide who be what. Besides, it ain't like we want to be livin' in the Seelie Court anyway." Mop's eyes filled with disgust. "Bunch of self-righteous whore mongers. We UnSeelie may not be the most attractive Fae, but least we be honest 'bout what we are."

"And what is that?"

"Honest," he said, and then waved a hand at me. "Don't worry yerself 'bout us. Ye need to be gettin' in there to get Hatter."

"But won't they be able to tell I'm human? Chess and Teeth did right away." I was stalling. I knew I was. I really didn't want to go in there and pretend to be one of them. Acting was so not in my skill set.

"Ye'll be fine. They're far too full of themselves to pay ye any mind. Just grab a glass of whatever they be servin' and act like ye belong. When ye get close enough to Hatter just say Hare be waitin' on his tea. He'll understand."

I ground my teeth together. It wasn't that I didn't have faith in Mop, though my faith was in short supply lately – he hadn't let me down so far – but up until this point, I hadn't really been alone. Going in that room and facing all those Fae by myself, I couldn't imagine it going any way but bad.

I glanced down at Mop once more. "What do I do if someone figures it out?"

Mop sniffed the air around me in a curious manner and then nodded his head. "They won't."

I cursed under my breath. What were the chances I would get in and out in one piece? About as likely as my sister stepping into a library – slim to none.

C H A P T E R

THE SEELIE COURT

BLENDING IN WASN'T as hard as I thought it would be. I assumed I would be the only one showing so much skin, but I was more clothed than most of the occupants. Male and female Fae danced in various stages of undress. Some of them were wearing what could barely be constituted as underwear while others were fully dressed like me with bits of skin showing. It made blending in a lot easier and me a whole helluvalot less self-conscious.

I grabbed a champagne flute off one of the passing trays and scanned the room around me. There were doors along the walls that led out to balconies, giving a view of the darkening sky. Could it be so late already? I hadn't been there long enough to go through a whole day.

155

Shrugging at another Underground oddity, I turned my attention back to the glass in my hand.

The liquid inside bubbled a dark golden hue. Didn't they know any other colors? I sniffed the top of the glass but jerked back when the contents singed my nose. I took a tentative sip. The drink was sweet and fruity, but it had a bite that caused me to go into a coughing fit.

"Are you all right, dear?" The hand belonging to the concerned voice sat on my arm.

"I–" I coughed and then croaked out, "Yes. I'm fine."

I glanced up at the Fae woman towering over me in stilettos taller than my boots. She had dark brown hair that fell around her shoulders in waves and magenta-colored eyes. Her outfit, if you could call it that, was a golden string bikini that left the majority of her flawless cocoa-colored skin bare. Her chest was the size I always wished I had. Not small enough to be flat chested, but not so large she wouldn't be able to leave the house without a bra. It made her top seem more modest than if I had worn it.

"Not a big drinker, I take it?" The woman's full lips were painted a dark gold and were curved down in a frown as her curious eyes scanned me up and down. Her sultry features made the expression seem more seductive than inquisitive.

"Oh no. I drink all the time. It just went down the wrong pipe." I coughed once again as I lied.

I hated drinking. A bad night of drinking lost me most of my female friends and had a dozen guys calling me at all hours wanting to 'hang out.' I could safely say I didn't drink much anymore. But she didn't need to know that.

"Right." The woman dragged out the word, disbelief on her face. "Well, drinker or not, I'm Magenta. You know, for the account of my eyes." She splayed a hand across her face, framing her startling magenta-colored eyes. "But you can call me, Mags."

"I can see that." I took a tentative drink this time as I was prepared for the burn. "They are very lovely."

"Aren't they, though?" Her lips quirked up. She was clearly proud of herself. "And what do they call you?"

"K – Lady." I caught myself before I gave her my real name, using the alias that I had gained since I had entered the Underground.

"Lady? Why would they call you that?" She looked me over once more before leaning forward and sniffing at the air around me.

I fought the urge to sniff myself just to see what the fuss was about. Did I forget to put deodorant on?

"I don't know. That's just what they call me." I took a big gulp of my drink, looking anywhere except at her.

"Oh! I get it!" She exclaimed clapping her hands together. "I was trying to figure out where I'd smelled your scent before. It's been awhile since I had my turn. I'd almost forgotten what he smells like."

"What?" I tilted my head to the side. I didn't have to lie this time. I had no idea what she was talking about.

"Chess, of course!" Mags giggled looping her arm through mine. She leaned into me like we had a shared secret. "You don't have to play coy with me, dear. Anybody with half a nose can tell you're one of Chess' play things."

"What?" I asked again, my eyes went wide at the mention of Chess. I searched the room to see if anyone had heard her, but no one was paying us any mind.

"Oh, don't be so shy, Lady." She gave me a playful little shove, dropping my arm. "Almost every Fae here has had a turn at being Chess' flavor of the week."

"Really?" I frowned, a little perturbed.

My mind flashed back to my kiss with Chess. Had he done that with other women? I was beginning to feel like I wasn't as special as I thought I was.

"Of course, silly. It's like a rite of passage. And besides," she lowered her voice to a whisper, "we have to keep the mediator happy or you-know-who will…" Mags made a cutting motion across her throat.

I nodded like I understood, my teeth grinding against one another. If she called me silly one more time I was going to punch her in the throat. I grabbed another glass from a passing tray as I tried to wrap my head around the new information.

Who was the mediator? Chess? Why did they need to keep him happy?

I searched out Hatter again, planning on returning to the task at hand. I could ask Mop about Chess' playthings later. Much later.

"It was nice to meet you and everything, Mags, but I really need to–" Before I could excuse myself to find Hatter, Mags started waving her arms in the air like a crazy person, yelling into the crowd.

"Jewels! Gab! Over here!" She motioned a male and female couple over. "Come meet Chess' new playmate!"

As the two approached, a sinking feeling began to grow in my stomach. I had never been one for attention and Mags' outburst had caused more curious eyes to focus on me. If I wasn't careful this chatterbox was going to blow my whole plan.

"Well now, aren't you delicious?" The male wrapped a strand of my copper hair around his fingers, his jewel-encrusted nipple rings flashed in the light. This must be Jewels. They sure were a creative lot in the Underground.

Unfortunately, the nipple rings weren't the main attraction of the male Fae invading my personal space. My eyes darted down to the thick muscular thighs surrounding the golden speedo barely covering his special parts. My face flushed when he angled it my way, pretending to bump against me.

"Hands off." Gab smacked his hand away and gave me an appraising glance. "You know she belongs to Chess right now."

Jewels pouted, his long blonde hair fell over his eyes. The two must have been twins. They both had the same shade of long pale blonde hair that reached their waist, and their eyes were the exact same shade of cerulean blue. But while Jewels was hard and muscular, Gab was soft and feminine.

She had large breasts and a curvy figure, and while Mags wore less clothing than the female twin, Gab's clothing was far more obscene. Her voluptuous figure was incased in a skin-tight, *sheer* golden dress that skimmed her mid-thigh. While I had opted to wear a bra under my sheer top, Gab had no inclination.

When my eyes scanned her completely, and I realized she had also decided to go commando, I took a large burning drink of my glass and hurried to grab another one as the tray passed by.

"So..." Gab's eyed Mags and then turned back to me.

"Lady." Mags provided, not at all bothered by the other woman's public nudity. Their bar for inappropriate had to be very, very low.

"Lady?" The blonde female's brows crinkled. "I don't believe we have met before. I thought I knew everyone who is anyone in the Seelie Court, especially one of Chess'."

She flipped her long shimmering hair over her shoulder, skimming a hand down her figure and smirked. "Our cat is very fond of me. And he's usually more particular about his playmates." She picked up a piece of my hair with a grimace before dropping it and giving me a condescending smile. "Usually."

Great. Meaning I didn't fit the bill. What was her problem? Based on her need to downgrade someone she had just met, I'd have said she was threatened by me. Not that I could compete with them on any level. I didn't even have the energy to try. Was it just me, or was the room getting a little warm?

"Jewels and I were with Chess just last month if you want any tips." Mags frowned at Gab's jab as I almost choked on my drink.

"Are you all right, love?" Jewels patted me on the back, pressing himself against my side as I coughed the burning liquid back up.

Waving him off, I swallowed. "I'm fine." He moved his hand to my lower back and pulled me close to his side. I glanced between the twins. "Together? You mean, like at the same time?"

The blondes nodded, an identical smirk splaying across their faces at my reaction, Gab's more delighted than her brother's. I wasn't naïve. I knew people had ménage à trioses, but I had never met anyone that was in one, let alone siblings. It made me think less of Chess in some way.

"Chess has quite an appetite." Jewels drew out the words to match the rhythm of his fingers that were stroking my waist.

"He's very talented with his hands and his..." Gab paused for emphasis. "...tail." She smirked, delighting in making me uncomfortable. "For a half-breed that is, but you would know that as his lover, wouldn't you?"

I didn't like the way she asked that. I didn't like any of it to be honest. My stomach rolled at the thought of Chess with any of them. So much for thinking I was special. I was just one of many. He was probably laughing at me right now.

"You know, it's awfully warm in here." Jewels fanned himself with a hand before turning his heated gaze to me. "Maybe you'd like to get some air with me."

As he said the words, my face became warmer, and I felt myself wanting to go with him. I didn't know if it was all the alcohol or if it was my insecurity about Chess. Maybe Jewels was working some pheromone mojo on me, and I barely heard myself say, "Okay" before I let him usher me toward the balcony.

"Lady!" Gab and Mags gaped at me.

"You can't." Mags pulled me away from Jewels. "You're Chess' until your time is up."

"That means you can't get involved with other Fae." Gab shook her head, frowning at her brother. "Honestly, did you forget the rule?" She lifted a brow at me. "When is your time up?"

"Yes, when?" Jewels eyes flashed in anticipation.

Instead of answering their question, I chugged the rest of the drink in my hand. I could hardly feel the burn of it as it went down. They were tasty once you had a few. I could drink them all night.

As I stared down into my empty glass, a dark shadow fell over me. A warm hand slid around my waist, pulling me close. I knew it was the prince before I turned my head up to see his pale blue eyes gazing down at me. His presence wasn't one to be forgotten quickly, even as fluid as I felt.

The circling vultures turned their attention from me to the royal, bowing in unison. "Your highness."

"Come now." He waved a pale hand at them to get up. "This is a party. There is no need to be so formal."

"What are you doing here?" I blurted out without thinking. The feel of his warm chest on my back caused tingles in my stomach that had nothing to do with the alcohol I had downed.

"Lady!" Gab gasped. "You can't speak to his highness that way. He may be UnSeelie..." she glanced up at the prince. "Pardon me, your highness." Then glared at me. "But he is still royalty."

"Of course." His understanding voice didn't match his hard eyes and the grip that tightened at my waist. The swirls that decorated the side of his face glowed briefly before his demeanor became playful.

"Please excuse Lady. She does not hold faerie wine well." He plucked the empty glass from my hand and shoved it into Jewels' hands. The blonde male pouted at the possessive hold the prince had on my waist. Not that I was particularly upset with the fact, but I was happy for an excuse to be away from the leering twin. The prince was right on time for once, and I found myself wondering what was in it for him.

A sense of relief passed over the group at my apparent inebriation. They were quick to accept my lack of knowledge was due to my drunken state and moved on to reminisce about their time with Chess. I opened my mouth to protest my ability to drink just as well as the rest when a large hand covered my mouth.

"I better get this spit fire some air before...." he trailed off as they all nodded in unspoken understanding.

Before what? Before I embarrassed him more? Before I made a fool of myself? Or before I lost my head to their ice bitch queen?

I let him usher me away from the group, my eyes taking in his clothes in an effort to keep the room from spinning. I was happy to find he was completely clothed, but a little out of place compared to the others. His previous dark clothing was gone, and in their place was a blood red poet shirt that had billowing long sleeves and opened at the neck. It was as sheer as my own, allowing me to finally confirm that the symbols did indeed run down his chest and into the top of the dark brown pants tucked into his knee-high boots.

"Hey, you don't match!" I laughed aloud at the discovery. Not a cute laugh, but a barking

'HA' that even in my inebriated state made me wince.

"Would you be quiet?" His voice was harsh in my ear as he led me to a balcony near the dais. His markings pulsated in an angry beat before leaving him with a teasing smirk on his face. "What could a silly thing like you be doing here?"

"What am I doing here?" What was I doing here? Wasn't I supposed to be looking for someone? I could really do with another one of those fruity drinks.

"What are you doing here?" I pointed a finger into his chest, falling over at the effort. "Oops." I giggled.

"I was invited. You, on the other hand, were not." The prince held onto my arms dragging me out the balcony doors.

My head was spinning so much I didn't know what was what. All I could think about was how good the prince smelled and how warm his arms were. I wondered what shampoo he used. Giggling at my own thoughts, I didn't know he had asked me a question until his fingers tightened on my arm.

"Ow! What was that for?" The pain helped clear my head as anger set in.

"Did you hear a word I said?" He growled, his eyes flashing dark blue.

I stared up at those ever-changing eyes. Those dark blue eyes reminded me of my time in the past. The way he had pressed against me as we kissed. My face heated at the thought. Did he remember that? Of course he did, but not with me. He thought I was that Lynne person. Had my trip there caused any damage to his timeline? There were too many unanswered questions, and they were making my head foggy again.

"Um, no." My eyes struggled to focus on his lips as they moved again.

"Do you know what will happen if someone finds out what you are?" His lips pressed together in a tight line.

My brow furrowed as I tried to think of what could happen, but all I could come up with was how thin his lips were. They were pressed together so tight they were almost nonexistent.

He gave a rough sigh when I didn't answer. "How did you even get in the Seelie Court in the first place?"

That answer I knew.

"Chess!" My voice echoed out into the darkness beyond the edge of the balcony. My voice shouldn't have echoed like that. I had the urge to yell out again to be sure it had, but I was more afraid someone would answer back than I was tempted.

For some reason my declaration caused the prince to pull me close and bury his face in my hair. My body tensed as his nose trailed along my skin. Inhaling deep, he cursed and shoved me away from him.

"Why does everyone keep sniffing me? Do I smell that bad?" My laugh caught in my throat as he brought his face close to mine again.

The blue of his eyes was so light they were almost translucent. He sniffed around my mouth. His eyes seemed to cloud over as the markings on his face gave an angry flash.

"You smell like that damn cat!" The dark prince growled deep in his throat. "I told you to stay away from him."

"You also said no Seelie Court," I reminded him, giving a girly giggle much to my horror.

"Obviously that was disobeyed as well, because here you are." He stared at me as if trying to see inside my brain. "Do you have a habit of causing trouble in your world as well, or is it just here?"

"Oh no, I'm chock full of trouble. Enough to go around." I swung my arms wide to emphasize but stumbled when I became dizzy.

"Well, it is no wonder his harem thought you were one of them." The jovial tone in his voice barely covered up the fury hiding in his eyes. The glyphs may have been able to change how the prince acted, but it couldn't stifle all of his personality. "What were you doing with that naughty cat to make you smell so?"

"What do you care?" Baffled by his sudden interest, I gripped his forearms in an effort to stay upright. All of the wine had caught up with me in a bad way. My whole world was spinning out of control, and the only way out was down. "Oh God, I'm going to be sick."

"Oh dear, oh dear." His dark hair fell over his face as he shook his head. "How much faerie wine did you drink?"

"Uh..." How much did I drink? At least two. Maybe three? I didn't drink often, but it shouldn't make me this drunk. "I don't know." I took deep breaths as I tried not to vomit all over the golden floor. "I lost count."

"Dammit, Kat." He rubbed a hand over his face and pulled me deeper onto the balcony.

"Not so fast." My feet stumbled as I tried to keep up with him.

My eyes widened as his large hands grasped my face between them, his lips hovered over mine. Was he going to kiss me? It would be my second kiss from him in less than an hour. My mother would have been so proud.

I fought the snorting laugh that threatened to spill out of my mouth as I let my eyes flutter close. I'm not the kind of girl, who would get involved with more than one guy, but the sting of finding out that Chess had a harem was still fresh and my befuddled mind only wanted to soothe it.

I waited for his lips to descend onto mine, but they never did. I peeked my eyes open when his thumb pressed down on my chin to open my mouth. Barely a sliver of space existed between our lips as he inhaled. When I exhaled, a glittery blue substance floated out of my mouth and into his.

What the hell?

The fog in my head lightened. The more substance he pulled out of me, the clearer my head became, and thankfully, my stomach settled with it as if I had never drank any of the faerie wine to begin with.

"What did you do?" I was grateful to be my sober self again but cautious as to why he was helping me. Mop had warned me about receiving help without expecting to pay for it later. The prince was the kind of Fae I really didn't want to owe.

"You, my dear Kat." His voice had gone soft, and his hand was still on my face as his thumb stroked my bottom lip. "Are human. Faerie wine is full of magic, which makes it far too strong for your little human body to handle. I simply took the magic away." He eyed me for a moment. "It is actually surprising you did not pass out after the first glass. Tell me, do you drink so heavily in your world?"

"Of course not!" I flinched as my voice came out louder than I meant. I glanced down at my feet, feeling foolish. "I got nervous. They were asking too many questions. Then they started talking about how everyone does it with Chess at one point or another and, I don't know." I shrugged. "It freaked me out."

"Why?" The prince chuckled. "Did you think you were special?"

"Well, no. I just thought–"

"What? The cat kissed you because he wanted you? Maybe even liked you?" I didn't like his condescending tone. He spoke to me as if I were a child that was thinking silly thoughts.

"I don't know, maybe." I wrapped my arms around myself to ward off his questions. I had thought I was special. That Chess had found something in me that he desired. Was that so wrong?

"Why else would he kiss me or stay behind to face the shadows while I got away if he didn't care for me?" I winced. I sounded desperate.

"Poor. Sweet. Kat." He punctuated each word while his hand trailed down the length of my hair, stopping to twirl a strand between his fingers.

What was with the touching?

"He only kissed you to cover up your stench. Your human odor would have given you away the moment you stepped into the ballroom." He brought the strand up to his nose, gazing up at me beneath long, thick lashes as he inhaled my scent.

It made sense, but it made my chest hurt. That was why Mop had sniffed the air before I entered the ballroom. Why Mags had decided I was one of Chess' play things after smelling me. Mop was right. Chess did always have another plan, even if that plan was to help me. But would I have to pay in return? I hoped not.

"Even if it's true, he didn't have to stay behind to let me get away." I jerked my hair from his grasp.

"Shadows don't care about him. He's nothing but a half-breed. Besides," he moved toward the balcony doors, "Chess can pass between worlds without a mirror."

"How's that possible?"

"He's a half-breed." He gave an impatient sigh when I frowned. "He is half-Seelie and half-UnSeelie. He does not belong to either court." His eyes watched the crowd as he talked, his shoulders tight as if he'd rather be anywhere but there. "He is not bound by the same rules."

"Is that why he has a full name and you don't?" I had wondered, but I hadn't had a chance to ask with all that was going on. Now that someone was offering up information, I wasn't going to waste the chance.

"I have a name." The glyphs flashed his irritation. "And it is quite rude to ask for a Fae's name. Only someone the Fae trusts completely would know it – like a parent or a spouse."

"But you know my name." I knew it was a stupid statement as soon as I said it. Of course he knew my name. I'd all but shouted it since I arrived.

"That is because you give it out too freely. Though, I have wished for the shadows to take you, it does not seem to have any affect. Another curiosity I have yet to figure out." His lips turned down into a tight frown, and I followed his eyes to where Gab was whispering to the White Queen. When the ice beauty locked her gaze on us, the prince turned to me, his hand outstretched. "Dance with me."

CHAPTER

DANCING & QUEENS

IT WAS MORE a command than a question. Usually I would have responded with a snarky remark or even a question, but I could feel the push of his Fae mojo pressing down on me. It wasn't as strong as it had been when I'd first met him. I didn't have the urge to throw myself at his feet and beg for mercy, but I couldn't stop it when the "Why?" on my lips morphed into a breathy, "Okay."

My hand slid into his, and before I knew it, I was on the dance floor with his arms wrapped around me. The press of his pheromones lessened and my anger flared to life, overpowering any nervousness I would have felt from dancing in public. Smart ass I was; dancer I was not.

"That's cheating. You could have asked." I fixed him with a scorching glare as the room spun around us. The many faces of the golden Fae blurred into one as he led me around the room. I focused my eyes on his left shoulder so I wouldn't become dizzy from the spinning.

"Would you have said yes?" He pressed me closer, his breath hot on my face.

"Well, no. Probably not, but it's still polite to ask." The anger in my voice lessened as I tried to ignore the feel of his body pressed against mine.

It was a formidable task. I'd have focused on making sure I didn't trip over my own feet, but since he was an accomplished dancer I couldn't use that as a distraction. Any other time I would have marveled at the feat, but I was neck deep in Seelie Fae and the only Fae I could worry about was the one before me making me feel weird emotions that were more terrifying than anything else in the room.

"I thought you weren't supposed to take things without permission? We didn't make a deal." I grumbled into his shoulder, trying to hide the way my heart pounded against my ribs.

The pressure of his magic slid across my skin as the dark-haired prince shifted his stance so he could look at me. The intensity in his gaze caused me to swallow hard. "For once in your mortal life, do not think, feel."

Oh, I felt it all right. It sizzled down my spine, along my heated skin, and settled deep in my stomach where it curled up and purred like a cat in a warm sunspot.

The music changed from a happy upbeat tone to a dark and sensual beat. It caused a tickling sensation that left me feeling both alive and breathless. The press of the prince's large hands against my waist and hand didn't help my ability to think straight, nor the zing I felt each time our bodies brushed against each other. I chanced a glance up to his face and smiled a little as his eyes flickered between light and dark. At least I wasn't the only one affected.

As he weaved us between the other dancers, I glanced away from his overbearing gaze to watch those around us. Some of them were too lost in each other to pay us any mind, but others openly stared at the redheaded girl dancing with the UnSeelie Prince. Their faces were full of curiosity and – hostility? The hostility wasn't directed at me, though. The disdainful glances and thinly veiled sneers were all for the dark prince holding me.

"Why are they looking at you that way?" I gripped his shoulder as if I could protect him from their animosity.

"Such concern for me now? How generous of you." The chuckle reverberated from his chest and into mine causing my face to heat.

I didn't care about him. Not really. It was just for curiosities sake and maybe for the fact that he was the only thing standing between me and a horde of Seelie Fae. If I kept telling myself that maybe it would be true.

"Is it because of Lynne?" I tried to take the focus off me but regretted the words when his entire form stiffened, stopping our promenade as he ripped himself away from me. Thankfully, his abruptness didn't seem to disrupt the other dancers. They simply stepped around us as if we weren't standing in the middle of a dance floor staring at each other.

"Where did you hear that name?" His eyes were full of an angry dark blue, his real eyes peeking through as the glyphs flared to life.

I realized my mistake as I stuttered for an answer, "Oh, you know. Around."

"You are lying." The prince grabbed my wrist in a pinching grasp. The teasing was gone from his face. Rage and suspicion poured out of him as his pheromones beat down on me, commanding me to tell him the truth.

"I'm not lying." I gritted my teeth against the urge to tell him where I'd really heard the name. I didn't think he would be too happy to know I was poking around in his past any more than he would be to know that I was the one he was kissing at that time.

"You are!" He growled, causing the dancers closest to us to pause in their dance. Seeing he was drawing attention to us, he pulled me back in his arms, keeping a tight but distant grip on me.

"I am not." I hissed at him, choosing to match his anger with my own, instead of giving in to the fearful pulse beating down on me.

He pulled me close as if to whisper naughty thoughts in my ear. "The only ones who know that name are the Seelie Queen, King, and myself. All other memories of it have been eradicated." His hand on my waist tightened further, bruising the skin beneath my sheer top. "So, either we missed someone, or you are not who you say you are."

I opened my mouth to protest but he cut me off, "And before you lie to me again. Know Fae do *not* make mistakes."

Eyes on anything but him I muttered, "I don't know what you are talking about. How can I be something that I'm not?"

"I do not know, but believe me when I say, I will find out." He grabbed my chin and forced my face to look at him. "You had best remember who you should be trusting here."

"And I can trust you?" I scoffed at the suggestion. I trusted him as much as I trusted that the tightness of his pants was causing some kind of neurological damage to his brain.

"Girl, here I am the only one you can trust. Their smiles are lies, and they will not hesitate to devour you in an instant." His voice lowered as the music stopped and the crowd around us opened up to reveal the Seelie Queen and Chess' harem.

Mags seemed uncomfortable to be there. Jewels wasted no time pinning me with a hungry leer, licking his chops like a wolf ready to eat his meal. Gab, on the other hand was the one I was most worried about. Her face was the definition of triumph. Nothing good would come from this interaction.

The dark prince didn't even bat an eye at them as he put a charming grin on his face. "Ah, your majesty, how can I be of service?"

"My darling Gab says that this is the half-breed's new playmate this moon." Her cool eyes washed over me, chilling me to the bone. "I swore she must have been mistaken because this is the mourning moon. If you do recall?" Her cold eyes locked with the prince's, causing him to tense up beside me.

"Of course, your majesty. How could I forget?" His voice held all the formality required of him, but his body gave away the building anger inside.

"Well, you do have issues with remembering items of importance." Her mouth curled into a cruel smile. "I believe that is the reason behind this celebration to begin with, is it not?"

"Yes, your majesty." I watched as his jaw clenched and the glyphs pulsed softly as if he was trying to control his rage.

"Now, now." The Queen patted the cheek with the glyphs. "Don't be cross." Her laugh stung like razor blades against my skin. "Not that you have a choice."

I gulped when she turned that cruel smile to me. I knew from the moment I saw her that I didn't want to be on her bad side. Too bad that didn't stick. I forced myself not to take a step back as her towering height loomed over me.

She bent at the waist so we were eye to eye. "Do you know what the mourning moon means, sweetness?"

"Uh..." My mouth became dry. "That we're in mourning?"

"Exactly!" She clapped her hands together pleased with my answer. "So tell me, why did you say you were the half-breed's toy this moon if this is the only moon in which he does not get a tribute?"

"But I didn't–" I blurted out. "I mean...that is to say." I pointed at the harem waiting eagerly at her back. "They assumed I was. I just didn't correct them."

"Oh?" Her eyes lit up. "And why is that, my dear?" She placed a long finger under my chin. "Could it be that you have something else to hide? Why would you smell like the half-breed, if not to disobey the rules?"

My eyes darted between the members of the group. Mags watched me with pity in her eyes. Gab was simply beaming at my lack of an explanation, reminding me why I didn't have girlfriends. Too many jealous bitches. I avoided the hungry gaze of Jewels and searched the crowd for something to inspire me.

Why did everyone think I was lying? Of course, I was up to something. I was trying to get home without being eaten, or worse date raped by Fae magic. My mouth opened and closed as I floundered for something, anything to satisfy the Seelie Queen.

"It was me."

All eyes jerked to the prince beside me. While I was relieved the attention was off me, I couldn't believe he would put himself in the line of fire for me. After the way Mop and Trip had described his sense of justice, he wasn't likely to be the one to take the fall, especially not for a human.

"What was you?" The Queen's words seemed more like a warning than a question.

"She was with me. Not the half-breed." His face formed a playful grin. "It has been a while, and the outskirts do get boring after a while. Am I not allowed my own play thing?" He slid an arm around my waist, his hand lying dangerously close to my butt. I didn't have a chance to react to his touch before the queen gave a vengeful cry.

"No you are not. Or did you forget that too?" She turned and addressed the watching crowd. "My children, hear me and be witness. The

UnSeelie Prince has once again caused offense to our court. Not only for his previous transgression, but to seek pleasure in the arms of one that is not his betrothed and on the anniversary of her demise."

The Queen's words stung my ears as the crowd gasped and shouted. The glittering room that was so full of merriment just moments ago was now full of anger and malice. My mind spun with questions.

The celebration was for the mourning of the prince's ex-betrothed, which apparently meant he was tied to her until death? What was he thinking? How was announcing me as his lover a good idea? I would have laughed at the complete disaster I was in if I wasn't so terrified of what the Queen was going to do next.

The prince stepped away from me and toward the Seelie Queen. "What could you do that you haven't done already? I am exiled from my own home. I am a slave to the courts and forced to be happy about it." The dark prince's rage pressed down on the room as he fought against the symbols influencing him.

"I have had to attend this gathering every year for decades." His voice filled with pain, the light coming from his face blinded the room from the force of his rage. "I lost her too, and I'm not even allowed to mourn her. So tell me, your majesty." He spit the words like venom. "What else could you possibly do?"

"Do?" The queen's voice was bitter and filled with sadness. Perhaps she cared more for the prince's pain than she let on. Then she seemed to remember herself as her eyes became hard again and found me once more. "I'm not going to do anything to you. Your companion, on the other hand, will get the same fate as the last one." She snapped her fingers in the air. "Guards! Seize her."

Two large gold-plated guards grabbed me by the arms before I could wonder where they'd come from. I pushed against their tight grip, my heart pounding in my chest. The manic look in the queen's eyes was all I needed to know of my fate even as her words sliced into my skin.

"Off with her head!"

CHAPTER

BOTH WAYS

MY MOTHER WOULD be horrified to see me in jail. A Fae jail, more of a dungeon really, but jail all the same. She wouldn't even question whether or not I was guilty, only that I was making her look bad. I could imagine exactly how that conversation would go.

"Katherine Marie, what am I supposed to say to the neighbors? How am I going to show my face on Sunday morning with all of them knowing I have a criminal for a daughter?" Her voice would start to have that screechy pitch to it whenever there was a threat to her public face.

"Who said you had to tell them?" I shot daggers at the floor of the cell, the cold stone biting into my hands where I sat.

"They're my friends. How can I not tell them?"

"Ha! Some friends." I snorted, rolling my eyes because she wasn't there to chastise me for it.

"You would understand if you'd leave the house more than to just go to work. Then maybe you would have more friends. Maybe that Ziegler girl? She seems nice."

"You only want me to go out with her brother." I wasn't naïve enough not to see through her schemes; years of experience had hardened me to that truth.

"So what? He's a good looking boy and a lawyer too!"

I scoffed. "You mean a bully."

There were only three items on my mother's checklist to make a good husband: a good job, good looks, and no scandals. The majority of the time I didn't know if I was talking to her or some character out of a Jane Austen novel. She was a poster girl for the 19th century. Not that she would know what that was.

"Now, Katherine, you don't know that."

"I do to. I...why am I even arguing with you, you aren't even here!" I jerked back, banging my head on the wall behind me. I closed my eyes and rubbed the sore spot. "No wonder everyone is crazy here. Much longer and I might not know where home is anymore."

"Talking to yourself, dear Kat?"

"Chess?" My eyes popped open at the sound of his voice.

There, peering through the bars of the cell door with an amused grin; was the delectable Cheshire S. Cat. I jumped up and raced over to the door. I was still mad at him, but it was a relief to see a friendly face.

"Hello, my lovely." He rolled his face against the edge of the window, looking very much like a real cat in that moment.

"What are you doing here?" I stood on my tiptoes to meet his gaze.

His head tilted sideways at my question. "To rescue you, of course."

Suspicion filled my eyes. I stepped back from the door and crossed my arms. "Why should I trust you? I'm only in here because of you."

"Now, is that any way to talk to your savior?" Chess moved out of sight, leaving me to stare at the door across the hall.

When he didn't poke his head back up after a moment, panic overcame me. "Chess?"

I grabbed the edge of the window and tried to peer out into the corridor. Did he leave me? I should have kept my complaints to myself. I turned back to my little cell, about to have a fit, when I saw Chess there lounging on the cell's little cot.

"Wha–? How?" I pointed between the door and the smug cat peering up at me.

"Besides, it's not my fault you got distracted," Chess continued as if he hadn't just appeared out of nowhere.

"How did you do that?"

Chess shrugged his bare shoulders. His previous ensemble had been switched out to a more golden variety, which of course, made him look even more delectable than before.

His pale pink hair hung loose over his shoulders, framing his shirtless chest. His array of belts was still wrapped around his waist, but his dark pants and boots had been replaced with ones almost identical to mine. Braided ropes wrapped around his bicep, tight enough to make his muscles bulge over them, that or his arms were more impressive than I had previously thought. I must have been staring for longer than I thought, because a growl rolled out from deep in his throat.

"What do you mean distracted?" I forced my eyes up to his and tried not to blush at the heat in his gaze.

"If you'd gone straight to Hatter like you were supposed to, you wouldn't have drawn any attention to yourself. I wouldn't have given you my scent if I had known you were going to blow it." His leering dimmed a bit at my failure.

"Fat lot of good it did me. Your play things sniffed me out." My eyes kept straying to his chest and the faint scars there. My fingers itched to touch them. To ask him how he had gotten them.

I glanced at Chess' face. His lips curled into a smile, the tips of his fangs peeked out over his lip. He knew exactly what affect he had on me. Gab's face popped into my head, reminding me I wasn't the only one who had his attention.

I balled my hands into fists and turned my face to the wall. Touching would be bad. No need to give him more ammunition to take advantage of me.

"Ah! You're jealous." Chess' excitement was abundant. I watched from the corner of my eye as he stalked his way over to me.

"I am not." I stared hard at the wall. "I just don't like being mistaken for one of your prostitutes." I tried not to shiver as his tail wrapped around my waist. The feel of it should have freaked me out, but I was slowly starting to expect it and even hoped for it a little bit.

"They are hardly prostitutes." His voice caressed my ear. "They come from noble families."

"High-end prostitutes, then." My heart jumped into my throat when his lips whispered down the curve of my jaw.

I let out a shaky breath as his clawed hands turned me to look at him. The feral glint in his eyes made me take a step back. And then another. The Fae mimicked each step I made until I found myself bumping against the hard stone of the cell.

"The guards will be here to check on you soon." His lips hovered over mine. "Wouldn't you – in your last moments – like to find out what all the fuss is about?"

"Um." My tongue felt heavy and clumsy in my mouth as I fought for an answer.

It was tempting. If our kiss was any indication of what it would be like with him – deep, wild and all consuming – I had no doubt that his lovemaking would be the same.

Though, I had never been a casual kind of girl, I had a feeling Chess only ever did casual. If that wasn't enough to deter me from accepting his offer, icy blue eyes attached to a dark head of hair popped into my mind. Those eyes were like a dose of cold water to my libido.

I turned my head so his lips brushed my cheek instead of completing the kiss. He pushed back from the wall, confusion and maybe a hint of hurt etched on his face. I almost apologized, but he recovered quickly, giving me his usual cheeky grin. Guess he wasn't that hurt after all.

"Enough dallying, let's get you out of here." He moved toward the door, his tail swishing behind him.

I stayed where I was against the cell wall and watched him approach the door. My eyes widened as Chess poked his head through the door. It reminded me of what the dark prince had said earlier about Chess not being bound by the same laws.

"What do you mediate exactly?"

"The worlds, of course." The green-eyed feline pulled himself back into the cell. Reaching down, he pulled a metal clip from his boot. "I'm what you'd call neutral." He popped his upper half back through the door.

"If you can pop though walls why do you need to pick the lock? Can't you just, I don't know, pop me through too?" I tried not to let my eyes focus on the swaying of his behind as he worked on the lock.

"It doesn't work that way, Kitty Kat." His tail's movements became more exaggerated as if he knew I was watching. "You belong to the human world. While I–" The lock clicked and Chess opened the door with a mischievous grin. "–can go any way I please."

"I just bet you do," I muttered as the thought of him and Jewels jumped into my head. "Don't you live in the UnSeelie Court, though? That's not very neutral."

"The willow is actually an extension of the Between. It doesn't exist in either court." He gestured for me to go to the right. "And only I can let anyone in or out."

Chess led me down the dimly lit corridor, passing several doors that were full of moans and groans. It was hard to tell if it was from pain or pleasure. For all I knew it could have been both. One room emitted a little squeak that was enough like Trip's to make me worry.

"Did you find Trip and Mop? Did they get captured too?" I grabbed Chess' shoulder; his skin was warm beneath my hand. "We have to save them."

"Don't worry that fiery little head of yours. They are safe and sound in my humble abode and awaiting your return. You, on the other hand, have a Hatter to get to." Chess' tail pushed me along the corridor.

"Won't the queen find out you were helping me?" I shoved a hand at the fur stroking my lower back. My refusal before apparently hadn't dissuaded him from trying his luck again.

Chess wrapped his tail back around his waist, and for the first time, his face showed irritation. "She will if you keep dawdling, Katherine."

"Hey! How do you know my full name?" I pointed an accusatory finger at him.

"I know quite a many things." He paused as we approached a split in the corridor. "Not all of them pleasant. Though, if you didn't want anyone to know, you shouldn't talk to yourself like no one is listening." His eyes searched around the corridor. "Someone is always listening. Now, if you are finished wasting time, I can hear the guards moving around above."

His ears twitched on his head as if listening to some noise I couldn't hear. "More than likely getting ready to remove that pretty little head of yours."

He turned down the right corridor with a little less swagger in his step. I supposed he couldn't be cheerful all the time. I wasn't in much of a cheerful mood myself. I was in a world I didn't know with people who could turn on me at any moment. No one at home knew where I was, and I doubted they'd be able to find me even if they knew I was missing.

Nothing was like I had read about. Even the White Queen was all backward. I thought taking people's heads for small offenses was only something the Red Queen would have done. Though, to her, I supposed it wasn't such a small offense. Not that I wasn't sympathetic to her loss, but I liked my head right where it was, and the thought of losing it didn't sit well with me.

I took a few big steps to catch up with him but stopped again when a small voice called out.

"Hello? Is anyone there?"

There weren't any doors down this way so it couldn't have been a prisoner. But both sides of the corridor were lined with curtain-covered frames. The majority of the curtains were brown and frayed, but some of them were vibrant red and blue. Did the different colors mean something or did they just run out of brown ones? I gave a curious glance at each of them, but I kept my distance in case something unwarranted jumped out at me.

I waited a few moments, straining my ears to find where the voice had come from. I almost walked to where Chess was waiting, tapping his foot with impatience when the voice called out again.

"Hello?" The voice came from behind one of the red-covered frames next to me.

I stepped up to the frame, observing the cloth covering it. The blood red cloth was thick enough to provide adequate coverage but thin enough that the embellishments on the frame bumped up beneath it.

I reached a hesitant hand up to pull the curtain back. My heart beat in my throat. This wasn't the beginning of a horror story at all. All that was missing was suspenseful music. And just as my hand was about to close around the cloth, a clawed hand captured mine, causing me to jump.

"You don't want to be doing that, Lady." Chess laced his fingers with mine and tried to lead me away, but I wouldn't be discouraged.

"Who's that?"

"No one of importance." He huffed, placing himself between the frame and me.

"Then why does it matter if I see or not?" I tried to glance around his shoulder, willing the curtain to let me see the contents of the frame.

"Is anybody there?" The voice was feminine and low as if they were trying not to be heard. "It's so lonely in here. Please help me."

"Chess." I placed my hands on my hips giving him my best stubborn stare. "I'm not leaving this spot until I see what is in there."

"Believe me, Lady." Chess placed a hand on my own. "Anyone who is in there deserves it."

"Like I deserved to lose my head?"

"This..." He gestured to the hallway filled with cloth-covered frames. "...is the Hall of Mirrors. This is where all the very naughty Fae are kept."

"Oh." Well, that changed things. I couldn't imagine leaving someone asking for help, but I also didn't know what kind of Fae could warrant them a place like the Hall of Mirrors. For all I knew it could be a trap. I let myself be led away when the voice cried out again.

"But I'm not a Fae! I'm human!"

"What?" I jerked my arm away from Chess. He cursed and tried to grab at me.

It was too late. I had already gotten ahold of the curtain and was yanking it free. The red silken cloth fluttered to the ground like liquid fire and revealed someone I'd never thought to see.

CHAPTER

HALL OF MIRRORS

THE MIRROR WAS square and surrounded by an iron frame. Even in the dim lighting, I could make out the swirling glyphs, similar to the ones on the rabbit hole and on the prince's face. The mirror didn't reflect my face or the dungeon behind me. The surface was filled with an inky black substance, which surrounded the person inside. If I hadn't already been searching for her, I probably would have never been able to tell who it was.

"Alice," I breathed out.

Or what I thought was the head of Alice. Her long blonde hair floated around her as if she were submerged in water. A dull, blue bow still adorned her head, though it was a little worn around the edges. Pretty marble blue eyes gazed out at me from the grown up face of the beloved childhood heroine.

"Yes, that's my name. Alice Liddell." Her voice tinkled like little bells full of innocence.

I turned to Chess, bewilderment on my face. "How is this possible? The book came out in 1865. She should be dead, but she looks to be younger than me!"

"Well, I'm certainly not dead. I'm right here talking to you, aren't I?" Alice's brow furrowed. "Unless I am dead and this is my punishment for running away so often. Mother must be so worried."

Worry etched her pale face for a mere second before she beamed at me. "But the tea party was such fun! We would laugh and eat. Oh and the rhyming! I love the rhyming, though, I can't think of any rhymes right now. I really should go visit them again."

Alice looked to Chess with a pout, her eyes lingered on him longer than I liked. "Can I come out now? I promise to be good. I would like to say goodbye before I have to be home for supper."

Suspicion began to inch onto my face as I watched Chess shift in place, clearly uncomfortable with the young woman's pleas.

"Chess?" I prompted him to answer her. I wanted to know myself. Why would she ask him?

"It's not my decision. I didn't put her here."
He crossed his arms and turned his eyes to the
end of the corridor. No doubt keeping an eye
out for the guards he heard earlier.

"Then whose is it?"

"The one who put her here, I just said that,"
the feline growled, his eyes still on the hallway.
"Don't you want to know why she is here? In
the part of the dungeon meant for the worst of
the Fae? The ones not even trusted enough to
be cast out to the Shadow Realm?"

"But she's not Fae. She's human!"

How could they do this to their own people?
It was inhumane. I couldn't imagine being
stuck in a mirror with no one to talk to, no way
to tell the time or day. It would make anyone a
little mad.

"Yes, I'm human. I don't belong here!" Alice
echoed me. Her head bobbed up and down
from inside its frame.

Chess' eyes flashed with the first hint of
anger. "She's no more human than I am."

"What do you mean?" Why was he so mad?
Did Alice touch a nerve somewhere in the
teasing feline? I had so many questions and
every answer brought on more.

"Alice, as you've pointed out, is quite older
than she looks." He finally made his way to the
frame, his eyes trained on Alice's face. She
stared back at him, the picture of perfect
innocence. "But what Alice forgets to mention

is that she has been with us for a long time. Longer than I have been the mediator that is for sure. Haven't you, Alice?"

"Have I? Perhaps I have, it is a little difficult to tell time in here." Sarcasm dripped from her words, making her seem much older than I thought before.

Was I a fool to be tricked so easily? I should have learned by now that not everything was as it seemed, and sometimes it was even worse. But my poor judgment aside, something was still bothering me.

Mop had implied many times that Alice had lost her head. Was this what he meant? A collection of heads incased in mirrors seemed creepy even for Fae standards. At least the little standards that I knew they had.

I turned to Chess and questioned, "Why keep their heads?"

"She's not just a head." Chess scoffed and gestured to the mirrors along the wall. "The head is all you're able to see. You could think of it as a window into her cell."

"So there's more of her?" I craned my neck to try to see around her, but all I could see was blackness.

I had already learned nothing good came out of the darkness. The creeping whispers that resided in the edges of the light promised horrors beyond even my imagination. But from the laughter coming from my flirtatious savior, it couldn't be all bad.

"Of course there is more of her. Do you think we just cut off people's heads?" A slight gleam of amusement glittered in his green eyes.

"Well, yeah." I shrugged. "When they said you'd lose your head I thought it was literal."

How could I not think that when everything there was taken so literally? How was I supposed to know the rules if everyone kept changing the game? I needed a 'Hitchhiker's Guide to the Underground.'

"Not so." Chess stepped up to the glass of the mirror tapping it with a claw, causing Alice to flinch back and cry out in protest. "The inside of the mirror resides in another realm."

"Another realm? I thought there was only the three?"

"There are, aside from the human world. Think, Lady." He tapped the side of my head, causing me to wince and swat at him. "Where would the Fae put their trash so no one will find it?" The words sounded bitter coming from his mouth.

Once again I had the urge to ask Chess about his past. Why was he the mediator? If he was half-Seelie and half-UnSeelie, where were his parents? Why did he have scars all along his chest? So many questions to ask and not one of them easily answered. But one of my questions he had already answered.

"The Between."

"Brains and beauty. A terrifying combination." Chess flirted but his heart wasn't in it.

"But the Between I saw didn't look like any of this." I gestured to the empty space around Alice's head. "What I saw was all white and empty and went on and on."

"Exactly." Chess tilted his head, the silken strands of his pale pink hair spilling over the side of his face. I had to clench my fists to keep myself from running my fingers through it. "You are still thinking like a human and not like one of us."

"What do you mean?" I asked, distracted by the magnificence of his hair. My own tangled mop would never cascade like that. I found it hardly fair that a cat had better hair than me, Fae heritage aside.

"You are thinking of the Between as something tangible, as a place you can mark on a map and be done with it. It is everywhere and nowhere all at once." He held his hands out, bobbing them up and down to illustrate his point.

"But that doesn't make any sense." I knew it was a stupid statement the moment it came out of my mouth. When had any of this made any sense?

"Of course it does. When traveling between worlds there is a line you have to cross that melds one world into the other. That is the Between." He gestured to the contents of the mirror.

"So the area with the doors, before I entered the Underground, was the Between that separates the human world from the others?"

"Right again, my pet." He smiled, gesturing for me to continue on my thought.

"So then your home, the willow tree, is the Between that separates the Seelie and the UnSeelie?" My brow furrowed in confusion. "Where in the Between is Alice then?"

At that moment Alice piped in, terror making her voice quake, "They whisper in the dark, such horrible suggestions. All the things they want to do to me if only I would let them in."

"The shadows," I whispered, barely loud enough to be heard. Who knew if they were listening? I didn't want to take the chance.

"They know what you fear the most, what will make you scream and quiver." Alice's eyes filled with tears. "I didn't mean to do it. I swear. It was an accident. Please don't let them get me!"

"It would serve you right," the feline growled at the sobbing head, all teasing cast aside. "You wanted to be Fae, and you got it. I'd think you'd be a little more grateful."

"What's the point of living forever if I'm stuck in here?" Pretty tears glistened on her face. I had never cried so pretty.

"That's not my problem. And we have dallied enough. Let's go, Lady." Chess stuck his nose in the air, turning on his heel to go further down the corridor.

"Chess, we have to let her out," I called out to him. "Nothing could be bad enough for this kind of torture. We don't even use the death penalty in my world anymore and that was reserved for serial killers."

"How do you know she didn't kill anyone?" Chess turned back to me. "Or worse? Would you just let them all go without a thought to why they were put here to begin with?"

"Well, no." I frowned. "But some of them have to be innocent. After all, the White Queen was going to put me in one of these."

"White Queen?" Chess held his stomach as he laughed. "Oh, she would love that. Believe me, Lady, her majesty is anything but pure."

"I didn't say she was pure. I am only speculating on what I see and what I know of the original story. But if the White Queen is as horrible as all that, I can't imagine the Red Queen would be any better. Or would that make her the nice one? Everything is so backward from the *Alice in Wonderland* I know."

"People talk about me? What do they say?" Alice's blue eyes gleamed at the prospect of her popularity; all thoughts of the shadows were gone from her voice. How much of what she had said was real, and how much of it was just to get sympathy for her case?

"Why can't they just put them in a regular cell?" I ignored the blonde in the mirror. "It can't be safe to have them so close to the shadows. What if they attack them?"

"What makes you think they aren't already?" A cruel gleam sparkled in his eyes.

The look on his face was like a punch to the gut. Was he really just as cruel as the rest? It was hard to believe it to be true, but then again, I'd only known the feline for a few hours. How was I to know what was real and what was all for show?

"But Alice is right here talking to us." I gestured to the girl pouting at being ignored. "If she has been in there as long as you say, shouldn't they have attacked her by now?"

"If you are starving what do you eat if you can't have your first option?" His fangs gnashed against his lower teeth.

I gulped at the sight. All thoughts of his mouth ever going near my body were gone in an instant. "You mean to say they are feeding on their dreams? But isn't that cannibalism? If Fae feed on the dreams of humans, I would think the dreams of Fae would hardly be a meal. Besides, you can't just live off of the dreams of mortals. I saw lots of them eating and drinking at the mourning party."

"Feeding on other Fae is not the same as feeding on a human. It's like you are permanently on a diet. Just enough to survive, but not enough to satisfy the hunger." His voice rumbled as if thinking of more than just food.

"What's the point in feeding them if you are trying to get rid of them?"

"Fae are immortal. Food and drink is more of a want than a need. We can't starve to death; it is harder than you think to kill one of us." Chess frowned. "You have to remember they used to be one of us until they were cast out. It is hard for us to kill one of our own, even if they are evil. The only way to keep them from overtaking our worlds was to provide them with an alternative to feed on."

He glared up at the girl in front of us. "And we wouldn't need to do that if someone hadn't ruined it all."

"I told you I was sorry!" Alice cried out, but her face didn't show an ounce of remorse. "I didn't know what I was doing. It's not my fault you Fae are so secretive about everything. You are a cat. You should know how tempting it is to discover the truth."

"Curiosity has never plagued this cat, that's for sure. I know when to keep my nose out of it." He sniffed, pointing his nose in the air.

"I didn't know what I was doing, or what it would do to the rest of the worlds," Alice pleaded with the feline. "I was only trying to help!"

"Help? Chess, what is she talking about?" My frown deepened as I took in their exchange.

"Now don't give me that 'I didn't know' nonsense." Chess brushed my question off, continuing to chastise the bobbing head. "You knew exactly what you were doing. They didn't need your help, and you butting in only made the situation worse."

"It always worked in books. She was supposed to get jealous and admit her feelings to him, not go commit suicide!" Alice scoffed.

"Who committed suicide?" I glanced between the two but was ignored again.

"That's the problem with mingling with humans. You always forget we are Fae, not human. We don't respond the same way to emotions as you do." Chess finally glanced my way as if I were to blame.

"I know that now." Alice huffed. "You bunch are stubborn and arrogant to the end. It's always a competition of who cares more. You can't just tell someone you fancy them and be done with it."

Her blue eyes turned to me in warning. "Be careful you don't make the same mistake in trusting them to be reasonable, or you'll end up in here too."

"Why are you telling me?" I crossed my arms and tried to look haughty. She couldn't know I was a human, could she?

"I might be a little crazy, but I'm not stupid." She rolled her eyes. "I know very well what you are and how you got here. It may have been a long time ago, but I haven't forgotten." Her eyes became sad and distant. "Not much to do but remember here."

"If they are feeding off your dreams, why aren't you dead yet?"

"It not like they are physically injuring us. It's like a piece of our souls are being eaten away one tiny piece at a time. It is quite a long process." She glanced off to the side as if she were examining her nails.

"Wait a second." I put a hand up. "You are telling me that you guys are torturing them to appease the shadows? That's barbaric!"

"Hardly! It's survival. We could just kill them all and be done with it. This way they are giving back to their community. Besides," he gestured at the other frames, "this saves so much more space, don't you think?"

I wanted to punch the stupid grin off his face. I kept forgetting that I was dealing with Fae and not humans. Giving back to the community he said. Ha. It was torture. Didn't they have any compassion for their fellow Fae? Apparently, not.

"That's not funny." I placed my hands on my hips and glowered at him. We humans had to stick together. Never mind that Alice didn't constitute as human anymore.

"I agree. As one of those sacrifices, it is neither amusing nor practical." Alice poked her lower lip out in a pout.

I began to ask her how long she had been in there when I heard shouting coming from the direction Chess and I had come from. The guards. They had found my empty cell.

"Time to go, Lady." Chess grabbed my hand, trying to lead me away from the mirror.

"Wait!" I yanked my hand back. "What about the key? Mop said I needed a key to get to the orchard. And Alice," I pointed at the startled face, "has it."

"Key?" Her blue eyes lit up. "You mean the faerie key?"

"Uh, sure." I didn't know what the faerie key was, but Mop said she had a key so that must be it. Besides, how many keys could she possibly have?

"I have it right here with me." She rummaged around somewhere inside the mirror. "Ah! Here it is." She gazed off to the side at something we couldn't see. There was no way of knowing if she had the key or not. Not without being in her cell.

"Great. Can I borrow it?" My eyes darted to the corner we had come from, expecting the guards to be on us at any moment. I so didn't want to get caught and thrown in one of those mirrors. I wouldn't last one day being syphoned on by the shadows.

"Well, of course you can." Her face scrunched up, frowning at the mirror. "The mirror does pose a problem, though."

"Hurry up, my pet." Chess gave my hand an anxious tug.

I glared at his impatience. Couldn't he see this was my chance? I couldn't go home without that key. Finding Alice had been a Godsend. I could skip the whole step of finding Hatter just so he could tell me she was here in the dungeon. But how was I supposed to get the key from her without having to go into the cell myself? I didn't want to get anywhere near the Shadow Realm if I could help it.

I spoke what I had been thinking aloud, "How do we get you out?"

"Like the cat said, only the one who put me in can let me out." Her voice took a condescending tone. So much for playing the innocent victim.

At that moment, a triad of guards spilled around the corner. One of the guards spotted us in an instant and pointed a finger in our direction. Fuck.

"There she is! Stop her!"

"No time for pleasantries, kitty Kat." My rescuer pulled me away from the mirror and toward the end of the hall.

"But what about the key?" I gasped, trying to keep up with him. If I'd known I'd be running from more than my lack of social life I would have bought that treadmill my mother suggested.

"It's not going anywhere." Chess led me up a flight of stairs, stopping in front of a metal door. He didn't open it immediately but stood there as if waiting for something.

"What are you waiting for? Open it."

"I can't." He reached out to touch the handle, but then pulled away with a hiss as if it burned. "Iron hurts Fae."

"Of course it does." I moved past him and grabbed the handle, not expecting the tingling heat I got in return. Ignoring it, I shoved the door open. We spilled into the golden hallway as the guards hit the stairs. I slammed the door, trapping the cursing guards behind it.

I stood there trying to catch my breath as my other hand nursed a stitch in my side. The first thing I was doing when I got home was joining a gym. My stomach growled in protest. All right, the second thing.

I gave a cursory glance down at the hand that had opened the door. A pale pink, almost red rash had spread across it as if the iron door had caused some kind of allergic reaction.

Curiouser and curiouser.

Putting the mystery that was my hand aside for later, I glanced down both sides of the corridor in search of an exit. Unlike the first time I stepped into the Seelie Court, there weren't any tables or decorations of any kind.

Why did everything look the same? One could easily get lost in here. Seeing as it was where the door to the dungeon was, I imagined it was exactly what they wanted to happen.

"Which way?" I glanced down both of the identical halls.

"This way." Chess headed down the right side, his tail swayed behind him as if he hadn't just been running from the guards.

It was getting hard to keep up with the emotional rollercoaster that were the Fae men. The women I understood. They were all perpetually pissed off by one thing or another, but the men didn't seem to know how they felt. It had to make that time of the month a frightening experience for everyone around.

The hall was quiet. We didn't see guards or any other Fae as we made our way down the corridor. Maybe the reason there weren't any guards was because they knew there was no way out. It wasn't a settling thought.

With no guards on our heels, it made me worry that perhaps they were stuck in the dungeon too. Certainly they had a way to communicate with those above? The White Queen wouldn't leave them down there. Would she?

"Don't worry, they'll get out." Chess spoke up as if he read my thoughts.

"How did you know I was worried?"

"You get a crinkle between your brow right here." He stroked a finger between my eyebrows. As usual, the gesture was more sensual than it really needed to be. "When you are thinking too hard."

"You don't know me well enough to have figured that out yet." I crossed my arms under my breasts, causing them to push up, and Chess' eyes to wander down to them. I quickly dropped my arms back to my side with a slight blush.

"I don't have to. Anyone could have figured it out if they paid enough attention." He stopped in front of a mirror that was similar to the one in his house and turned to me, leaning in close with a smile on his lips. "And I pay *very* close attention."

"Or I just think too much." I leaned back from him, so I couldn't breathe in his scent.

The big feline gave a masculine chuckle. The sound swept through me making my toes curl. He slid a claw down the side of the mirror, activating it. The surface rippled and gleamed like quicksilver.

"After you, Lady." He swept his arm low in a bow, pretending to be the gentleman he wasn't.

"Where are we going?" I stepped up to the mirror but didn't go through. "I need that key, you know."

"You'll get your key, but first, we have to see Seer." Chess laughed at his own pun.

I gave him a flat look. Everybody thought they were a comedian. It was hardly the time for jokes.

"And the seer will help us get Alice out?"

"Among other things." Chess gave me a mysterious smile.

I frowned at him. I didn't like that smile. It meant he was keeping secrets from me, either for some mysterious agenda, or his own amusement.

"Come, come now, my peach." He placed a clawed hand at my waist. "Have I ever steered you wrong?"

"Not yet, but the night is still young." It sounded cynical even to me. Had I always been like that or was it another result of being in the Underground?

Nah. It was just me.

I stepped into the mirror, the silver surface caressed me like an old friend. I wondered how the mirrors worked. How did it know where to go? Did Chess have to just think about it and it knew, or were there more mirrors spread throughout the Underground? Did certain ones only go to certain areas? I tried to turn back to ask him, but the liquid kept me on a fixed path forward.

No going back now.

CHAPTER 14

DREAMS & SATYRS

I STEPPED OUT of the mirror expecting to be back in the willow tree, but instead found myself back in the green hedges where I had first met the UnSeelie Prince. My eyes scanned the area taking in the little alcove surrounded by thriving hedges that stood at least ten feet tall. The hard cobblestone beneath my feet was broken and cracked. A potential tripping hazard, especially with the ridiculous boots Chess had dressed me in.

Somewhere off in the distance was the sound of water falling. It wasn't loud enough to be a waterfall, but unless there was a stream flowing through the middle of the maze, which was easily possible, it was probably some kind of fountain. Music blended with the sound of falling water.

It sounded like it was coming from some kind of pipe instrument. The tones were deep and probing as if they were trying to find out who was listening. I could feel them deep in the pit of my stomach. It was a little unsettling.

Ignoring the music for a moment, I turned back to the mirror. My reflection was the only image visible in its surface. The cool, solid glass pressed against my fingertips as I touched it.

Where was Chess? Had he gotten caught? Or did he expect me to go at it alone? Didn't he say *we* needed to find the seer? I glanced around the small enclosed area and realized how utterly alone I was.

Since the beginning of this adventure I'd always had someone beside me leading the way. I prided myself on being independent, on never needing anyone to take care of me, but here in this unfamiliar place, I wanted someone beside me. I never would have guessed I would miss my reluctant companions until this moment. I'd have given anything to hear Mop complaining about what a nuisance I was or Trip clinging to me as if I were his only friend.

But they weren't there. I was on my own. I could either wallow in it or move forward like I had always done.

The problem was I didn't know where to go. I needed to get the key from Alice, and to do that I had to find the seer. Whoever that was. I didn't even know where to start. I could get lost in the hedge maze forever and never be any closer to finding the seer. How did I find someone by name alone?

The music from the pipes changed from searching to urging. It urged me forward to find it. My feet began to move.

I gritted my teeth, digging my nails into my hands as I tried to stop myself from moving. But the music became more persistent. It whispered inside my head.

If I found it, I wouldn't be alone. Someone had to be playing the music, and I could ask them where the seer was. It was a good idea. It was even a rational idea, but it wasn't the asking that was the problem. It was the thought of who could be behind that music. If they could make me come to them just from the sound of the pipes, then what else could they do?

Unfortunately, I didn't have any other ideas at the moment. The urging had become annoyingly insistent, like a buzzing in my ears, but I was able to keep my feet firmly planted where they were. After a few moments, the player seemed to give up as if I wasn't worth the hassle.

Of course, now that I was free to decide for myself, I wanted to know who was trying so desperately to get me to come to them. I hoped they were willing to help me find my way. Happy with my plan, I exited the alcove and headed north toward the sound of the pipes.

The green walls of the maze became a blur with each turn I took. Besides the occasional opening, every wall and pathway looked the same. The next turn left me staring at a dead end.

Growling at the wall, I plopped down on the stone floor. I could hear the sound of the pipes on the other side of the dead end, just a gigantic hedge away from me. I wanted to lean back against the hedge, but a flash back to a particular movie, where the foliage ate people kept me at a cautious distance. I settled for laying my head on my knees, and I tried to think of a plan.

The music became a soothing melody. It made me think of swaying palm trees and swinging hammocks. The night's adventure began to weigh on me. My eyes felt heavy and threatened to close at any moment.

It'd been well past nine o'clock when I left my house. I felt like I'd been in the Underground for days, when in fact, it had probably only been a few hours. My body told me it was well past my bedtime, not that I could tell by the sky.

Time must work differently in the Underground than at home. There was no sun for me to calculate the time, but the short time I had been in my cell had been enough for the sky to brighten to blue again. I wished I'd had the forethought to grab my phone before I left, then I could at least tell the time.

I glanced down at the ground and pondered how safe it would be to take a nap here. At least I was somewhat hidden away from view. I didn't want to be out in the open and wake up inside somebody's stew.

I wasn't sure what to do next. I couldn't get to the person playing the music. I didn't know how to get out of the maze, and it didn't look like anyone was going to save me anytime soon. Not that I needed saving. Maybe if I just laid here for a minute something would come to me.

I lay back on the hard stone, the coolness sinking through the thin material on my back. Staring up at the sky, I wished there were some kind of clouds to watch float by. My eyes grew heavier with that thought. I vaguely remember the hedges behind me starting to shudder. My eyes fluttered open and then closed, and then there was nothing.

I WAS DREAMING. I don't know how I knew I was dreaming. It felt more real and vivid than the hard stone I had fallen asleep on.

The dark forest lay before me. I was in the clearing where Hatter's tea party cackled and writhed, except this time there was no laughter or rhyming Fae creatures obsessed with tea. The table lay barren. The seats empty and table cleared. Only the ripped and stained tablecloth remained. How that made any sense was beyond me, but then again, this was my dream.

It seemed so long ago – a lifetime ago – that I had been sitting at that table watching them fight over the tea that may or may not have been drugged. I recalled Bat's gleaming eyes as he ruined each and every ploy his companions tried to use.

Back then; the creatures of the forest, the ones that hid in the shadows, had frightened me. But now in my dream state I relished in them. I stifled the laughter building up my throat as they whispered to me.

"Hurry, before he catches you."

That's right, I was running; running from someone.

My skirt swished around my ankles, the weight of it heavy against my waist. The sleeves of the dress wrapped around my arms left my neck and shoulders bare to the night air. With every step I took the bushes and branches blocking the way seemed to clear a path for my slipper-covered feet. My heart beat a rapid cadence in my chest, but not from fear. It was excitement. As if it was all a game. The point wasn't to get away but to be caught.

Running past Hatter's Tea party and into the woods beyond, I dashed behind a large tree. I pressed my back against its base as I tried to catch my breath. My chest heaved up and down, pressing my breasts up against the pale blue top of my gown.

I could hear him now. His footsteps were heavy on the ground, even though I knew he could be quiet as a mouse if he wanted to be.

"Come out. Come out wherever you are." His voice was filled with a dark promise of events to come, the kind no one dared speak of in polite circles. The ones only lovers did in the cover of night. I wanted what he promised. My blood thrummed in my ears, adrenaline pumped in my veins, and my body ached for it.

Time stopped as he approached my hiding spot. I held my breath, waiting for him to find me. I wanted him to find me. The thrill of it made the blood in my veins pound deliciously against the surface. My thighs pressed together at the thought of what he would do when he found me, of what we would do.

He made a small sound of pleasure, no doubt smelling the difference in my scent. Did he want me as much as I wanted him? Did I make his palms sweat? His heart race? His scent, like his face, never gave away his true feelings. The only way I would know for sure was if I were to come out and face him.

The last thought wasn't my own. He was projecting into my head, trying to get me to give in to him. But that wasn't part of the game. It was a match of wills.

Whose was stronger? Who could last the longest? I couldn't give in so easily. I couldn't be the first one to admit it, even if my body betrayed me.

"You can't hide forever, my love." His words were a deep caress beneath my skin that settled low in the pit of my belly.

He was closer now. On the other side of the tree. I was sure of it. I could probably reach my hand around and touch him if I wanted to. And I did. I wanted to touch him more than anything in the Underground, but I couldn't be the one that started it.

It had to be him.

He didn't though. He didn't move from his spot on the other side of the tree, the only barrier between us. There always seemed to be something between us: politics, people, and realms. Something always got in the way, but not tonight. Tonight it was just us.

"Who's hiding?" My voice was a soft whisper, though I knew he could hear me. I closed my eyes and leaned my head against the tree, angling it to the side, listening. Would he make the first move? Did he know he was supposed to?

After what felt like an eternity, he breathed against my neck, "I found you."

His hands slid around my waist as he brought my body in line with his. The swell of my breasts pressed against the hard plains of his chest. My eyes fluttered open to look up into the dark blue eyes set in an unblemished face.

They were darker than usual, almost so black that the pupil swallowed the iris. It could have been because of the night shadows, but I knew it was from something far more primal. If I had had a mirror, I was sure my own face would have shown the same look.

I kept my hands against the tree, not daring to touch him back. My eyes flicked from his gaze to his mouth and back. I moistened my lips with my tongue. His eyes fixated on the movement. A single clip held back his dark hair but threatened to slip free as he angled his face to mine. His face hovered above mine, teasing me with his lips, just a breath away from kissing me.

The forest's occupants quieted their whispers. Their urgings became a held breath in the wind, waiting for someone to break and close that final space.

I'd like to think he moved first, but in all honesty, I think we both did. My fingers tangled in his dark tresses, pulling his mouth closer to mine. There was no pretending anymore. Nothing keeping me from showing him how much I needed him. We melded our mouths together as if we were trying to climb inside the other.

Eventually, when kissing wasn't enough, he lifted me up by my thighs, pressing my weight into the tree's base. I came up from the kiss gasping at the new sensation of him pressed hard between my legs. Our bodies began to rock against each other, slow and building until heat radiated from where our bodies met through the material of our clothes.

His eyes locked with mine before he pulled the bodice of my dress down, exposing my chest to his hungry gaze. Moving his eyes from mine, his mouth fell on the flesh there and was hot against my skin. I cried out against him, the pleasure building up until my body began to quake.

"Close," I whispered into his hair while breathing in the smell of him. He smelled dark and rich, like a triple-shot mocha latte, and I couldn't drink him up fast enough. As if reading my mind, he lifted his face to mine and captured my lips in another searing kiss.

Keeping our mouths locked, he moved and slid a hand between us to unfasten his pants, causing me to make a small sound of objection in my throat. His other hand took the brunt of my weight. I wrapped my legs around him to help ease the effort, not caring that we were out in the open and had an audience. All I could think about was how I needed more skin.

Before long, my gown was around my waist, and he was deep inside me. The bark of the tree bit into my back as we moved with swift determination, each of us seeking our own pleasure. The sounds of our lovemaking echoed through the forest, our audience quiet with anticipation.

I could feel it as it built in the air. Not the pleasure that flowed through our bodies, but something more tangible. It made the air thick and heavy as if it were a swelling, pulsating organ ready to burst at any moment.

Magic.

Our coming together was nothing short of spectacular, and the Underground responded by opening itself up just as I had opened myself to him. My gaze found his, awe reflected in his eyes. Each stroke made the magic press against our flesh, making each movement, each touch, more intense. It pushed until I was once again on the edge and couldn't hold back any longer.

My legs tightened around him as I cried out. His voice echoed mine. It had been what the magic was waiting for. It gushed over us in a tidal wave of energy, alighting each nerve from the very ends of my hair down to the tips of my toes.

When we caught our breath we glanced at each other and laughed. We were high on the feel of each other's skin and even more so on the pulse of magic still clinging to us. Who knew such a thing would happen? We certainly didn't.

He adjusted his grip slightly, getting ready to put my feet back on the ground no doubt, but that slight friction was all the magic needed to push against us again. In that moment we weren't spent anymore, we were ready and willing to go again and again. If that was what it wanted.

Now I'm not against multiple orgasms in one night, let alone ones that are the result of a dark dream fantasy, but when the magic built us up again for the third time, making what was a leisurely, pleasurable act into a painful frantic need, I knew something was wrong.

I pulled my mouth away from his, tightening my grip on his hair to keep it that way. He didn't even pause or open his eyes to question me. His hips just kept moving in the tantalizing rhythm I had come to fear.

"No. Stop." My voice sounded distant and echoed in the dark forest but was completely ignored by my fantasy prince.

My mind fought against the need, even as I reached that edge again. I tried to drop my legs to keep my hips from moving with his, but I was frozen in a dance that wouldn't end until the magic released me, or I broke the dream.

Since I didn't believe for one second they would just let me go, I tried to think of something else. Anything else that would douse the flame inside me. Meat-jelly sandwiches. Moss-covered gnashing teeth. Mrs. Jenkins wearing a golden string bikini.

The last thought made me shudder and the blood in my veins began to cool, but the sound of a pipe playing in the distance surfaced in my brain. I focused on that sound, pushing at it with my new control. I didn't drift out of my dream as much as I got ripped from it.

My body still throbbed where the prince had been. I could feel my clothing, what little of them there were, pressed against my heated flesh. The music I'd heard in my dream had long since stopped, and in its place was the sound of a male voice chattering around me.

My mind was still a bit garbled from my dream, even as my brain began to panic, though a small part of me wished I had stayed with the blue-eyed UnSeelie prince.

What was up with that anyway? If I was going to have a fantasy about anyone I would have thought it would be Chess. Not the prince, who besides a tension-filled dance and a heated kiss, had been a pain in my ass from the get go. I was never going to be able to look him in the face again.

"Shut up, stupid! You're going to wake her up!" The gravelly voice smacked the other male, and was followed by a languid, "Sorry."

I groaned and shifted, finding my arms pulled taut above my head and my legs spread out to either side. My panic began to build into full out hysteria. Oh, fuck. Oh, fuck. What do I do? What do I do!

"Now see what you did," the first voice chastised the other. "Don't struggle. You'll just make it worse for yourself." He tsk'd, his warning doing nothing to pacify me. "You should have stayed asleep. Enjoyed your little fantasy. You would have missed this whole part."

I forced my sleep-encrusted eyes open and screamed at the creature staring down at me. It was a satyr, nearly seven feet tall. His broad shoulders and bulging pectorals did nothing to hide the fact that he was naked, save for the fur covering his legs and hooved feet. His chocolate brown hair was pulled back in a tight ponytail. The same hair trailed across the edges of his jaw and chin. His human face was attractive in the strong, Adonis kind of way, but the black lust-filled eyes beating down on my visible skin was as much of a turn off as the protruding horns on his head.

"Please don't scream. I have a hard time performing when a woman screams." His voice was smooth and buttery. Very gentlemanlike as if he had just stated the time of day. It was nothing like the one before, which meant someone else was there, hiding from my view.

I tried to glance around to see where the other voice was but could only see the hulking monstrosity blocking out the rest of the world. He leaned on one hand against the stone I was tied to; his other was tugging on the thickness hanging between his legs. I would have blushed at the sight had I not been so frightened, my prudish sense of decency null and void.

"That doesn't make me want to scream any less." I opened my mouth and screamed as loud as possible. The satyr before me covered his ears, bending over enough to let me see my surroundings. As I continued to scream, I took in where the satyr had taken me.

I was in a large, square courtyard surrounded by tall green hedges. I was still in the hedge maze. That was good to know. In each corner of the courtyard were tall trees that reached up and above the top of the leafy walls. If I cranked my head back enough, I could see a fountain against my back. The water sprayed out of the mouths of scantily clad women just out of reach.

"Make her stop, Piper! Make her stop!" The becoming even less and less attractive satyr shook his head at my pained screeching.

I paused to take a breath and watched as a smaller satyr popped his head out from behind the crying giant. There was nothing remarkable about him. He had the same coloring as his larger companion, but he wasn't near as handsome. He was the average Joe of satyrs. Not that I had more than him and his crying friend to compare them to. I wouldn't have given him much more thought than that had it not been for the panpipe in his hands.

He must have been the one playing pipes that I had been following in the hedges. I wished I'd never heard those pipes to begin with. It was my fault for being naïve enough to think someone would help me.

Piper, as the other satyr had called him, brought the mouthpiece of the panpipe to his lips and began to play. Calming tones floated out of the panpipe, ceasing my panic mid-scream. All the tension in my body rolled off me.

Why was I screaming? There was nothing to fear. I was safe. The satyrs would take care of me. I sighed into the stone beneath me, not at all bothered by the restraints holding me in place.

"That's a good girl." My eyes rolled up to the larger of the two that was stroking himself in time with the pipe. I wasn't so worried about the girth of him now. In fact, I was eager to please him. I arched my hips off the stone beneath me, trying to get closer to him.

The satyr gave a throaty laugh. "Hold on there, girly. All in good time." He bent down to the top of my pants and tried to pull them down my hips, but the positioning of my legs kept them from moving more than a few inches. The satyr frowned at his friend playing the pipes. "Why won't they come off?"

They weren't the brightest Fae in the Underground. They caught me easily enough but were too stupid to take my clothes off before they tied me up. When Piper stopped playing to argue with his friend, my head cleared once again, and panic seeped back in. Part of me still wanted the satyr to touch me, while the other half urged me to start screaming again.

I fought against that urge so Piper wouldn't play the pipes again, taking my free will away. I was on to their little game and would let them think I was still affected.

As I tried to think of a plan, my eyes couldn't help but be drawn to the large appendage hanging in front of me. Even if I was willing, there was no way that thing wouldn't hurt. It reminded me of this one guy in college I dated, Travis.

He majored in sex therapy and thought he was God's gift to women. One drunken night I had let him talk me into exploring my unbridled sexuality. It sounded like a good idea at the time. That was until he shed his pants and let me see what I'd be working with.

Though he wasn't as long as the confused satyr in front of me, the girth of him was about the same. It had taken a whole lot of foreplay, and almost a whole bottle of strawberry-flavored jelly, to make it even bearably comfortable. In the end, he still had to fight for every inch. I doubted the satyrs before me would be thoughtful enough to have brought lube – strawberry flavored or otherwise.

Not willing to take the chance, I shifted my hands in their bindings, judging the knots there. They were tight, but not so much that I couldn't wiggle one hand out if I had the time. Thank God for sloppy workmanship. If I could get the piper away, I could get one hand free while lug head was distracted.

Gulping my fear down, I tried to channel my inner porn star. I winced when my voice came out more running a marathon breathy, than ready for a good time breathy. "Untie my legs and then you can get them off."

The two quit arguing to stare at me. Piper frowned. "If we untie you, you'll just try to get away."

Fuck. Not as dumb as he looked. I tried to channel every bad porno I had ever seen as I bucked my hips up with an exaggerated moan. "But I need you now!"

"She won't leave, Piper." The larger one smirked down at my writhing form. "See. She wants me."

"I don't know. Maybe I should play some more." Piper brought the pipes to his lips, but at that moment, my curiously absent feathered friend swooped down and snatched his pipes away. "Hey! Give that back!"

I watched as Piper ran after the owl to the tree on the other side of the fountain. He hollered over his shoulder in between cursing the blessed bird. "Don't do anything before I get back, Romp."

Romp, the larger satyr above me, snorted and bent down to untie my legs. "Damn voyeur. Like I need him to fuck." He grinned up at me. "I'm going to fuck you real good before he gets back."

I bit my lip to keep from crying out in protest as he cupped me between the legs. "If you don't bleed too much, I'll let him have a go at you before I fuck you again." I chewed the inside of my cheek until it bled as he stroked me through my pants. "If you survive we'll keep you around, maybe even make you our wife, but if you don't..." he shrugged his shoulders as if he weren't talking about rape and murder. He stroked my face with his large hands and smiled. "I really hope you survive."

Oh joy. I was going to be raped not once but three times. And if I didn't die I would get to be their little wife forever, or until I died of internal bleeding, which was more possible than me ever being their wife. But at least I was in my right mind now, if he would just hurry up with the ropes before pipe brains got back.

While Rump focused on the ties on my legs, I twisted my one hand in its constraint, wincing as the rope rubbed my hand raw. Once it was free, I began working at the knot on the other one. I kept glancing down at my, hopefully not-soon-to-be-husband, giving him what I hoped was a come hither look. He responded by groping one of my breasts, stopping his work on my remaining leg. I don't care what my sister says; I'm a great actress.

Though, the fact that I was more concerned with what my sister thought of my acting abilities than the danger I was in was more disturbing than I could process. I was going to need to see a shrink when I got home. If I got home. One problem at a time, Kat.

"Don't stop now. We're almost there. Quick, before he comes back." If he was smart he'd realize he could take my pants off with only one leg loose. I was betting he wasn't that smart.

"I'm trying." He grunted as he pulled on the ropes. "There we go. Now let's–"

As soon as the ropes gave, I kicked out one heeled boot into his low hanging bits, causing the satyr to cry out before doubling over in pain.

"You bitch!" Romp coughed out, grabbing his wounded parts.

Thank you, Chess! I was never going to complain about wearing high heels again. Or at least, not until I wasn't in a *Beauty and the Beast* does rape situation.

I pulled on the remaining restraints on my wrist while peeking over my shoulder for Piper's return. It wouldn't do to get caught right after I got free. I couldn't imagine how much worse they would treat me after my attack.

When I was finally free, I jerked my pants back into place and stepped up to the groaning giant lying on the ground. I didn't even hesitate when the heel of my boot connected with the side of his head, knocking him out cold. The human part of me felt guilty for causing another being pain, but another part of me, a dark part, held a deep satisfaction for the blood that trickled out of the wound my heel had made in his skull. It was a part of me I couldn't deal with right now.

Walking around Rump, I searched for the nearest exit, which as luck would have it, was right next to where my feathered savior was playing keep away with the panpipe.

I inched my way toward the exit keeping Piper's back to me. There was no way I was going to be able to get out without him seeing me.

Piper tried to climb the tree, but his hooves just didn't give him the leverage he needed to get him up it. As I approached the tree, the owl dropped the pipe when he saw me. I held my breath as the satyr grabbed the pipe off the ground, shaking an angry fist up at the owl.

"You better stay up there! I'll feed you to Romp for dinner!" He turned around grumbling under his breath. When he saw me, he opened and closed his mouth, gaping like a fish. "You!"

The hand holding the pipes moved toward his mouth, but this time I was ready for him. I grabbed ahold of the other side of the pipes, but the little devil held on fast. A tug of war began over who would get the pipes. I used my other hand to dig my nails into the back of Piper's hand until he jerked his hand away with a yelp.

"Hey, give it back!" He cried out, jumping on his short legs to reach the pipes I held just out of his reach.

I cackled and waved the pipes above my head. "Not so tough now are you?" I turned the pipes over in my hand, contemplating smashing them. "What should I do with you now?" I brought the pipes up to my mouth and gave it a test blow. I winced at the high-pitched note that sounded.

"Stop that!" Piper screeched, grabbing his ears. "Are you trying to kill us all?"

"It would serve you right." I gripped the pipes in my hands, so tight that my knuckles began to turn white. The fact that I had almost been raped had finally sunk in as I stared down at the wooden instrument in my grip. They had almost–if I hadn't gotten free–

"To try and force me to," I screamed the last part out loud. My anguish clear in my voice as the wood cracked beneath my hands.

"Careful now! That's mine." Piper gave a frantic cry, his hand outstretched. "Give it back."

"How do I know you won't use it again to try and attack someone else?" My throat was raw from all the yelling.

"I won't! I won't. I promise. Just give it back." His eyes pleaded with me to believe him.

The forgiving part of me would have believed every word the little satyr said and would have urged me to give him a second chance. After all, he hadn't actually done anything to me, but not from the lack of trying. Romp, on the other hand, deserved every single thing he had gotten from me and more so. But the cynical part, the part that had grown more and more since entering the Underground, whispered to me. How do you know he didn't already do this to countless others? If he was willing to do it once, he would most certainly do it again.

"I want a blood oath," my voice came out hard and unyielding. "I want you to blood oath you will never use this pipe for evil deeds on pain of death."

"What?" Piper's eyes became wide. Not quite believing I would invoke such a thing. "But I–I won't do it again. There's no need to swear to that!"

"Then you will have no problem swearing to it." I tightened my grip on the pipes, the little cracking noise made my lips twitch. The sound of breaking wood quickly became one of my favorite sounds.

"Yes!" Piper screamed, his eyes fixated on my hand.

"Yes, what?" I held the pipes to my chest, his beady eyes followed.

"I swear it!"

"Say it."

"I swear on my blood, Piper's blood, that I will never do an evil deed using the pipes again. If I do, let the Shadow's reaper have me and send me to the never-ending darkness." When he finished he held his hands out, tears brimming his eyes. "Now please, please let me have my pipes."

"All right." I pulled the pipes away from my chest, but instead of handing them to him, I snapped the pipes at the seams, and then dropped them to the ground. My lips curled at the satisfying crunch it made under my boot as I smashed it into tiny wooden fragments.

"No!" The small satyr cried out as he fell to his furred knees. "Why? Why?" He asked through choking sobs.

I stepped back as he crawled across the ground toward the remains. My smile turned into a disturbed frown at the pathetic mess he had become as he cradled the splinters in his hands. I shook my head from side to side as I backed away from the crying satyr.

I didn't do this. I wasn't capable of such cruelty. Even if they tried to rape me, I'd never– I'd never do something like this. I had to get out of here. I turned on the heel of my damn boots and fled through the archway.

"But I swore! I swore." The sounds of Piper's cries and the owl's hoots chased me down a path of despair.

CHAPTER

THE SEER

I RAN UNTIL my chest burned and my feet ached. I ran until the hedges became nothing more than a green blur. I didn't have a destination in mind. I just knew I needed to go. Get away from it all. Too bad I couldn't run from myself.

When I finally slowed down, I found myself surrounded by fungi. It was as if I had walked into the mushroom city. The colors varied as any city would. From dull pale yellow to bright neon green, and it didn't stop there.

There were mushrooms the size of houses, with thick stalks and large looming tops. Mushrooms the size of Buicks and ones with short stumpy bases, and tops so wide, I feared they'd fall over. If the tallest were the buildings, then the smallest were the people and children. There were tall ones with skinny stalks and short ones that were so fat around the middle I wouldn't have been able to fit my arms around them.

Had I shrunk? I hadn't drunk from any bottles with the words 'Drink me' on them. Or maybe it was another misnomer from the original telling?

I plopped down on a patch of cushy grass next to a deep maroon-colored mushroom with football-shaped black spots to catch my breath. My eyes were heavy and begged for rest. But no matter how tired I was; I didn't dare close them. I wasn't sure I'd ever be able to close them again. The thought of it filled me with a paralyzing terror. Is this what PTSD is like?

"What do you think?" I glanced up at my blue-eyed friend that had followed me from the maze and into the mushroom forest. "Do I need therapy?"

The owl shuffled in place on top of a bright pink mushroom with a strange inner glow. He cocked his head to the side as he hooted.

"I'll take that as a no." I sighed, picking at the grass beneath my fingers. My head was beginning to hurt from lack of sleep, and if that wasn't enough, its friend residing in my abdomen decided to make its presence known.

I placed a hand on my stomach, frowning at its emptiness. I hadn't eaten since dinner. Though, I didn't usually eat in the middle of the night, which it was bound to still be, I also didn't usually do much physical activity, sleeping or not, if I could help it.

"What do you think, Mr. Blue Eyes? Are the mushrooms edible?" I asked my feathered companion once more. The owl wrinkled his feathers in response. "I suppose not. With my luck they're poisonous, or worse, hallucinogenic."

Or carnivorous.

I felt a little weird about there being so many mushrooms. It was like they were watching me. I half expected them to talk like the flowers back at the beginning – with hushed voices as they kept tabs on the goings on around them.

I pushed myself off the ground, my feet still aching in my boots. These boots were definitely not made for walking. I almost took them off to go barefoot, the cool grass would feel nice against my sore feet, but I was wary to be without a weapon. It was hard to be intimidating when you only had five feet and two inches to work with, not that the boots made me much taller, but at least I had a sharp, pointy end that would make someone think twice. Or at least a quarter more.

I opened my mouth to ask my unhelpful shadow which way I should go when a sickly sweet smell floated through the air. First, a small strand of smoke floated by, and then a huge honking cloud smashed into my face. I sneezed as the strength of it hit my nose.

Mr. Blue Eyes hooted and took flight in the direction the smoke came from. I frowned, and against my better judgment, followed suit. It couldn't be much worse than what I'd already faced.

My body gave an involuntary tremor at the thought of something worse than Piper and Romp. Thinking about them made panic rise up. It made my eyes burn and my throat constrict. I wouldn't cry. I knew if I started I wouldn't be able to stop. I had to keep moving, or I'd fall apart where I stood.

I made my way through the thick smoke, unable to see more than one foot in front of the other. I had to use the sound of Mr. Blue Eye's flapping wings as my guide. After a few moments, the smoke began to wane. We came to a stop before a circle of dark navy mushrooms that reached a foot above my head.

They were clustered together, their edges lined up against their neighbor. Atop one of the mushrooms was a large, rather plump, fuzzy blue figure. The figure's back was turned so I couldn't see his face, but ringlets of smoke billowed up from where he was perched.

"Excuse me." I coughed, my voice hoarse from breathing in smoke. It shifted as if angling its head to listen. "I'm looking for the Seer. Have you seen him or, um, her?"

My new plan was to kill them with kindness, and if that didn't work, I could always throw my boot at them. I could be the boot ninja. I'd have a different pair of boots for every kind of weapon. Maybe even a blowtorch feature. I wondered how much something like that would cost?

"The Seer?" My attention locked onto the low, sultry voice coming from the figure. It was an unusual sound coming from the big, blue blob.

"Yes. Have you seen him?"

A slight chuckle shook the figure on the fungi; it paused to suck in a drag from its pipe. "Not today, but then again, I haven't been up long enough to find a mirror."

I cocked my head at the new information. This was the Seer? Well, it kind of made sense. The hookah pipe and the blue fuzzy exterior had all the makings of the caterpillar, and he was supposed to be old and cranky. I didn't expect to get much help from him if any at all.

The seer gave a languid stretch, and the fuzzy blue exterior fell to his waist to reveal a smaller figure. Large, vibrant butterfly wings fluttered on his back as he stretched and turned in his seat.

My jaw dropped. Mr. Caterpillar was not a mister at all, but a petite, albeit blue, miss. The bluish hue that spread across her skin fanned out into six pale white hands. Dark long lashes surrounded large eyes the color of obsidian. Full, hypodermic blue lips curled into a secretive smile on a strong but delicate face. Her hair, a periwinkle blue, was cropped short in a stylish pixie cut. There was nothing in her form that screamed masculine. If her face wasn't enough to determine her gender, than the slight curvature of her breasts hidden behind a dozen or so necklaces hanging down to the bottom of her ribs would have.

Besides the necklaces, the only other clothing covering her form was a tattered, multi-blue-hued skirt. The skirt spread out across her crossed legs as one foot hung off the edge of her mushroom perch. Next to her was a large hookah, almost as tall as her seated form. One of the six hands held onto the pipe attached to it and brought its tip to her mouth.

Taking a large inhale from the pipe, her eyes surveyed my disheveled appearance. "Though, I have to say, dear. I can't look anywhere as bad as you do." Her lips formed a teasing smirk as she fondled the tip of the pipe with her lips. "You're late by the way."

"Late?" I lifted an eyebrow at her, my eyes drawn to the pipe in her mouth. I admit it was an alluring sight. Unfortunately, my distaste of anyone that chose to smoke outweighed my intrigue.

"Yes. Late." She pointed the pipe at me as she annunciated each word. "I expected you hours ago, but who'd have foreseen you attacking the satyrs?" Amusement glittered in her eyes.

Her mention of the satyrs made me cringe. I stared hard at the ground as my guilt and fear ate at me. I still hadn't come to terms with what happened to me or what I did to them. Let alone what I was becoming.

"Now, now don't look at me like that. Those satyrs had it coming." She tapped the pipe against her hand, crossing her other four arms over her abdomen. "If it wasn't you, it'd be someone else. Fae or human, it doesn't matter to them, so long as they have some where to stick their cock." She gave me a private grin as if we were best friends gossiping about boys. "But isn't that the way with men? Always thinking with their little heads; it's no wonder they have no room for much else in their noggins."

"I guess so." An awkward silence followed.

I was still a bit stunned that this chatty little thing was the Seer. She wasn't anything like what I had read about. Wasn't she supposed to be mean? And old? Though, as a Fae, old was measured by years, not the lines on their faces. I stared up into her blue face, trying to decipher how old she really was.

"Do I have something on my face?" She pressed a hand up to touch her cheek.

"No, no. Sorry. You're not exactly what I expected. So, you're the seer?" I gave a nervous laugh, tucking my hair behind my ear.

Three of the hands waved me off. "Not *the* *seer*. Just Seer. And don't worry about it. I get that all the time." She held up one of her arms examining the smooth skin there. "This is my thirteenth metamorphosis. I'm still not used to this new body. The last one was some old mean coot. After the incident with *her* I said to myself, 'Seer, you need to be more hip with the younger generation.' I was counting down the days until I could cocoon myself again, but enough about me. What about you?" I could feel her eyes as they studied me. "I don't always get the whole picture, so I can't say for certain what I expected, but I hadn't thought you would be so..." Her blue eyes lingered on my exposed flesh.

"Slutty?" I offered up, crossing my arms over my midriff.

"Enticing," she finished, which wasn't much better in my book. "And you seem to attract the most unusual company." Her eyes lifted to my feathered friend that watched in silence.

"Though, I am surprised you have tamed our feathered beast here. He's not the nicest of Fae to be around. All those fleas to deal with." She smiled at some inside joke I didn't get, but Mr. Blue Eyes certainly did, and his hoot of irritation only made her smile more.

"Oh." I blinked, not quite sure what to think of her heated gaze. I'd never been hit on by a woman before.

What is with these people? I was hardly the most beautiful human. They have had to have seen better ones. Is it because they haven't had any around in a while? I suppose if I wanted a double decant chocolate cake, but only had the choice of vanilla ice cream; I'd take what I could get. I thought it was just the males, but apparently female Fae were just as sex driven as the rest. I wanted to ask her, but it didn't seem to be the time.

Seer gave a good-natured chuckle at my discomfort before she jumped. Her wings caused her to float, rather than fall down from her mushroom bed. If I had tried that I would have twisted an ankle. Wings were a definite necessity when leaping from large fungi. I'd have to put an order in for a pair of my own.

While she descended down to the wingless rabble, her skirt flared up, letting me know just how little she was wearing underneath it. I turned my head and blushed.

Yikes.

She reached out with one of her many hands, and I tried not to flinch as she caressed my face. "Don't worry, my dear, you already belong to someone else, and no matter how tempting, I don't take what doesn't belong to me, at least not without permission."

"Well, that's nice." I pretended to ignore the dark glint in her eyes saying she really wished I'd give her permission. I didn't want to be anyone's, but if it was going to keep her from touching me more, then I wasn't going to say otherwise.

"Come now, Lady. I know exactly what you want." She took my hand with her dominant set of hands. My body gave an involuntary jerk when one of the lower hands pushed against the small of my back as she led me deeper into the mushroom forest. Mr. Blue Eyes followed in silence above our heads.

I watched Seer from the corner of my eye. Not without permission, she'd said. I had to make sure I didn't give her permission, however that may be. I gritted my teeth as the hand on my back inched down closer to my butt than was polite. The multiple hands were going to take some getting used to.

She brought us to a stop in front of a large mushroom. It wasn't much bigger than the others, but unlike the vibrant colors of the rest of the mushroom city, this one was black and charred. It emitted a dark hue around it that made my hairs stand on end. Weeds and vines crawled up its sides droopy and browning where it touched the mushroom, but in the center of the decaying plants was a mirror.

I didn't like it. There was no reflection. No light gleaming on its surface, only a black emptiness. It was close to the darkness that surrounded Alice in the Hall of Mirrors, but this darkness was so much darker. If there was evil in the world – and I surely believed there was, who else would invent decaf coffee – then this mirror was the window to that evil.

I had the sudden urge to run back the way I came, but my eyes wouldn't leave the mirror. The longer my eyes stayed on the mirror, the more it drew me in. Voices whispered underneath its surface, pushing to get free. They promised what no one else knew I wanted. Desires even I had never admitted to wanting.

They could help me find my way home. If only I would let them out. I didn't need Alice and her stupid key. I could do it on my own. I'd be back home and curled up in bed before I knew it. All I had to do was let them out.

"Ow!" A sharp stinging pain pulled my eyes from the mirror to new crescent-shaped marks on my hand; blood welled up from each wound. I scowled at Seer. "What was that for?"

"Look." She gestured with her second set of hands as she licked the blood from beneath the nails on her fingers. I cringed at the sight but glanced around myself.

My insides rolled. Seer had stopped us some ways back from the mirror, at least a couple of yards, but now I was only a few feet away from it. I backed up from the mirror, not daring to give it my back, but kept my eyes on Seer. I didn't even remember moving.

"What happened?" I asked even though I was fairly certain I knew the answer. I could still hear the voices whispering in my head, urging me to look back at the mirror. I fought against the urge and stared hard at Seer's nonchalant face. How was she so calm? The presence coming from the mirror alone was setting me on edge.

My guide gave me a knowing look, as if she knew I knew the answer to the question, but shrugged and indulged me, "You want to save her, don't you? To get the key?"

"Well, yes." I dared to peek at the mirror out of the corner of my eye. It felt like it was listening to our every word. "But I can't go through there."

"Of course you can."

"Even if I was willing, which I'm not, I'm not Chess. I can't just go through mirrors all willy-nilly." I jerked my thumb in the direction of the mirror. I took another cautious step back. I couldn't be farther away from it. Another planet was more preferable.

"Ah, yes. Cheshire." She smiled as if remembering a fond memory. With what I knew of Chess and his reputation with the other Fae, it was probably a perverted memory. I needed to ask him about that when he stopped shoving me through mirrors. "Why do you think he is able to use mirrors as portals and the rest of the Fae can't?"

"I don't know." I shrugged a little frustrated. Why couldn't anyone just answer me straight out rather than make me figure it out? I didn't have all night to play 20 questions. "Something to do with being the mediator?"

"But *why* is he the mediator? What makes him so special? Well, besides the obvious." She giggled a bit like a schoolgirl with a crush. Apparently I wasn't the only one smitten with the feline.

"He's a half-breed," I answered rather cross. "So, he's allowed to pass between worlds."

"That's right. The reason he can go between worlds so easily is because he doesn't have to obey the same rules as the rest of the Underground." She drew out a short smoking pipe from God knows where and teased the end of it with her lips.

"And what rules are those?"

"Rules are rules." She waved me off, her answer not helpful in the least. I glared daggers at her, and she made a frustrated noise. "You humans are so impatient, always with the questions. It's more fun finding the answers than the actual knowing, but if you are going to be that way, I'll tell you."

"That would be a nice change." Sarcasm dripped from my mouth.

Seer floated onto a low toadstool, her skirts spreading out around her as she sat down. "The only way in or out of a world is with a key."

"I figured as much since that's what I'm trying to find. How–"

"Do you get a key?" She finished, giving her pipe a vicious tap. "You have to apply for one. There is a form and everything. If you get approved you are provided with a key that will allow you in and out of the Underground for a certain amount of time, when time is up, the key returns to the vault."

"That sounds all very..." I paused, scrunching my brows. "Civilized."

"Of course it is. We aren't heathens. We have rules and processes that must be abided by just like anyone else. But you." She pointed the pipe at me. "You broke those rules by coming here. You shouldn't have been able to see the entrance, let alone get into the Underground without a key. Do you see what I mean?"

"I think so. But how did I get in in the first place? I'm not a half-breed like Chess. I don't have any Fae blood in me. I'm just...just me." I paused for a second, remembering the irritation that had shown up from touching the iron door. It was faded now, but it was still a bit pink. I spoke low to myself. "I am, aren't I?"

"That remains to be seen. But if you gather all the evidence, it would point to the fact that you might not be entirely as you seem." Seer stood from her post, leaning in close as she searched for something in my eyes. "Could be that one of your ancestors had a Fae lover."

"If they did I never heard of it." The thought of any of my family being with a Fae was ludicrous. They were all as prim and proper as my mother. Dad was the only one of the bunch that I could even marginally relate to with our joint obsession of books, but even he held the same high opinion as the rest of them. Though, grandma had always been the black sheep of the bunch. Perhaps she had one? It was something to add to my growing list to research when I got home.

"So, I'm a half-breed like Chess?" I quirked a brow at her.

"Hardly." She snorted, her necklaces jingling with the movement. "More like a 16th, if not a 24th. Possibly even only the smallest iota of Fae blood in you."

"But that doesn't mean anything. I'm sure you get people like me in here all the time. How else would Al–, I mean, *she* get in here?" The entire no-name-saying bull was getting tiresome. Couldn't they just be like normal people?

"That's the question, isn't it?" She crossed one leg over the other, her wings fluttered behind her, causing her to hover off the toadstool. "That was years and years ago. Back then anyone could come and go as they pleased. No key required. We don't get many of your kind anymore. None in fact. You would be the first one in over a century."

"But how can that be?" I tugged on the blonde part of my hair, wrapping it around my finger. "Surely, there was someone else? Someone else had to have seen the rabbit hole. A child maybe?

"No. Just you," she said in a sing-song voice.

"Why all the hassle? If humans were allowed before why not now?" It seemed all a bit stupid to me.

"It all comes round to someone poking their nose in where they didn't belong and now." She swept her arms about her. "Here we are. Everything was much simpler back then, none of this mind-your-tongue nonsense." She waved her pipe in the air to iterate her point.

"What happened?"

The blue Fae gave a petulant sigh. "You could say we were put on house arrest for the action of one."

"That doesn't seem fair." I frowned, catching sight of my feathered companion. Mr. Blue Eyes seemed forlorn at my words. Could owls even feel human emotion? It was a Fae owl, so for all I knew, he could probably talk and just wanted to make fun of me for talking to myself.

"Of course it's not, but that's just the way it is," she said as if she had accepted their fate long ago.

"So, what did they do that was so bad that they had to punish everyone else?" Was this what Chess and Alice had been arguing about? She said she didn't know what would happen. She was just trying to help. It was all very suspicious and conveniently aligned with the sudden ban on humans. "It wouldn't have to do with a certain blonde-haired, blue-eyed girl, would it?"

"My, you are quick." Seer beamed with pride, giving the owl a peculiar wink. "I can see why you are so taken with her."

My owl blinked its blue eyes at her in response.

"But as with many ways of the Fae, it is far more complicated than all that." She tapped the pipe against her lip in thought. "I suppose it would be easier to show you."

Mr. Blue Eyes hooted in erratic aggravation. I eyed him while asking, "Show me what?"

"Well, I'm not telling you all this for free. Think of this as my payment for helping you out." Her lips curled up in a mischievous grin.

I didn't like where this was headed. I wanted to know what the big mystery was, but not bad enough to make a deal with another Fae. I was still left wondering when the prince was going to show his pretty head demanding retribution for sobering me up back at the Seelie Court. Though, I'd think he would owe me one after he got me arrested and almost thrown in one of those mirrors. Fair was fair after all.

"And how do you benefit from showing me? Doesn't that just make me double in your debt?"

"Not at all." She placed her feet on the ground, my eyes hypnotized by the swaying of her hips as she approached me. She slid a set of hands around my waist and another set caressed my arms as she slid the end of the pipe along the line of my lips. "You see, to show you, you'll have to dream and–"

I knew where this was going. "You'll get to feed off my dreams. Right." Everything was about food for them. Well food and sex, but when wasn't it?

"Good. You have been paying attention." Her eyes flicked to my lips as if she were contemplating stealing a kiss.

My body was a rigid statue against hers. I was afraid the slightest movement would give her unwanted permission, and in turn, cause her to pounce. I wasn't homophobic by any means, but she was pushing me so far out of my comfort zone even Sherlock wouldn't be able to find me.

"Um, so I go to sleep and that's it?" I muttered the words to keep from drawing any more attention to my mouth.

"Well, no. Not it, per se. I have to direct your dreams after all, or what is the point?" She took a step back, finally allowing me to breathe easier.

"Right," I drew out the word. "What do I have to do? It doesn't involve music does it?"

I didn't think I could handle anymore musical adventures. I wasn't sure I'd ever be able to listen to music ever again. At least not anything the general masses approved of. Death metal sounded good. There were no pipes in that, right?

"No." She laughed at the panic on my face. "There's no music involved. So, tell me, Lady…" She pulled something from inside a pouch at her waist.

Seer stuffed a pinch of some kind of dried herbs into the end of the pipe. With a flick of her wrist, a small spark ignited it, causing lavender smoke to billow out the end. My stomach clenched in fear at the smell, even as my muscles began to relax.

Her black eyes glittered as she smirked at me. "Do you smoke?"

AFTER A FIRM, "No, absolutely not." I sat glaring at the pipe dangling between my thumb and pointer finger. I gave it a tentative sniff, which in turn caused me to sneeze. My face scrunched up at the pipe.

Smoking. I hated smoking. It stuck to clothing and it took forever to get the smell out of one's skin and hair. I tried smoking once. My allergies were all kinds of fucked up for months. The heady effects were not worth the extra discomfort. Not to mention, cancer. No thanks.

"It's not going to bite," she remarked, not even having the decency to pretend she wasn't laughing at me.

I gave her my best death stare. The kind I gave to the teenage couple who thought they could hide in a corner and make out and no one would see them. Really? How dare they? The library was a sanctuary for the studious and those in need of a vacation from real life. Not for swapping spit. That's what the back of their car was for.

"You have to understand my hesitance after what happened. Let alone the disgust factor. How do I know I will be safe?"

The thought of being vulnerable after recent events would put me in therapy for years. It was quite sad. I couldn't see myself being able to see another well-endowed male specimen without flashing back to Romp's swinging in front of me.

How did one overcome a fear of large male genitalia? Would there be flashcards? Then after I was able to stomach those, we'd work our way up to dioramas, and then after many, many hours of dissecting every aspect of my aversion to large penises, there would be a parade of endowed men all for the purpose of healing my delicate sensibilities.

I found my ability to make light of my near-rape experience a good sign. Or I was trying to overshadow my terror with humor and sarcasm.

"I'll be right here." She gave me what she thought was a comforting smile.

"Oh, that makes it all better."

Sarcasm it is.

"Look." She sighed. "You won't even be asleep. It will be more like daydreaming. Not as satisfying as a deep-sleep dream, but I will take what I can get, and you will be able to get out of it at any time. I'll only be directing the dream. You will be in complete control. I'll even stay all the way over there." She fluttered her wings, lifting her off the ground and over to a neon green mushroom the size of a Hummer. She sprawled out across the top of it.

I gave her lounging form a suspicious glance. "How will you feed from there? Don't you need physical contact or something?"

"Why would you think that?"

"That's your thing, isn't it? The touchy feely, any chance to cop a feel?" I eyed the hand that had descended onto her stomach and was making a circular motion along her skin. My eyes jerked up to her face as one of those hands crept up to trace the edge of her breast beneath her necklaces.

Geez.

The butterfly Fae, or whatever it was she claimed to be, laughed at the heat that crept up my face before dropping her hands innocently to her lap. "We aren't all touchy feely as you put it. You're the first of your kind to step foot in the Underground in a long time. Not all of us have the privilege of visiting your realm whenever we like. So, you'll have to excuse those of us who are unable to contain ourselves by your presence. Your scent is kind of..." Her eyes darkened as she breathed in the air. "...intoxicating."

I shuddered at the thought. "So, you're like a recovering alcoholic who just had their first drink after ten years of sobriety?"

"Think more like an opium addict." Her eyes filled with hunger as if I were her next hit.

"But Trip and Mop didn't act like I'm the very air they breathe. Don't they feed on dreams too?" I gulped, not sure I wanted to know after all.

"They're lower Fae," she answered like it answered everything. "We are wasting daylight. Are you going to do this or what?"

"Just wait a couple of hours it will be daylight again," I muttered, but then said to her, "What is up with the time thing anyway?"

"Are you trying to stall?" Seer's black eyes narrowed. "The outcome won't change, besides, I thought you wanted to know what all the fuss was about?"

I gave a disgruntled sigh and glared down at the somehow still smoking pipe. My eyes strayed to the watchful blue eyes of my feathered friend, wondering how he felt about all of this, but he just tilted his head as if to tell me to get on with it already. Frowning, I placed the tip of the pipe to my lips and grimaced at the taste of the burning herbs.

The smoke burned as it went down my larynx and into my lungs, causing me to break into a coughing fit. As my vision glazed over and my body relaxed into a trance-like state, an awful thought came to mind. What if she lied?

CHAPTER 16

QUESTIONS & ANSWERS

THE SMOKE SPREAD out in front of me, taking up all the edges of my sight. It was as if I were inside an IMAX theatre. If the smoke was the screen, then my eyes were the projectors.

The mushroom forest was gone. Seer was gone, even though I could still hear the tinkling of her necklaces bumping against each other and the sound of her wings twitching on her back. There was one thing.

The mirror.

I couldn't see it, but I could feel it. Its presence pressed down on my mind, begging me to let them out, but my mind was on the screen of smoke before me. Figures began to form. Their outlines became clearer as I focused on the smoke.

"Let's start at the beginning, shall we?" Seer's voice cut through the hazy fog in my head and the White Queen became clear on the screen.

She was as I remembered, except less hard, less cold, but with a determination that would scare the primly pressed pants off my mother. "We can't let this go on any longer. The humans are starting to suspect."

"What do you suppose we do?" A black-haired woman formed in the smoke with dark blue eyes and sharp cheekbones. "You've rejected my suggestion. Quite spitefully I might add."

"And with good reason, Mab!" The White Queen glowered at the woman. Was this the UnSeelie Queen?

"Cousin, you know the rules! No names. Not even in private." She searched the room as if looking for an eavesdropper.

"That's ridiculous, Cousin." Indulging in the other queen's request, however silly she thought it.

"You won't find it so ridiculous when one of yours is called into the shadows one night never to be seen again. I might have power over air and dark, but even my power has its limits."

"You are admitting to not being all powerful?" The White Queen scoffed, but when Mab was silent she stiffened. "Truly? You're afraid of the dark?"

"Not the dark, the shadows. Don't change the subject. If you would let us kill them rather than cast them out into the abyss, we could fix this whole mess." She slashed a hand through the air, the black-netted lace of her sleeve whipped around her arm.

"We can't just start killing our own kind." The White Queen gave Mab a stern look as if chastising a child. "With the rarity of children amongst us Fae, there are hardly any of us left."

"And whose fault is that?" she hissed at her. "Who's the one who didn't want her precious Seelie to cross breed with humans anymore?"

"They were diluting our magic. It had to be stopped before the Fae became nothing more than humans themselves. Excuse me for trying to save our race."

Mab gave an unqueen-like snort. "You didn't save us. You just delayed the inevitable, and now those precious Fae that you couldn't kill, no matter how dark and demented, are going to destroy both our worlds on their way to an all-you-can-eat buffet where human is all that is on the menu."

"Not if we stop them first." The White Queen smiled mischievously.

"Cousin, what are you thinking?" Mab eyed her with a curious frown.

The White Queen's smile widened, and in that moment, she was the most beautiful creature I had ever laid eyes on. The surface of her skin sparkled with the intensity of that smile. Her eyes alighted with a victorious joy as she said, "Have you met my daughter?"

Before I could hear Mab's response, smoke covered the scene.

"Wait! I wasn't done with that," I called out to Seer.

"I didn't do it." Seer's voice made me jump when it came out next to me. It was filled with concern and a hint of curiosity. "You have to come out of it on your own. Try clearing your mind."

"I am trying."

I really did try to do what she said. I attempted to clear my mind, to picture the mushroom forest, Seer with her multi-hued wings, and the mirror that chilled me to the bones. It didn't matter what I did, the figures kept forming before my eyes.

Instead of being a spectator in the next vision, I was the star of the show. Their thoughts were my thoughts. Their feelings became mine. Until whoever I was had been lost.

"Did you hear? The UnSeelie Prince arrived today." A familiar blonde walked arm and arm with me along a path in the garden. Instead of feeling irritation at seeing the female twin, I felt a comforting companionship with her. It was weird to think of the vindictive blonde in such a way. My mouth moved on its own to answer my – friend?

"I had heard such news." A sinking feeling overwhelmed me at the thought of the Prince of the UnSeelie Court.

Gab chuckled beside me. "Don't sound so excited about it. Someone will start to think you care about your betrothed."

"Hardly." I snorted, playing with the ends of my pale blonde hair. "Everyone knows that this is a marriage of convenience. Nothing more."

"Sure it is, but have you seen him yet? Don't you want to know what he looks like?" Smiling at me, Gab trailed a hand along the metal fence lining the garden path.

I quirked a brow at my friend's mischievous grin. "Why would I want to do that? I'm to marry him whether or not I approve of his appearance."

"Well, I would want to know whose bed I'll be warming for the rest of eternity." Gab stopped in her tracks, pulling me with her. "And as you are my best friend and confidant, I did a little reconnaissance on your behalf."

"Of course you did." I rolled my eyes. The younger Fae always needed to know what was going on with everyone in the palace. It was for her own pleasure and hardly a selfless act in the name of friendship.

Gab sniffed. "Well, if you're going to be like that I don't think I'm going to tell you what I found out." She stuck her nose in the air, pretending to be cross.

"Yes, you will. You can't help yourself." I dropped her arm and continued down the path, my attention half on the flowers around us.

Having never left the palace, I'd seen them all hundreds of times over. I'd never even seen all of the Seelie Court, but I was supposed to marry a complete stranger, and live with him all for the sake of solidifying our defenses against the Shadow Realm.

The hope of leaving the palace was the only reason I even agreed to the sham of a marriage to begin with. It gave me the chance to be free, to see new places, and to finally walk through the halls of my own home without the fear of who would lose their heads next. I didn't need to know what my husband looked like. I'd marry him all the same.

"Oh all right, you've talked me into it." Gab gave an exaggerated sigh and hurried to catch up with me. "You know all you had to do was ask."

"But I didn't ask."

Gab ignored me and continued babbling, "So, I went down to the guest wing where they keep all the important people. Not that UnSeelie royalty is all that important, but anyway, I got stopped by one of his brute guards..."

As she told her story, I could feel the excitement radiate off her in waves. She always got this way when she had some juicy tidbit that she wanted to share. It was nearly impossible for her to keep a secret.

"...and then I said, I have as much right to be here as anyone." She scoffed. "Can you believe that? He actually thought I was a servant! Me! The thought of me cleaning." She shuddered.

"Maybe he didn't know." I shrugged my shoulders, pretending to show interest in her distress.

"Ha! Do I look like a lower Fae? No. Look at these cheekbones." She gestured toward her face. "Fae have killed to be as pretty as me."

I rolled my eyes. "Gab, that was one time, and they didn't die. They only ended up scarred."

"She might as well have died. I would have committed suicide if I had to go the rest of my life disfigured like that." Gab made a face at the thought.

"Not everyone cares about appearances." I offered and then tried to change the subject. "I thought you were going to tell me what he looks like, not his guard."

"I'm getting there." She waved me off. "So, I got passed the nasty guard and into the prince's sitting room and low and behold, there he was lounging on the couch like some half-breed. Really now, does he have no decorum? It is no surprise he wouldn't think twice about letting his guard down where anyone could walk in on him."

"He was in his private rooms, though. No one should have been able to walk in on him," I pointed out.

"But I did, so anyone else could have as well. I'm just saying; he should be a little more mindful of where he is, even if he is a guest. He is still UnSeelie. He could have…" Gab stopped mid-sentence catching sight of something in the garden. "Oh pooh, I was just getting to the good part."

I followed her gaze my eyes landed on a dark-haired Fae sitting on a bench with a book in his hand. With his attention focused on his book, my eyes trailed down his exquisite form. All thought of not caring about looks was smothered by a sudden undeniable need. When he glanced up from his book, my breath caught in my throat.

Eyes the color of the glittering night sky locked onto mine. The fierceness in his gaze froze me in place. There was anger there, but also a hollowed emptiness. I knew at that moment I'd go through with the engagement.

Not because I craved freedom, or because he made my insides melt, but to make sure those beautiful eyes never gazed at me with such loneliness again.

The image of the prince faded from my mind as I slowly drifted back into my own head. For a brief moment, I was me again. I could hear Seer arguing with someone a few feet from me, but since I still couldn't see past the smoke all I could do was listen.

"I can't stop it," Seer explained to the unseen person. "I only started it. Something happened, something not in my control." She huffed, her frustration apparent. "It's not up to me now. It's up to her."

"She shouldn't have been here in the first place." A deep voice tingled down my spine.

I would know that voice anywhere. The sound of his voice as we made love was still fresh in my mind, causing my face to heat up. Hopefully they were too involved in their fight to notice.

"What did you think you were doing? You had no right. I should take your head for this," he growled at Seer. His words echoed, causing a new vision to form in the smoke screen.

Alice as she was now, adult sized and prettily arranged in her seat, sat as he berated her, tears glistening in her eyes. "I was only trying to help. They said I could be one of you and I am. Look." She tried to extend a hand out to him, but he was too blinded by his rage to give her a second glance.

I watched from between branches and peach-shaped fruit that shone like starlight. I was a spectator once more. My thoughts were thankfully my own as I looked down from the branches of the tree to those below me. The area was dim and surrounded by a stone wall, closed off to everything else except one door-shaped hole in the stone where two guards stood awaiting the prince's command.

"I'm quite aware of your new found abilities, Alice." When he said her name it sounded like a curse on his lips, and it caused the young girl to cringe. "Did you think for a moment that they could have lied? That they would tell you anything you wanted to hear? Just so you would do what they wanted?"

"But why would they want to keep you apart? Surely they could care less about your marriage?" She stuttered as she tried to rationalize her actions.

"You couldn't be more wrong." His laugh was bitter and heavy. "They have as much invested in my marriage as I do, except I have more to lose."

"Why? What do they gain from breaking you two up?" Alice cocked her head like a child trying to understand grown-up things.

"That's the question, isn't it? And you will have plenty of time to think about the answer.

Guards!" His voice rose as his anger spiked. "Everything that happens from here on out is on your shoulders."

His words caused Alice to crumble into a heap of blue on the ground. Her cries racked her body and only grew louder when the guards wrapped their hands around her arms and dragged her away. The prince was left standing staring at the base of the tree.

"Where she lay buried beneath our roots. The boy cannot feel her, but his soul knows she is there. It will always know she is there," a voice whispered in my head.

A voice I recognized. It was the same one that had kept urging me to come home. I wanted to ask it why was I here. What did it want from me, but I couldn't get the words out as it continued whispering.

"It isn't true. It isn't the human child's fault. The fault lies on those who came long before her, older than him, older than any of the Fae, or the humans. In a time when there was no love. No sadness. No hate. Only want. The want to have what one cannot." Its voice was warm and oaky as its words caressed my skull.

"That's why we gave the human child what she wanted. They think merging the light and dark together will destroy the shadows, the nightmares even the darkness fears. But they wanted. Oh, how they want what they could not have."

My physical body shivered at the dark warning in its voice, but I kept my ears open as it whispered words only I could hear.

"So, we let them take our fruit. We granted the human child and the daughter of light's wish, and hope the seeds we planted will be enough to save them. To save the humans, to save the Fae, to save us all."

The smoke cleared from my eyes, slowly at first, fading around the edges until I saw double. On one side, a forlorn, but angry dark prince mourned his bride beneath a glowing tree. On the other, was the current prince, flickering glyphs marring his otherwise beautiful face as he scolded Seer.

I sat there for a moment, gathering my bearings, not mentioning to the arguing Fae that I was back from my vision quest. I observed the prince's new attire. The blood-red shirt he had worn to the mourning party that caused him to stand out from the golden Fae was gone, and in its place was a black on black button-up shirt and fitted vest. It still bugged me that the Seelie would wear such an ostentatious color for a remembrance party. It was like they were declaring to the entire realm that yes their princess was dead, but they are still wonderful beings in need of worship and adoration.

Now knowing what I did, it was no wonder. Maybe they were ashamed of their princess.

She committed suicide after all. Though, why was it still a mystery? I know it had something to do with Alice and the shadows.

Oh.

And the glowing tree.

I got the part about Alice wanting to be a Fae. She made a wish that the tree granted and somehow her wish caused the princess to kill herself. That was the start of the whole 'no humans' rule.

I also couldn't forget about the shadows that helped Alice get to the tree in return for breaking the couple up. I wasn't quite sure why the shadows cared so much about their marriage, but the White Queen and Mab, the Red Queen I assumed were planning on using them to beat the shadows.

That brought me to the no-names rule.

Mab was afraid of the shadows. She said some of her people had been called into the shadows and never seen again. Were they killed? Turned into shadows? Eaten? As more information appeared, I seemed to have more questions than answers.

"Lady, you're awake." Seer noticed me staring at them first as she rushed to my side.

Damn. I had been spotted.

"Are you all right?"

"Of course she's not all right. Look at her!" The UnSeelie Prince yelled, gesturing a hand at me.

Was there something wrong with my face? I didn't feel any different. I still felt like I could sleep a month and still be tired. I was still craving a double quarter pounder with cheese and a large slice of chocolate cake. I was still creeped out by the mirror, which seemed even more aggressive than when I went into my vision quest.

Seer placed a hand on my face and frowned. "She does look a bit pale."

Her other set of hands went to work taking my pulse and generally poking and prodding at me. The Fae must have been genuinely concerned because she didn't once try to grope me or take advantage of my disoriented state.

"I'm fine, really." I pushed my arms out in front of me, causing her to back up and give me some space.

"You are not fine." His royal pain in my ass glowered at me.

Towering over me, his markings glowed hard enough that his eye was twitching. He must be in pain from fighting the spell. Why was he keeping it from changing his personality? What did he have to gain from being mad at me?

"Calm down. No need to pop a blood vessel." I reached a hand up, tucking the blonde hair that had fallen across my face behind my ear. I froze. My eyes widened as I stared up at a curious Seer and a smug prince, my face filling with horror.

Blonde?

I lifted the strand of hair I had just tucked out from behind my ear. No, it wasn't my imagination. My hair was blonde. I grabbed another section of my hair and felt an ounce of relief when my usual bright orangish-red hair glared back at me, but growled when I grabbed another section, and it was blonde as well.

What the fuck?

I stared at the blonde chunk in my hands, not quite believing what I was seeing. I was used to having a random section of blonde. The hair I was holding was exactly the same color as the one at the nape of my neck.

It was a blonde so white it was near impossible for me to color my natural fiery red to it. I wouldn't have cared so much if it had changed all of my hair, but to only change bits and pieces? I dreaded seeing it in the mirror. With my luck, I looked like some punk rock reject.

"How did this happen?" I questioned the no longer twitchy prince. His smug smile showed he had finally let the magic on his body smooth over his personality. I honestly couldn't decide which way I liked him better. Both sides of him made me want to deck him.

"Why don't you ask your new best friend, since you seemed perfectly all right with her watching over your mind, body, and soul?" Though his face held the usual teasing grin, his voice held the biting heat of anger. He kept his icy blue gaze on me as he addressed Seer. "Go on, tell her."

Seer crossed her arms, all six of them over her torso. "I hate to break it to you, your highness, but I didn't do this."

The prince's attention jerked to her. "Of course you did. You know the risks of feeding directly from a human." His eyes flashed dark. "Or has it been so long you have forgotten?"

"Like I would lose control like that? I'm not some lower Fae." She seemed offended he would even suggest it.

"Then how do you explain that?" He pointed at my whitened hair, making me grip the pieces as if to defend them.

I scowled at them. What was the big deal? Yes, my hair was a mess, but what did that have to do with Seer feeding from my dreams? I wasn't as worried about my hair as I was the mirror – its presence felt like a two-ton truck was crushing me.

"Would someone tell me what's going on?" My voice became a bit breathless. How did they not notice that thing?

The UnSeelie Prince grabbed my arm, jerked me to my feet and pulled me to the mirror. I dug my heels in as he tried to drag me to it. I so did not want to be any closer to it than I had to be, but his damn Fae strength far surpassed my own. Not that it was hard to do. Working out for me mainly consisted of lifting stacks of books to put back on the racks and walking to the fridge.

The closer I got to the mirror, the harder it was for me to breathe. I focused on my breathing, keeping my eyes on anything but the mirror, which ended up being the Fae prince himself. I couldn't help but compare this version of him to the one in my visions.

His face was hard with anger and determination, and if I had to guess, he was a bit afraid. What was he afraid of? The glyphs on his face didn't take away from the beauty of him, especially since I knew what he looked like without them. His eyes were flirting between the dark and icy blue.

The icy blue made me think of the White Queen, since she placed the spell on him it was no wonder she had given him her trademark blue eyes as part of his punishment. I was more partial to the dark blue color. They contrasted so much better with his pale skin and dark hair.

"Look," he demanded, his eyes locking with mine. While I was caught up in watching him, he had done something to the mirror. Waved his hand in front of it, sprinkled it with faerie dust, or whatever. I'd been fighting not to pay attention to the mirror, but as he watched me watching him, I chanced a glance at it.

It wasn't black anymore. The frame was still charred, but the mirror was clear and reflected back what I had pretty much guessed I looked like, a punk rock wannabe. My face was paler than usual as if I was suffering from a cold. My hair had more of the white blonde than red to it now, as if I had streaked it red and not the other way around. But the part that mystified me, the part that caused me to lean in closer to the mirror to get a better look, were my eyes.

My eyes, which were usually the color of a newly cut Christmas tree, weren't completely my eyes anymore. Bleeding into the green was an icy blue, causing a weird ring around the middle. In any normal setting, I would think it was pretty awesome. People had completely fucked up their eyesight by wearing color-changing contacts, and I now had my very own set of freaky eyes, but how they got that way was disquieting.

"How did this happen?" I asked, still staring at my new eyes as my foot took an involuntary step closer to the mirror. The pressure from the mirror had eased up for some reason. Not that I was complaining, it made it easier to breathe.

"It's a side effect of the feeding, which I never got around to because someone..." The blue-haired Fae glared at the prince. "Jumped in just as it was getting good. Only a lower Fae would be careless enough to lose control when feeding directly from dreams. It's unheard of in us higher Fae. We have more control than that." She smirked at the scowling prince. "Well, most of us anyway."

"Who else if not you?" Accusation rang in his voice. "There isn't any other Fae, or do you think my abilities are not up to par?"

"I would never insinuate that, your highness." Though, her voice implied that was just what she had done.

If they didn't do it then who did? I placed a hand on the mirror as I leaned in even closer to gaze into my eyes. The instant my hand touched the mirror the whispers were back tenfold, and the heavy weight of the mirror crushed me to my knees.

I tried to pull my hand away, but it was stuck in place. The blue in my eyes grew larger the longer my hand was there as did the blonde color of my hair. The red had all but become inch-wide streaks along my scalp.

My eyes darted around to the others, frantic that I couldn't let go. Seer and the UnSeelie Prince finally stopped fighting enough to notice what was going on. The fear that had crept up their faces, even as they fought to keep calm, set me on edge.

"Lady," Seer coaxed as if the slightest movement would cause me to go into hysterics. "Let go of the mirror."

I gave a tired chuckle. "Gee, why didn't I think of that?"

"You don't understand," the UnSeelie Prince stated in a calm and reassuring manner. "Opening yourself up to be fed on this close to the Shadow Realm has allowed them to hijack your life force. That's why you're changing so quickly. They're trying to drain you. Someone should have known better." He glared at Seer who had the decency to look ashamed.

He knelt next to me, placing his hand on mine. I could feel his breath on my face. I would have been embarrassed to have him touch me, especially after my little fantasy he had starred in, but I couldn't think past the whispers in my mind.

His hand was warm and engulfing on top of mine. He gave a firm tug on my hand as he commanded the mirror's occupants. "You know the rules. Let her go." The prince's own magic pulsated down my hand and into the mirror.

The whispers turned to screams in my head, causing me to wince. They didn't like being told what to do. Not one bit.

In that moment, they decided to give up their façade. The darkness in the mirror didn't so much as creep back into the glass as appear. It had only pretended to let the prince control it, so they could get me closer. Now that they had their teeth in me they weren't going to let me go.

They whispered how good I tasted. They hadn't tasted someone so powerful, someone so old, in centuries. They were tired of barely getting by on the dreams of their fellow Fae. They wanted fresh dreams. Human dreams. My dreams.

I didn't have the energy to fight them. I'd been awake too long. Too many life-changing events had happened. I was exhausted both physically and mentally. I only wanted to sleep and they jumped on that want, pressed their magic into it, causing my eyes to droop.

I couldn't stop it. Even as the Fae prince shook me, even as he yelled in my ears to fight it. Their voices were barely a hum above the whispers in my mind urging me into the darkness.

Their whispers were a menacing lullaby that promised everything and nothing at all. As the edges of my vision darkened, my hand slipped through the mirror and I tumbled face first into the Shadow's Between.

CHAPTER

THE SHADOWS

IT WAS COLD. Even as I slept I could feel it down to my bones. An icy breath crept along my skin. If I had been awake I was sure I would find someone hovering over my body. A large looming figure, so dark in my mind's eye I couldn't quite comprehend what I was seeing. Its presence, even as I slept, pressed upon me, drinking me in, leaving me frozen and empty inside.

Its voice, no longer a whisper, burned my ears. Neither male nor female, but both at once. "We don't know how you got in. The Fae queens claimed to have closed off the human world from the Underground, but here you are." It seemed amazed at such a feat. "We have been here, forgotten in the dark for many centuries as they go about their endless lives."

I knew my body was asleep, but I tried to ask it with my mind. "What are you?"

"We are the Fae who have been cast out by the courts. The court of light with its need for perfection and disgust for anyone different would not dare sully themselves with our deaths." It gave a bitter laugh. "And the UnSeelie court, where even the most gruesome Fae are welcome, wouldn't even give us sanctuary."

It shifted its massive body above me. It was close enough for the hairs on my skin to rise up at the cold. "We've been waiting here in the dark, waiting for someone who would help us, feed us, and set us free. We never expected our savior to be such a puny human, but you will do." Their laughter echoed through the blackness.

"How can I save you? I'm just one person. One human." I questioned it in my mind. "I can't imagine I'm enough to sustain all of you?"

"Ah, but you are not like the others." As if sensing my confusion, it went on. "You are like us. Of this world, but not. You do not belong to either world and they do not claim you as their own. It is a rarity indeed."

"But I'm human, not Fae," I protested, my fear growing to a substantial size. "I can't save you. I can't even save myself."

It tsk'd, its many voices coming together as one. "Let there be no lies between us. You are human yes, but more. We were there listening at the mirror's edge. What's said is said, no going back now." I flinched as dark formless fingers tried to caress my face. "Do not fear us, for you will be our Lady, and we your people. We can give you everything you desire. Power."

An image was thrust into my mind. I was a mighty queen. No, a goddess. My hair burned around me like a fiery crown of glory. I had the world at my fingertips, and it quaked at my every whim.

"Wealth," they whispered as another image filled my head. I was adorned with jewels of every shape and size as I lounged on a bed of furs.

"Love." This time, the vision didn't just fill my mind, but it filled my body with a pulsating need. I could feel the hands of each and every Fae that had been lost in the darkness as they caressed me and touched every inch of my being inside and out. Each touch promised undying love and devotion. My heart would never be empty. My bed would never be cold. I would never lack companionship.

The last image made me realize something. This wasn't what I wanted. It's what *they* wanted. They had been cast aside, powerless, and unwanted. Yes, they wanted revenge on the courts, but they weren't evil by nature, only necessity. The shadows were exactly that, shadows of the Fae they once were, but they were still Fae, and Fae had rules.

"A place to belong, as we crave to belong. You will be ours, and we will be yours." Their voices pressed upon my skin, urging me to accept them, to be with them.

It's not like I wasn't tempted. Who didn't want unlimited power, more money than you knew what to do with, and people that would always love you? Even the most holy of men would have been tempted. But there was always a price, and with the Fae, the price may not be something I was willing to pay.

"You claim you are the Fae forgotten, but faded or not, you're still Fae." I could feel their curiosity pique at my words.

"Yes." The simple word hissed along my skin.

"Then you still have to obey the rules." I made it a statement, not a question.

The shadows shifted their massive form as displeasure filled their voice. "The Fae magic still holds us captive, but you could fix that. You could be the new law of the world. Of all the worlds." It tried to change the direction of the conversation back to me, but I wouldn't be deterred.

"But for the moment the law still stands." I was proud the voice in my head didn't quiver with fear as I neither denied nor accepted their offer. "And that means you have broken that law."

Shocked and disgruntled voices rose up around me. "We break no laws, Lady."

"Then tell me, when exactly did I give you permission to feed from me? I don't remember us ever making a deal." My voice hardened with my accusation, even as my fear fought to suffocate me.

The voices began to argue. They knew I had not given permission for them to feed off my dreams, and the Fae were all about permission. Evil Fae or not, rules were rules.

"But you wish to save the Fae pretender, do you not?" The shadows questioned. "We have brought you to her, so it is a fair trade to let us feed from your delectable dreams." It purred as it tried to placate me, its voices now back in agreement. "The winged Fae could not fulfill your bargain." They laughed. "She could not bring you through the mirror. She is too tightly bound by the UnSeelie Court."

So, she had been lying after all. Or maybe, she knew that this would happen. The prince said no Fae in their right mind would try to feed off a human's dreams so close to the Shadow Realm, and Seer didn't seem the stupid sort. Did she know the shadows would take the bait? That the only way for me to get into the Shadow's Between was to be dragged there by one of them? Even if she did, the shadows still broke the rules.

"That all may be true, but the deal was with Seer, not you. You can't pass off a deal from one Fae to the next." I was full of shit. I didn't know if you were allowed to pass them between one another. Hell, I barely knew what was going on half the time in this cockamamie world. I could only hope that I was right and they were in the wrong.

Their displeasure rolled off them in waves, their voices so loud my eardrums felt as if they would burst. I thought they would strike me dead then for daring to question their reasoning, but they didn't. They made sure that they were not touching me at all as they reveled in their anger. I was thankful for it, because as much pleasure as their caress could give, I'm sure they were much more skilled in pain.

The shadows' anger calmed after a few moments. Their voices lowered to a dull drum and their fingerless form reached for me once again. They petted my hair and rubbed my arms as if I were the one who needed calming.

"You are more worthy a leader than we thought. To see the logic and injustice of our actions," they praised me. "We shall make a new deal now, so there will be no questions about it."

"But you already stole your payment. A deal can't be made from stolen goods," I scolded them.

"You are here, are you not?" It growled at me, their anger leaking through. "We have already paid for the dreams we've taken without permission. A verbal transaction is all that is necessary to make it right."

"Rules are rules," I quoted Seer's words. "I didn't ask you to bring me here, and you didn't ask to feed from my dreams. You bringing me here was all on your own. If I'm to be your salvation, your lady, would you expect me to take such crap from a Seelie? Or even an UnSeelie?"

The looming shadows cried out in protest.

"Then why would you expect me to accept yours? As I see it, you owe me for the dreams you stole, and I demand equal payment. Only then will I consider being yours." I nodded to myself since my body was still inoperable.

They moved amongst themselves, debating my words, and whether they should agree to my terms. They would have to if they wanted me to cooperate. I still wasn't sure what exactly they wanted from me. I wasn't anyone's savior, let alone fit to be queen. All I wanted to do was get the key from Alice and get the hell out of dodge. I planned to sleep until next week, screw my mom and Sunday dinner.

"Very well." They came together at once. "We accept your terms. What is it you would have of us?"

I thought about it for a moment. What did I want? Being able to move would be good.

I must have thought the words too hard, because they asked, "And that would make us even?"

"Not hardly." I scoffed. "Why am I even unconscious anyway?"

"You were tired, your body needed rest." Their reasoning made sense, but once again they had done it without asking. Maybe that was why they got kicked out? They had problems with following the rules.

"Well, I am rested enough. Let me up." If they had heads, I would have sworn they exchanged glances as if they were not sure they should do as I asked.

"We admit you are not simply resting. After so many years of being in the dark, of living off the dreams of the headless, we have lost physical form. We are but a mass of energy on the wind. The thing in the dark that you dare not look at for it might look back. Thus, we are impossible to be heard to those who are not listening. We are able to communicate more clearly this way."

Their words reminded me of all the dark corners I had encountered in the Underground. They were the whispers that treaded along the edges of teeth, giggling in the dark at my naiveté as I questioned about wishes. I do remember the pounding on Chess' willow, so they must have some kind of abilities. They couldn't be completely powerless.

"You're Fae, can't you use magic? A glamour? Or I don't know, shapeshift or something?"

"If we could glamour ourselves, would we not have done so to blend in with the other courts?" Their voice rose to a shout, but a few whispered off in the edges. "We could take on the appearance of one of the headless."

"We could not do that!" The others argued back but soon changed its tone to question. "Could we?"

"Yes we could, but it would require a sacrifice. A death to make the magic work." The mass turned back to me at once in agreement with each other. "Do you wish us to destroy one of the headless?"

"What? No!" I couldn't let them kill another Fae just because I wanted to wake up. No matter their crimes. "There has to be another way."

They sighed. I could feel their frustration as well as the rage lurking just beneath the surface. They were becoming tired of my demands. The few that I had anyway. I knew they wanted me, no, needed me, but I could tell they were weighing the odds of dealing with me and getting what they wanted. Whatever that was.

"There is one who may die at any moment, what of them?" They inquired, apparently coming to a unanimous decision that I was worth the effort. A relief really.

"What do you mean? I thought Fae couldn't die of natural causes."

"We can't, but they have been here for hundreds of years. A Fae's dreams can only be fed on for so long before they are nothing more than an empty husk. This one is such a Fae. We would be taking pity on them, to end their life now rather than lay dormant, not much more than a lifeless doll."

I tried to weigh the pros and cons of their suggestion. I couldn't imagine living that way: a brain dead vegetable just waiting for death to claim me. Death would be kinder, but there had to be a catch somewhere. Death magic sounded dark and ominous – evil in every sense of the word. But I didn't see any other way out of my dream state. I couldn't lay there forever, and if it would bring someone else peace I could be all right with it.

"Fine. Do your death magic and let me up," I demanded before I could change my mind. I waited for them to start some kind of chant or to feel a magical pull, but nothing happened. "Well, are you going to do it or what?"

"It's already done." The voice that spoke was no longer filled with many voices, but with one singular voice. It was light and quirky with a hint of an accent I couldn't quite place, and it was decidedly male. Thankfully, it was nothing like the overpowering sound of the massive shadow. "Come, come now, all the fuss to wake up and you won't even open those pretty eyes of yours."

Ignoring the prodding to open my eyes, I flexed my muscles first. An arm. A leg. I wasn't 100 percent positive it was already done. Shouldn't death magic take more preparation? At least, some kind of dead language to call the Fae to their grave. Not that I was complaining. I could do with a little less complicated and a lot more straightforwardness.

When I was sure I was able to move my body, I placed a hand beneath myself and pushed myself upright. I peeked one quaking eye open.

I had expected many things when I opened my eyes. A blinding white room, like the first Between I entered, or a monstrous dungeon-like setting with chains, and maybe even a rack, or at least an iron maiden. I was kind of disappointed when I opened my eyes to a dungeon corridor, much like the one I had escaped in the Seelie Court.

"Not what you expected; is it?"

I jumped at the voice next to my ear and spun around, backing away on my hands and knees.

The man before me held up his hands in defense. A silly lopsided grin graced his slender face. Of all the prisoners to take the shape of, they had to pick someone that I would be attracted to. It wasn't like I didn't have enough of a problem with the prince and Chess.

He had dark brown hair that was tousled on top but short along the sides. The hair ran into sideburns that ended just below his ears, near the dark chocolate brown eyes that crinkled at the sides as he continued to smile at me. His hands were in the pant pockets of his black suit, and he rocked back and forth in a pair of beaten trainers.

"What exactly was the guy you are wearing guilty of?" I couldn't help the small smile that crept up onto my mouth. "Bad fashion sense?"

"Ah-hah." He laughed a much more carefree sound than before. "That's funny." He held a hand up, turning it back and forth as he examined his new body.

"I think he was some kind of time wizard. A funny lot they are. Academic hermit types. Always jumping about in time at a whim, never really paying any mind to the chaos they are ensuing in the other worlds. This one was the last of his kind. The Seelie Queen made sure of it when he was caught trying to change the outcome of our birth. Nasty business that was." His voice was so jolly and full of life it was hard to tell if he was serious or not.

I inched up from the stone floor, keeping my eyes on the man before me. Was this really the monstrous shadow that had me quaking in my bones just moments ago? It was hard to believe. It also didn't help that I was a sucker for a guy with great hair, which left me with the overwhelming urge to run my hands through his.

Why couldn't they have picked someone less attractive? It was going to be impossible to remember he was the bad guy, but then again, that was probably the point. Lucifer couldn't have persuaded so many to follow him if he was all terror and gruesome. Being enticing was part of the thrill of evil. Why would the Fae be any different?

"Now." He clapped his hands together, rubbing them in anticipation. "What would you have of us, Katherine?"

I stopped in my half crouch and waited. He knew my name. Something bad was supposed to happen if they found it out, wasn't it? My life force was supposed to drain away. My will taken from me. But as I crouched there, and my knees began to ache nothing happened.

He chuckled at my stance and shook a finger in my direction. "Now, haven't you been listening, Katherine?" My eyes met his when he said it again. "You aren't like the others."

I eased to my full height, what little of it there was, and watched him as a child would a distant relative: curious, but cautious all the same. Though he had a pretty face, I had to remember what dwelled beneath.

"So everyone keeps telling me," I grumbled, dusting the invisible dirt off my backside, so I could pretend I had something to do as I assessed him. "So, you know my name, what now?"

"Well, that's up to you." He circled me, his long legs stretching out before him with each step. He was so tall.

"Up to me?" I frowned at him.

"I demand equal payment," my voice rang out of his throat sounding strange and foreign to my ears. He smiled at my startled face, his eyes twinkling with mischief. "Or did you change your mind and letting you up was enough?"

"I haven't forgotten our deal. I'm just..." I searched about the corridor for some inspiration, "...not sure what to do next."

He moseyed – yes, moseyed – over to me and brought his face close enough to mine that I had to lean back to meet his eyes. "While we are your humble servants, may we make a suggestion?"

I took a step back as his third-party reference reminded me once again who was under that pretty face. "Sure."

He moved down the corridor and gestured at the many doors lining the walls. All of which seemed to be made of solid iron with no locks and no windows to peek out of. I supposed they didn't need a lock if the prisoners couldn't touch the door, let alone what awaited them outside of their cell. Though, in his current form, he didn't seem threatening to anyone.

"You came to find the pretender, did you not?" He stopped in front of one of the doors and pointed at a metal nameplate bolted into the wall. "What was her name again?"

"Al–" I started to say but caught myself at his cheeky grin. "I don't remember."

He frowned at my lie. "There's no use lying. We've been feeding off her and at one point we knew her name. But this guy's head," he wiggled his fingers at his head, "Has gotten us all jumbled up. It's hard to tell where his memories end and ours begin."

I marched over to where he stood, anger rising in me. "I thought you said he was a husk of a man. Nothing more than a vegetable? How did you get his memories if that were true?"

He scratched the side of his head with a finger, his eyes cast down to the ground. "Well, you see, it's a complicated process. Lots of long words to do with atoms and particle separation and–"

"Make it simple then," I growled, crossing my arms over my chest. I didn't like being made a fool, and while I was still wary of the Fae man, I'd rather be angry than scared any day.

"Fine." He narrowed his eyes at my command. "We are him. Or I am him. Every thought, every memory, and every feeling he has ever had is lodged right up here." He tapped the side of his forehead. "He exists no longer except when we are in this form."

I could only gape at him. It was impossible to process the enormity of what he had just admitted to. He, no, they hadn't just taken on his appearance; they had taken over his body, his very being, and made it their puppet. The Fae that had belonged to that wonderful face didn't get to pass over to the next world. He didn't get to die with dignity like they had led me believe. It was unacceptable.

"How could you do this? How could you just destroy another living being? One of your own? What have you done? What have I done?" I cried out, the horror of what I had allowed them to do stabbed at me.

It was my fault. I had told them to do it. I didn't even think twice about what it would mean to take on another Fae's face. I was only thinking about getting home.

"Now, now. There, there." He reached a hand out to pat me on the shoulder as the grief overwhelmed me. "What's done is done. No use worrying about it now. Unless..." he paused, his hand stroking the edge of his chin. "Unless his life was payment enough to make us even?"

"What?"

"You have to admit it seems like a fair deal. His life for your stolen dreams. More than fair I'd say." He gave a slight shrug of his shoulders.

I stood appalled that he would even try to get out of our deal by playing on my guilt. I was upset with what happened, but I wasn't stupid. I knew I had the upper hand, and I wasn't about to give it up for a mistake, no matter how regrettable it was.

"We will be even when I say we are even, and as far as I'm concerned, we are far from even." I pushed past him to get a better view of the nameplate. I growled at him over my shoulder. "Could you move back a little? I can't read anything in this light."

"Our apologies." I rolled my eyes as he placed his hand on his chest and gave me a half bow. He was as bad as Chess.

I squinted at the markings on the nameplate when his shadow wasn't blocking it. The name wasn't a name at all. It was just a set of initials.

"Who the fuck is J. S.?" I wondered aloud.

"Hey! Do you kiss your mother with that mouth?" He frowned before glancing down at the nameplate.

The fact that a being of ultimate evil, well, in those shoes ultimate was a questionable description, but for him to be scolding me about my language was laughable. Wasn't cursing a sin? Ranking in the evil category, technically, it would be a minor sin, but any sin I would think would be encouraged, not chastised.

"And that's the Fae in there. They only label them by initials, because they think it gives me less power over them. Not that they can keep from telling me their name for very long. I am after all, very persuasive." He gave me a lecherous smile that unfortunately had my insides tingling.

Damn my libido.

"How long are you going to keep that face?" I noticed he had started to refer to himself in first person, which must mean he was losing more of the collective thinking and becoming more like the time wizard he had absorbed.

As I walked down the dungeon hallway, I wondered how long it would take him to become the Fae completely. Would he no longer want revenge on his fellow Fae? I would hardly think it would be that easy.

He strolled down the corridor, glancing at each nameplate as he went. "As long as you require it of me." He paused in his search and tilted his head so some of his hair fell over his face in such a cute manner; I had to force my eyes to the door next to us.

"Do you not like it?" He held his hands up and twirled about like a model on a runway. "I could take someone else's form if you wish?"

The smile that was in the process of creeping onto my face went south. "No! I mean; you're fine the way you are now." I ended lamely, continuing to search for Alice's initials.

"Fine? Just fine?" He frowned, not at all happy with my response. "I took this form for your pleasure. I could have easily chosen someone else and all you can say is fine?"

"What do you want me to say?" I stared hard at the door in front of me. I wasn't here to pick up guys. I didn't want to be here at all. So his appearance was the least of my worries. "This is it." I pointed at the nameplate that had A. L. engraved into it.

"That you find me irresistible," he continued, disregarding my discovery. "Don't you?"

I glanced up into his blinking, brown eyes and wondered how in the world a mass of vengeful energy could be self-conscious. Why did he care what I thought? They said they wanted me to be their lady, but certainly they didn't mean in a physical sense?

Staring up into his eyes and seeing the intense hunger lying just beneath the surface, I realized they did. They had gone centuries without a friend or lover. No one to touch or hold them. Of course they hoped to have me – mind, body, and soul. Emphasis on the soul part.

"Yes, I find you attractive. Now, can we please," I gestured to the door before us, "Focus on the problem at hand? How do I get into her cell when there's not a door knob?"

I didn't know whether he believed me or not. He leaned a shoulder against the wall and nodded toward the door. "All you have to do is knock."

"Really? That's it?" My brow rose at the simplicity of it. "That's not very secure."

"To someone like you it's not, but to a Fae, that are deathly allergic to iron, a single touch would bring on such excruciating pain the very thought of it is enough of a deterrent. Besides…" His eyes filled with a wicked gleam. "The thought of me being out here terrifies them more than being trapped inside."

The reminder that underneath that silly grin was a force so fearsome Fae would rather be imprisoned forever than face them caused my own fear to spike. There was more to the shadows than they would lead me to believe.

He gave a curious sniff to the air and growled. "I thought we dealt with this already?

I'm not going to hurt you, so your fear is unwarranted. How can I get you to trust me?"

I took a deep breath and tried to quell my quaking insides. "Trust is earned, and it isn't fair to use my scent against me. Not to mention, disturbing."

"My apologies. I had forgotten how limited human senses are. It won't happen again." His head dipped down, but his eyes looked up at me through his lashes.

I turned from his ashamed face and knocked on the metal door. The heat against my knuckles was instantaneous. I jerked my hand back with a yelp and glared down at it. Unlike the door from the Seelie dungeon, which only led to a mild irritation along my skin, my knuckles turned bright red and stung enough to bring tears to my eyes.

I glanced up from my aching hand when the door began to whine and creak. I took a few steps back as the door inched open at a painstaking pace. I craned my neck as each inch revealed what lie inside.

Alice's bell-like voice tinkled from the cell. "What took you so long?"

AS FAR AS cells go, especially ones in solitary confinement, Fae had it far better than any human prisoner. The stone walls were draped with colorful curtains and pictures that depicted enchanted forests and faerie getaways. The stone floor was covered with a beige fur rug that looked soft enough to sleep on. Not that anyone would want to sleep on it when the overstuffed bed covered in pale lavender silk sheets was available to sink into.

The mirror, which gazed out into the Seelie dungeon, was covered once again, leaving the frame cloaked in red. Next to the mirror was a bookcase. It filled one entire side of the cell and was jam packed with so many books it would make any bookworm drool. Next to the magnificent bookcase, lounging on a long chaise with a book in hand, was Alice.

She was no longer a floating head, Alice's pale blue tea dress was draped over her lap, while a single barefoot dangled off the edge of her perch. Like her bow, her dress had seen better days. There were holes where moths had gotten to it and stains from what could have been grass, but had faded from time.

"Well? Are you going to stare all day, or were you here to rescue me?" Alice huffed, tossing her book down as she stood from her chair.

"I know why you were put in here," I blurted out without thinking.

Alice quirked a blonde brow, amusement sparkling in her eyes. "Oh, do you now? Is that why you took so long? Trying to dig up the goods on dear Ole Alice? And here all I was trying to do was help you?" She smirked as her eyes took in my disastrous hair. "Tell me, was it worth it?"

"Like you were trying to help out the prince?"

If it would end with me six feet under, I didn't think I wanted the type of help she could give. The shadow man gave a silent laugh as he stood just outside the door, and out of Alice's line of view. At least someone thought I was funny. The number of fans I had was dwindling by the minute.

Alice made a noise of disgust. "Of course no one told you the whole story. I can hardly be surprised. Fae just love their half-truths. 'Isn't it more fun to figure it out on your own?'" She imitated Chess' voice perfectly. So, Chess had spoken to Alice on more than just the one occurrence. It made me wonder what else he had bent the truth about.

"Well then, why don't you tell me what really happened?" I crossed my arms over my chest, tired of her games.

A slow smile spread across her face. It was one of those smiles that I had learned meant whatever she was about to say I wasn't going to like.

"Let's make a deal. I'll tell you my sad story and in return you get me out of here." She clapped her hands at the brilliance of her own idea.

"But I'm already letting you out in exchange for the faerie key." I frowned at having to remind her.

"Well, what do you want more? The truth or freedom?" She held her hands out as if to weigh the options. One hand was empty while the other held a small brass key with a red ribbon looped through it to be worn as a necklace.

I took an involuntary step toward the hand with the key, and she snapped it shut, holding it behind her back with a grin. Alice may have been human at one time, but now she was Fae through and through. Games, games, and more games. I wasn't leaving without that key, but I also wanted the truth so badly I could taste it, but how could I get both without offering up something more in return?

My own lips curled into a smile to rival her own as an idea formulated in my mind. Keeping my eyes on Alice, I called out behind me, "I've been horribly rude making you wait in the hall. Why don't you come on in?"

I didn't need to turn around to know when Alice saw him, the blood draining from her face and the slight step back made it easy enough to guess.

"You!" she stuttered, clenching her hands to her chest. "What are you doing here? I haven't been bad. I haven't been bad, I promise." When my companion did not answer, her eyes turned to me in desperation. "You can't let them take me. I've done nothing wrong."

"Ah, but weren't you just going to try and trick me into taking a different form of payment?" I turned my head to look back at the shadow man, who had an amused grin on his face. "I did hear her correctly, didn't I?"

"That's what I heard, love." The sound of his voice had taken a threatening edge that didn't match the smile on his face.

Alice searched between us, confusion on her face. "Wait. You're together?"

"Well, I wouldn't say that–"

"Yes, don't we make a lovely couple?"

I glared at the shadow man for interrupting me. "Not yet, we aren't."

"Ah, yet. That only means a when not an if, and I have plenty of time to wait. I'm a patient man after all." His voice was full of promises, but his eyes had not left the Fae girl before us. The hunger in his eyes had nothing to do with Alice's appearance and everything to do with food.

Alice gulped at the intensity of his gaze and turned to plead with me, "You can't trust them. They're liars. They don't want to help you–"

"And how is what you're doing any different?" I interrupted her with a shake of my head.

"But I was human once. I know what it's like to be tricked by them." She pointed a shaky finger. "They'll make you believe they can give you exactly what you want, but you'll end up regretting it in the end. Look what happened to me." Her fear turned to anger as she whipped her arms around the cell. "I'm stuck in this hell hole because I listened to them. I should have been a good little girl and went home to my mother." Alice buried her face in her hands and cried. "Being a Fae was supposed to be romantic and exciting, but it's not. It's boring and it never ends. I should have died a long time ago. I just want to go home!"

I sighed. I hated crying women. As a woman, crying was not something I liked to do. Tears were meant for children and mourners, not everyday problems. Especially when the tears were unwarranted, like Alice's were right then.

"Oh, pull yourself together." I crossed my arms becoming angry at my own discomfort. "It's been over 100 years, there's nothing for you to go back to, so there is no use crying over what can't be changed. You're a Fae now. Suck it up and deal."

"How can you be so cruel?" She sniffed, peeking up from her hands, her face puffy and red.

"Lady is right." I jerked my head to the shadow man, who had stepped into the cell, his presence causing Alice to take a few more steps backward. "She's not being cruel, she is being practical, but if you are really dissatisfied with your existence I could easily end it for you." He reached a hand out as if to touch her.

Alice shook her head, her eyes wide and once more filled with terror. "N-n-no. Don't come near me. Don't touch me."

I watched with mild fascination as she became more hysterical the closer the shadow man came to her. I could understand her fear, I had been before the masses and knew the sound of their collective voice, the feel of their touch on my skin and their breath on my face, but unlike her, I still had options. She could only die, and with her death, her key would be free for the taking.

"Please, no." Her eyes sought me out, begging me to help her. "Help me and I'll tell you! I'll tell you what happened. Just keep them away from me!"

I was half tempted to let him have her. I was tired of making deals, but I also wanted to know. Damn my curiosity.

"Stop," my voice rang out just as he was about to touch her golden head. "I still need her."

He turned to me with a frown on his lips. "Are you sure? I could just..." He held a hand out as if to touch her anyway.

"Yes. I'm sure. Are you questioning me?"

He frowned harder at the authority in my voice and something in his eyes flickered at being commanded. He didn't like my demanding tone. Not at all.

"No, but if you change your mind..." He dropped his hand and stepped back to stand beside me.

"I won't," I snapped, my eyes locking onto his, daring him to question me again. I liked being in charge and making the rules. I could get used to this.

I turned my attention back to the blubbering girl before me and grimaced. "He's not going to hurt you, so stop your crying. I'd like to get out of here as much as you." I exited the cell, not waiting to see if she followed.

"Which way do I go to get out of here?" I asked the shadow man. He put his hands in his pant pockets and rocked on his heels looking this way and that. "You do know how to get out of here, don't you?"

"Just hold on a second." He waved a hand at me. "There are many ways out. I am thinking of the best one. I wouldn't want you to end up somewhere unpleasant."

"No, you wouldn't want that," a sarcastic voice said from behind me. Alice had finally decided it was safe to leave her cell and stood in the doorway glaring at the shadow man.

"How did you change so fast?" I eyed her new attire.

No longer was she clothed in a stained and torn blue dress, but instead, she wore a black dress covered in red heart and spade patches. Her legs were encased in black tights with small red buckled shoes. She had small, red tea gloves and a miniature red top hat, adorned with a black feather.

"Isn't it lovely?" She held the knee-length skirt out around her. "I thought it up myself a while back, but hadn't had a chance to wear it until now."

"Did you make that?" Still a little in awe of her clothing.

"Oh, silly." She laughed waving me off. "Of course not. That's my gift."

"To make clothes?" I quirked a brow at her. That was a shitty power. If I was going to become a Fae, I'd want a better power than that. Like the ability to mute someone when they were being annoying. Or even to be able to eat anything I wanted without gaining a pound. Now that was a power I would give my soul for. There were so many possibilities, but changing my clothes at will, would not even have crossed my mind.

"I can do a lot more than that." She slid her hands up across her face and revealed my own face staring back at me but on Alice's head. "It's called a glamour."

I gaped and took a step back at the un-canniness of the face she had made. She had gotten every detail, down to the last freckle. Even her eyes matched the blue green clash that was my irises rather than my usual green. She slid her hand across her face again and Alice was looking at me once more.

"Now, tell her what naughty things you had to do to get the power you are so proud of," the shadow man hissed at her, causing her to step back, fear flashing in her eyes before she glared at him once more.

"I only did what *you* told me to. I am hardly to blame when I didn't have all the information – Fae and your half-truths. The lot of you can go to the reapers for all I care. Save the rest of us the trouble."

"Funny, you say so, when you wanted to be one of us bad enough to leave your world behind," he barked out, his lip twisted up in a sneer.

I rolled my eyes at them. We were going to be here forever.

"Weren't you figuring out what exit to use?" I offered up, turning the glaring Fae's attention back to me.

The shadow man frowned for a moment, clearly confused. "I already know which one."

"Well?" I gestured for him to lead the way.

"Fine. This way." He marched down the corridor, the carefree swagger he had obtained from the time wizard gone.

I took a step forward to follow him but stopped when Alice stared back into her cell. "Alice? Aren't you coming?"

She didn't immediately answer, and her voice was soft when she did, "I've been trapped for so long I'm a little scared to finally be free." She gave me a small smile. "Silly, isn't it?"

I watched her, not sure how to respond.

"Forget it." She shook her head and walked past me toward where the shadow man had gone. The heels of her shoes clicked on the stone floor.

I gave a cursory glance to the empty cell before turning on my heel to catch up with her.

What was it like to be imprisoned for centuries? Alone in a room with nothing but yourself as company? Did she get many visitors from the other side of the mirror?

I thought back to our previous conversation with Chess. She had pleaded with him first to be released, like she knew who he was and what power he had. Once again I wondered if they had met before.

"Alice?" I walked alongside the young woman.

"Hmm?"

"Have you and Chess met before?" I kept my eyes on our guide who didn't give any indication that he was listening to our conversation.

"What do you mean? I've been locked up since before he was born. Of course I've never met him." She scoffed, examining her hand as her gloves flickered between colors.

"But why did you ask Chess if you could leave back when we first met if you've never met him before?" I blew a strand of blonde hair out of my face, once again wishing for my hair tie that I had lost at the entrance.

She finally settled on a pale pink for her gloves, which spread out to her dress and hat. "I didn't say I've never talked to the cat, just that I've never met him. Seeing the cat with you was the first time I'd ever had a face to the voice."

"But he's in all the stories, so you must have met him before. Maybe you just don't remember?"

Alice gave a snort, rolling her eyes at me. "I think it'd be pretty hard to forget a delicious man such as Chess."

I couldn't argue with her there, the cat did leave an unforgettable impression.

"Besides, you know more about these stories than I do. I've been kind of busy being locked up and everything."

"Well, if not Chess, then some other cat? It doesn't make sense for it to be in the stories if it never happened." I frowned at the sarcasm in her voice.

The blonde tapped her chin as she thought about my words. "Well, there was that one cat, but he was quite rude. Very cryptic about everything, and he was just a big fur ball. Nothing at all like Chess' masculine physique." Her cheeks flushed at the thought of Chess.

I was so focused on her face that I walked straight into the shadow man that had stopped in his tracks. I felt myself falling backward and braced my hands for the impact. A hand wrapped around my wrist and pulled me hard against a warm body.

My shoulders tensed as my skin crawled where the shadow man touched me. He may have taken on a pretty face, but no amount of magic could cover the vengeful essence lying beneath his skin. The very feel of him pressed close to me made me sick to my stomach.

"Are you all right?" He tipped my head back, concern in his eyes.

I swallowed the bile that had crept up my throat. A bit breathless I spit out, "Yes, thank you."

My eyes locked with his, the dark pool of brown drawing me in. I could hear the whispers in my head again, but this time they froze me in place. I couldn't move or speak as I watched in horror as his face lowered down to mine. My eyes screamed for him to stop. For my face to move away. To do anything.

"Excuse me! This is no time for kissing," Alice piped in, causing the shadow man's eyes to tear away from mine, and with his concentration broken I was free.

I jerked out of his embrace, my eyes wide as I took several steps away from him. I had become too complacent with his presence. His aloof personality distracted me from the fact that he was Fae, and not just one Fae, but hundreds of vengeful souls merged into one being.

"Don't do that again." My voice was hard as my eyes burned with the heat of my rage.

He smirked at my words, then tipped his head back and laughed. "Can't blame a guy for trying."

"Yes. I can."

I pushed past him, my legs threatening to fall out from beneath me. Under my mask of rage was fear. A heart-stopping terror I couldn't let him see, because if he knew how afraid of him I actually was, I'd lose all my leverage.

"I said you couldn't trust them," Alice called out from behind me. "None of them. Every single one of the Fae are in it for themselves and would turn on you in a heartbeat."

"Is that what happened to you?" I kept my eyes forward as I felt the shadow man's presence against my back.

"I loved coming to Wonderland. The talking flowers, the rhyming animals sipping tea while Hatter sang fantastical songs about nonsensical things." Alice's voice became dreamlike as she reminisced. "And the handsome Fae prince was always so nice to me."

I ignored the fact that she had called it Wonderland. I was sure Alice knew she was wrong. "So what happened? You just up and decided one day this world was more appealing than ours?"

"Of course not. I'm not some delusional idiot." She glared at me. "I knew for all the beauty and fun to be had there was always a price." She eyed the man who was quiet as he trailed behind us only motioning which way every once in a while when we came to a junction. "Nothing and no one are what they seem here, and you can't trust your eyes or your ears." She eyed the shadow man. "Even for a pretty face."

"You've got that right." I snorted. I'd had my fair share of attractive Fae, and while appealing they may be, they still had their own agenda that had nothing to do with my well-being. "What happened then to make you change your mind?"

"I fell in love, what else?" Her lips curled up in a bitter smile. "He was my neighbor back home. He was so sweet to me, always wanting to hear about my adventures in Wonderland, unlike my parents who thought I was making it up. I thought he loved me."

"I had planned on coming back to Wonderland, I mean the Underground, to say goodbye because I had found my reason to stay. But..." Her eyes glistened with unshed tears. "It was a lie. He didn't love me." Her blonde hair whipped around her as she shook her head. "He was just like everyone else. He was only nice to me for the stupid book he was writing."

"The Adventures of Alice in Wonderland." I frowned, remembering something. "But when I mentioned the book before you seemed surprised?"

"Because he promised he wouldn't publish it, not after I..." She stopped and covered her mouth as a sob forced its way out.

"After you what?" I urged, but she soon was caught up in her sobs.

"Go ahead. Tell her," the shadow man finally spoke up, taunting her from behind us. "Tell her how you tortured him for days on end. Tell her how you changed your shape at will to the most hideous creatures imaginable. Until he was so afraid he wouldn't dare close his eyes for fear of waking to you standing over his bed, waiting to start it all over again."

My eyes widened at his words. Was she so heartbroken she would resort to such extreme measures? I'd never fallen in love. I couldn't pretend to understand what she was going through. If this was the result of love, I wasn't sure I ever wanted to be a part of it.

Alice turned her tear-filled eyes toward him, her despair turning to anger. "You have no right to judge me! I pretended to be her so it would look like he was cheating, because you said it would make her admit her feelings. But you lied."

The shadow man held his hands up and shrugged. "What can I say? Like you said, I'm Fae, and we are only in it for ourselves. Though, I had thought she would simply break the marriage off." He stroked his chin and then his lips curved up into a smile. "Killing herself was just a bonus."

My hands balled into fists at the smug grin on his face. The pieces were falling into place, and the picture it was painting was a grim one. How could anyone find their happy ending in this place when everyone was against you?

"I think it's time to go." I placed a hand on Alice's shoulder. My eyes locked on the monster before me. "No more stories. No more games. Where's the exit?"

He returned my glare with a growl. "You try our patience, human. But a promise is a promise." He turned the corner next to us and gestured to the wall. "Here is your exit."

I glanced around the corner to see the mirror he was pointing at. It was identical to the ones I had seen in the Seelie Court, glyphs along the frame and all. I reached a hand out to trace them with my finger and started when they came to life beneath my touch.

"You've always had the ability," he answered my question before I could ask it. "And now you have your exit. Take the pretender and leave this place." I didn't glance behind me as I ushered Alice through, but the shadow man caught my hand before I could follow. I narrowed my eyes at the hand holding mine. "I expect you to return to fulfill your part of the deal."

"I will." I jerked my hand out of his grasp. "Unlike you I don't go back on my word."

"Don't make me wait too long, or I'll come after you." He eyed me up and down, making my skin crawl with his gaze. "You won't like the result."

"What's taking so long?" Alice called out to me from the other side of the mirror.

"I'm coming." I responded as I backed into the mirror. My eyes never left his face as the cool liquid engulfed me.

CHAPTER

VEIL OF THE FAERIES

TRYING TO EXIT the mirror backward was as easy as trying to walk in five-inch heels – neither poised nor graceful, and I always ended up on my ass. So I wasn't entirely surprised when I fell out of the mirror and landed hard on the dirt. Didn't mean it didn't hurt all the same.

"Fuck." My hands had tried to catch me, but instead, I ended up scraping them against the ground, leaving dirt and little rocks encrusted in my palms.

"Well, aren't you graceful," Alice's snarky voice pointed out the obvious.

Looking up from my stinging hands, I searched out Alice who was seated neatly upon a rock formation. Her face was contorted in disgust, and a wary fear filled her eyes as her gaze darted around. I couldn't blame her. The mirror's destination was creepy as hell.

Dead grass and dirt patches pitted the ground. There was more rock than plants, and though there were trees and bushes, they were bare and twisted like they had been struck by lightning. It was as if all the life had been sucked out of the place, leaving nothing but a deserted wasteland.

"You really should have been more specific when you asked for an exit." Alice frowned. "Not that I'm complaining, mind you. I'm happy to be free, but this place has always given me the willies."

"Where are we?" I dusted myself off and moved to stand next to her.

She stood from her perch and swept out her arms to the area around us. "Welcome to the Veil of the Faeries. Where all your nightmares can and will come true."

Veil of the Faeries, huh. To me it was less like a veil and more like a graveyard, but who was I to critique someone else's décor? If I had to get through here to get home, then there really wasn't anything I could do about it.

"Well, I'm going to be going now." Alice clapped her hands together in finality. "Thanks for getting me out. Bye."

I grabbed onto the hand waving at me before she could poof away.

"What do you think you are doing? Unhand me," she cried out, struggling to pull her arm away, but I held tight. She wasn't going to get away that easily.

"I believe we had a deal." I held my hand out expectantly. My eyes narrowed when she glared down at my open palm. "Come on, hand it over."

She reached under the neck of her dress with a growl and jerked the key out from her bodice. When she fingered the key, making no motion to remove it from her neck, I tightened my grip until she winced. Finally, she huffed, ripped the ribbon over her head, and dropped it into my open palm.

The moment the brass key touched my hand I closed it with a snap. Still holding onto Alice, I glanced around us trying to decide where to go from here. I needed to get to the orchard, but I had no idea where that was from here. If only I had a map of some kind. Then again, I peeked back to Alice who was getting ready to dig the nails of her other hand into the one I had on her.

"I'll make you a deal," I announced, causing her to stop before she assaulted my hand.

"Another one?" She tilted her head to the side. Curiosity filled her face for a moment but then closed down. Her blonde locks whipped around her as she shook her head. "No. I'm done making deals with you. I just want to find somewhere I won't be recognized. I don't want to get thrown back in that cell after I just got out."

"Look." I sighed. "I don't really have a choice. I have no idea where I am or how to get to the orchard from here." I gestured to the dead terrain. "I need a little direction is all and then you can go crawl into a hole for all I care."

"Honestly? That's all?" She frowned, not really believing my words.

"Yes. Cross my heart and all that jazz." I crossed the hand holding the key across my chest.

"What?"

"Never mind." Obviously, my pop culture references would be lost on someone locked up for over a century. "Do we have a deal or what?"

"Fine. Go that way." She pointed down a worn path directly in front of the mirror. "And you will hit the palace. The orchard is on the other side, but you'll have to go through the Queen's gardens to get there."

I stared down the path she had pointed to. There was a weird light along the path, even though the night sky was void of any kind of moon. I shivered at the ominous presence coming from the direction of the palace. Did I really want to go it alone?

Before I could make my decision, Alice dug her nails into my hand. The sharp pain caused me to cry out and lose my grip, which the blonde used to release herself from my grasp. Rubbing her wrist, she backed away from me with a glare.

"Don't lose that key. I'll be wanting it back," she informed me before disappearing with a snap of her fingers. The sound radiated out into the darkness.

I looped the ribbon of the key around my neck, and made my way down the path, keeping a wary eye on the shadows in between the trees. Something made Alice afraid of this place. With each step I took, I was beginning to understand.

I could feel eyes boring into me like an itch along my skin. I jumped when a branch near me snapped. My eyes darted to the sound as I searched around in the dim light for the culprit.

Finding nothing, I quickened my pace along the path. My feet moved even faster as more branches and twigs snapped beneath what sounded like little feet. Giggles echoed out in the dark at my rising fear.

I stumbled as a buzzing noise flew by, giving a vicious tug on my hair. I spun around, but nothing was behind me. There was more snickering, and then there was another yank on my hair from behind me.

"Argh!" I stomped my foot. I heard tiny peals of laughter at my display of emotion. Someone was playing with me. I really didn't want to play any more bullshit games. Thought they were funny, did they? I'd show them funny.

I could be fucking hilarious.

I tensed myself for another attack, and the moment I felt a light weight on my hair, my hand swung out. I hit something solid. Yes!

My feet fell out from under me before I could do a victory dance. I glared at the cackling darkness when I crashed to my hands and knees. My already scrapped hands stung as I scanned the area for my attacker. I searched the air around me for what I hit before landing on a small moving figure on the ground.

Not more than four inches tall was a walking stick. No. Not a walking stick, a faerie. Its skin was brown and grey like the bark of a tree. Its wings thin skeletal spines with barely enough skin covering them to fly.

I inched closer to get a better look at it. Its arms and legs were as skinny as its torso, which wasn't much bigger than my pinky. Its fingers were bone thin as were its toes, and its scowling face was as thin as the rest of it. It had long, black wiry hair and no clothes or any distinguishing gender parts. Razor-sharp teeth snarled at me, and its big black eyes bore a hole into my face.

I stuck a finger out toward it, and it gnashed its sharp little teeth at me. I jerked my hand back with a girlish eep, causing the winged creature to snicker.

Growling at my own cowardice, my hand shot out and snatched the little shit up. It waved its fists in alarm, its voice a high-pitched noise as it yelled profanities at me in a language I didn't understand. I brought her, him, whatever it was, up to my face and snarled back.

"I don't know what your problem is, but you and your little friends..." I glowered at the twittering coming from the branches. Their little bodies and black shiny eyes became visible now that I knew what I was looking for. "Need to knock it the fuck off. I have enough Fae riding my ass. I don't need you little twigs adding to it."

I tried to toss the faerie down, but my little speech had pissed it off, and it latched itself onto my hand. I shook it with an impatient growl and then yelped when the little bastard bit me. It smiled up at me with its teeth still locked into my hand.

"Let go, you nasty little faerie!" I grabbed onto its body with my other hand and tried to dislodge it. "Who knows what kind of diseases you have!"

I fell back on my butt when it let go of my hand with a sudden pop. I turned to chastise it for biting me, but the words died on my lips as it licked its chops, smacking them as if I tasted like a double decker chocolate cake with whip cream frosting.

I couldn't taste that good, could I? I'd never tasted my own blood with much thought before. Chess had said I tasted old when we kissed. It definitely wasn't chocolate cake worthy. It must have found something it liked because the faerie leaped into the air with a small battle cry.

It would have been cute if it hadn't been a signal for a whole horde of faeries to come popping out of the surrounding shadows. There had to be at least 100 little brownish-colored creatures, each almost identical to the one who'd bit me, hovering just above their hiding spots. The only distinguishing feature between them was the length of their hair. Some had long hair like the offending nit, while others had short. The gender of the creatures was still a mystery.

They watched me with hungry eyes as the first faerie hovered a bit away from where I sat. The horde seemed to be waiting for some kind of sign. I wasn't sure I wanted to be around when the signal was called.

"Hey, come on now." I gave a nervous chuckle. "There's no need for violence." I searched around me, desperate for some way out of the faerie horde's focus. Where was a mirror when you needed it? Or a big can of bug spray?

I watched as the one who'd attacked me rattled on in its nonsensical language to the gathering faeries. The rise in its voice and the vigorous gestures of its hands was not foretelling a good ending for me. I had to get out of here before I became as dead as the terrain around me.

While the faerie inspired its fellow Fae, I inched into a crouched position. My eyes darted to those around me for any telling sign of attack. As the speech reached its crescendo, I took off in a knee-jerking run.

I didn't look back as the faeries cried out in alarm, or when I heard the rattling of their wings beating together as they chased after me. A few caught up to me, pulling my hair and nipping at any exposed skin they could.

I put my hands up, swatting at them as my legs began to ache from over exertion. Though I hadn't run far, my body was telling me it was at its limit. I really did need to join a gym. If not to stay in shape, then so situations like this didn't come up again. Then again, when was I ever going to be chased by a horde of faeries again?

Hopefully never.

I could feel myself slowing down as more of the faeries crowded around me. They bit and pulled at my arms and legs as they tried to knock me to the ground. The thing that got me, though, wasn't my exhausted legs or the nasty winged Fae, but a rock. A fucking rock hidden in the shadows.

When I fell, I fell hard. My knees hit the ground in an explosion of pain that rocketed up my back. The moment I was on the ground the horde came upon me. The weight of them kept me from being able to turn over to fight them off. All I could do was curl into a ball and try to protect as much of myself as possible.

Shit. Their teeth hurt. It felt like millions of tiny needles being jabbed into me at the same time, taking bits of me here and there. They were going to kill me, and there was nothing I could do about it. No Mop and Trip to talk their way out of it. No Chess to pop in and out again. Not even the UnSeelie Prince to save me.

Hell, I'd take Alice or even the shadow man at this point. Some kind of Fae intervention. Anything to make it stop.

Then it hit me.

I was Fae. Well partly. I could make it stop.

I stopped the satyrs, didn't I? I didn't even know I was Fae then. I wasn't a helpless damsel in distress who needed saving. Being part Fae had to mean something, didn't it? I had to have some kind of power, besides going between worlds. Otherwise why would the shadows want me to join them?

As I began to believe in myself, in my own ability to save myself, I could feel something rising up in me. The need to save myself. To make the faeries stop. It pressed against my insides trying to get out. It reminded me of the magic in my little fantasy about the prince. It pushed itself to the limits of my essence, and then all of a sudden, like a dam breaking, it rushed out of me, tearing a scream from my throat.

Tiny winged Fae were thrown across the dark, hitting the ground and trees with a thud. Though it hurt to do so, the moment the weight let up, I tried to move my body. My eyes peeked out to prepare for a counter attack, but the faerie didn't try again. The ones who weren't knocked out kept a wary distance as if afraid of my power and me.

Power. *My* power. I didn't know how I made it happen. If it was because I was under duress or because I wanted it to happen, either way I was getting out of here.

I grimaced as I pulled myself to a standing position. The bites were bleeding, my blood dripped onto the ground and my clothes. I glared into the grey veil; the watching faeries flinched when my gaze passed over them. Satisfied they wouldn't attack me again, I began to limp down the path toward the palace.

With the faeries at my back, it didn't take long to get to the end of the path and the beginning of another hedge maze. I plopped down onto the ground with a groan. Not another obstacle.

I was tired, sore, and hurt. I wanted to go home. Lick my wounds. Change clothes at least. Not fight my way through something else. Glancing down at the tiny wounds on my body, I decided to inspect the worst of the damage before trying my hand at the new area.

It wasn't as bad as I thought. There were mostly scratches and shallow bites here and there. Some deeper than others. They must have been trying to taste more than maim. It was good for me, but still a little disconcerting.

Would they come after me again?

I was pulled away from inventorying myself when rustling from the hedges made me tense. No more. There was no way I could endure another fight so soon.

As I prepared for another attack, I hoped my new power would come when called, but I sagged when a familiar brown and white face popped out from around the corner.

"What have ye done to yerself now?"

CHAPTER

PAINTING THE ROSES RED

I TRIED TO make my face contrite as Mop patched me up, but I didn't have the energy. Maybe it was the blood loss, or maybe I just didn't give two shits about what anyone thought anymore. It was probably a little bit of both. I did try to listen to Trip as he told me what happened to them after I was arrested.

"Trip wanted to stay and rescue Lady, Trip did!" Trip grabbed my arm, causing me to groan as he tried to make me understand. "But Smiling Cat showed up and said we'd get in trouble if the queen caught us too. Said we should leave it all to him, so Trip and Mop went back to the Smiling Cat's house, though, Mop complained an awful lot, Mop did."

I gave the opalaught a weak smile and patted him between the ears. "It's all right. I would have done the same. If you'd gotten caught as well then who would have been there to tell Chess to rescue me?"

"Fat lot of good that did." Mop growled, shoving his bandages back into a small pouch at his waist. "Look at the state ye be in! Tore to pieces by thems faeries, ye hair's a complete wreck, and where be that damn cat?" He waved his arms around. "Nowhere. Just like always. Not worth a lick, that's what he be. I told ye." He shook his finger at me. "I told ye he couldn' be trusted."

I waved him off with a hand as I moved to stand up. "It wasn't entirely his fault. He got me out of the Seelie Court, but where he went afterward I don't know. He never made it through the mirror. The rest..." I gestured at my hair and bandaged arms. "Is a series of consequences made from my own decisions. You can't fault him for that."

"But the Smiling Cat promised." Trip's face became serious, his tail rigid behind him. "And when Fae makes a promise, they have to fulfill it. Smiling Cat did not keep Lady safe like he promised, no Smiling Cat did not." He shook his head, and his eyebrows scrunched together at the cat's betrayal.

"I be tellin' ye before, when are ye going to learn?" Mop chastised Trip. "His word don' mean nothin'. That cat doesn't play by our rules, never has."

"Because he's a half-breed, right?" I intercepted.

The brownie raised a curious brow at me. "How'd ye find out bout all that?"

"I haven't just been getting myself in trouble, you know. I've figured some things out along the way." I rolled my eyes as I stepped over a root poking out beneath a hedge.

"Oh, yea?" Mop sounded surprised that I had been able to untangle some of the mysteries of the Fae world all on my own.

"You bet. I even got the key from Alice." I pulled the red ribbon out from between my breasts to show them.

"Shh!" Mop hushed me, glancing around with wide eyes. "Have I taught ye nothing? Don't say her name!"

"Might as well get over it, because I let her out." I gave a smug grin, and then grimaced when a particularly deep bite began to protest from all my moving around.

"Ye did what?" Mop covered his mouth at the loudness of his voice, once again searching for some unseen eavesdropper. He lowered his voice to a whisper and hissed, "Why'd ye go and do that fer?"

"Because it was the right thing to do." I placed my hands on my hips, daring him to argue. "Besides, it was the only way I could get the key from her. Though, dealing with the shadows was not something I had anticipated."

"The shadows!" Trip cried out, his fur sticking up as his eyes darted around.

"That what happened to ye hair? Ye be makin' deals with those monsters?" Mop growled at me.

"That was actually a misunderstanding I took care–" Mop grabbed my arm and jerked me back before I went around the next corner. "What?"

"Shh!" He put a finger to his mouth. "Listen."

I glared down at the brownie but did as he said. I angled my head to hear whatever had caused the pair to clam up. A voice. It was humming a sad and depressing tune, barely heard above the sound of water falling. The mixture of music with the sound of the water caused my mind to flashback to the satyrs.

My pulse raced and panic flooded my senses. Not again. I couldn't do it again. I was already going to be in therapy for the rest of my life. I'd break if I had to fight more of them off. I wasn't strong enough. I needed to get out. I needed to-

Mop tightened his grip on my arm when I tried to bolt. I glowered down at him, giving a violent jerk on my arm.

"Let go. I need to go. I won't deal with them again. Not if I can avoid it."

"Calm down, ye ninny. It's just the queen. This be her garden we be walkin' through." He reminded me, his eyes looking beyond the corner toward the sound of the humming.

"The queen? But we're in the UnSeelie Court, why would she be over here?" I kept my voice to a dull whisper.

"This is our queen." Trip's ears perked up to hear her song.

"The UnSeelie Queen? You mean Ma–" I caught myself before I could say her name. Wouldn't do to give away too much of what I'd learned. "You mean the prince's mother?"

Trip nodded his head, his face eager to see his queen.

"Why does she sound so sad?" I was curious to see Mab, the tall, black beauty I'd seen in my vision in person. What would cause such a fierce woman to sound as if the love of her life had died?

Mop scoffed, giving me an impatient look over his shoulder. "You'd be upset too if you hadn't seen your only child in over a century."

I angled my head to see around the corner, my eyes searching for the face that went with the song. What I found instead was a garden of outstanding beauty. I stifled a gasp as my eyes took in the rows and rows of flowers of all shapes and colors. I recognized only a few, and the rest were ones I'd never seen before.

I liked flowers as much as the next girl. Though, I'd rather have a book over a bouquet any day, I could appreciate the magnitude of what I was seeing.

The flowers were arranged so they made a circular pattern along a stone path. At the center of the circle was a large, marble statue depicting an image of Adam and Eve beneath the Tree of Life, but instead of a serpent hanging down from the tree as in most depictions of the story, there was another woman peeking around the base of the trunk.

What was a garden this beautiful doing in the UnSeelie Court? Wasn't it more of the Seelie Queen's style? And why did the Tree of Life appear eerily like the tree from my vision?

"Are you going to stand there all night?" A voice from behind the statue asked, and then I noticed the humming had stopped.

I glanced down at Trip and Mop for some guidance. They shrugged their shoulders. Well, they were a lot of help. I inched out from behind the hedge and made my way along the garden path.

When I came upon the woman whose voice had called out, her beauty once again stunned me. The vision did not do her justice. Her hair cascaded down her back in waves of inky silk, which blended into the black of her gossamer gown. The gown hung off her shoulders, exposing her pale, white shoulders to the moonless night. Her long fingers held the stem of a white rose, the tips of its petals bled into red.

"I have heard a lot of about you, Katherine."

I watched as she bent her ear down to the flowers as if listening to their whispers. So this is where the flowers reported. It's no wonder she knew my name already.

"Not all bad I hope." I tried to joke, but clamped my mouth shut when she turned her gaze to me. The sadness in her song was gone and had been replaced with a condescending tone.

"You have been a busy, busy little human." She stepped toward me, taking my chin in her hand to examine me as her son had done. "Breaking so many rules in so little time."

"But I can–"

"I am talking," she snapped, cutting me off. The commanding sound sent a chill down my spine. For all her beauty, she wasn't someone to be trifled with.

I clamped my mouth shut at her steely gaze.

"Not signing in. Piggybacking on into our world on someone else's key. Trampling all over that gruesome talking head's insides. Causing havoc at the Hatter's. Even crashing my dear cousin's precious party." She gave a dark chuckle. "In short, you have caused quite a stir in the Underground."

I opened my mouth to apologize but stopped. I had nothing to apologize for. I never meant to end up in their world, let alone cause so much strife. My initial curiosity had landed me in the Underground, but since then I had tried my best to play by the rules, ever changing as they may be.

"Do not misunderstand." Mab smirked at my solemn expression. "I find it all delightful news. My cousin has made life stifling with all of her rules. 'Do not say this. Do not do that.'" Her voice mimicked the White Queen. "It was high time for a change."

Her personality flip-flops were giving me whiplash. One moment she was cool and indifferent, the next she was a hot blaze of anger, and then she was happy as a clam. It made me wonder how much of the UnSeelie Prince's personality was inherited from his mother and how much was because of the spell?

"I'm glad I could cause you some amusement," I said, eyeing the dark queen for any signs of displeasure.

"The thing that makes your appearance in our world all the more fascinating," she continued as if I'd never spoke. "Is not the reaction from the Underground, but from that of my son."

Her gaze misted over at the mention of the UnSeelie Prince. "I myself have not seen or heard from my dear boy, but my flowers." She caressed the pelts that gave a sort of sigh. "They keep me up to date of his comings and goings. They had some interesting words to say about you too."

"He should have alerted the guard the moment you stepped foot in the Underground, but for some reason he did not." Her dark blue eyes surveyed me. "Why do you think that is?"

"How should I know?" I shrugged my shoulders.

I had no clue why he would do such a thing. He had no problem threatening Mop and Trip, and while he had threatened me as well, it was more of a playful poking than an actual real threat. The prince was as much a mystery to me as he was to his mother.

"He planted these for her, you know." Her long, red-painted fingers stroked the petals of the roses before her.

"Who did?"

"They were supposed to be a wedding gift, but well." She sighed, snapping the rose at its stem. "You know how that turned out."

I gave an awkward cough, not sure what she wanted me to say. Instead, I focused on the roses. "They are an unusual color. I've never seen a rose with white and red petals before."

"No, I cannot imagine you have." She gave a small sad smile. "They used to be as white as a newborn Opalaught's coat, but after that horrid incident, they began to bleed red. They've stayed that way for the last century or so, but for some reason," she held the rose out for me to examine, twirling it around between her fingertips. "They have begun to turn white again. Very curious, is it not?" Her eyes twinkled as her lips curved up in a peculiar smile.

I licked my dry lips. "Yes, very curious."

"Here, take it." She held the rose out to me. I stared down at the rose and then up to her eyes, which seemed to be searching for some kind of reaction.

"Oh no." I shook my head. "I couldn't."

Mab's eyes hardened, the curve of her lips pressed into a thin line. "Would you deny a gift from the Queen's garden, the garden you are currently trespassing on?"

I gulped. Well, when she put it that way, I couldn't refuse. I reached a hand out to grasp the stem in my hand, but the moment I touched it, a sharp sting caused me to drop it. Of course it had thorns. I should have known better.

"I'm sorry." I gave a quick apology as I reached down to pick it up. Before I could pick it up, the queen's lace-covered shoe stepped out and crushed the rose beneath her foot. I gave a wary glance up to the queen.

"Speak no more of it. There are plenty more. You must be more careful." She took my hand in hers, examining the blood swelling from the prick. "Blood like yours should not be wasted."

I had a feeling I knew what she was going to do, but before I could take my hand back, she pressed her mouth to the wound and licked the blood from my skin. I watched her face as it contorted between disgust, surprise, and then a knowing smirk.

"Well now, that is interesting." Her inquiry was more to herself than directed at me.

"What?" She wasn't the first one to find my blood appealing. Could she tell I was part Fae? Did she know I was human? Or did she find out something different altogether?

"Nothing of importance." Mab waved a hand, dismissing me. "Now get out of my gardens before I call the guards."

"But–" I started, but found Mop and Trip at my side in an instant, leading me back out of the garden. As I let myself be dragged away, my eyes darted back to the queen, who'd turned her eyes back to the roses before her. Something had transpired here, and even though I had been present, I was lacking the knowledge of knowing what it was.

"And, Katherine."

I paused at the exit. "Yes?"

Without turning to me, she spoke, "We will meet again. Have no doubt."

My brow furrowed at her cryptic statement. Before I could inquire further, Mop and Trip pulled me into the maze and out of sight. Curious indeed.

THE ORCHARD

THE HEDGE MAZE wasn't as much of a maze as an entryway into the orchard. Thankfully, it was nothing compared to the headache I endured before encountering the satyrs. A few more turns and I found myself standing at the entrance of what was without a doubt the orchard.

My confusion over Mab's final confounding words was pushed aside as I was drawn into the reality of where I was actually standing. The orchard. It had been a hard and mystifying trip, but I was finally going home.

The orchard was exactly what it sounded like, an orchard. Though, I'd never been to one back home, it was the same as most were in books and movies. There were a dozen or more rows of trees, all with different colored fruit. At the moment, there was nobody to harvest them. Actually, there was nobody around at all.

A light breeze blew my hair across my face. The majority of it was still white and I wondered briefly how I was going to explain that change, let alone my eye color. Would it change back on its own, or was I stuck with it for the rest of my life?

"The door's this way." Mop waved me over toward a stone wall that wrapped around the orchard, caging it in.

"Mop?"

"Hmm?" He moved along a path, which circled the trees. There were wheelbarrows and baskets sitting alongside the wall as if workers would come back any moment. For all I knew they would.

"I was wondering about my hair and eyes."

"Yea, what about them?" He didn't look at me as he answered.

"Well, am I stuck like this, or what?" I gestured to my hair, growling at his nonchalant attitude.

"Nah, the affects don't last. As long as you don't be lettin' anymore Fae feed on you that is. Ye should be back to normal after a few days." He paused and then shrugged his shoulders. "Probably."

"Probably?" Mop sped his pace up, ignoring my question. "Wait. Mop? What do you mean probably?"

"Trip likes Lady's hair."

I glanced down at my long-eared friend and smiled. He always knew what to say to make me feel better. I'd miss him when I got home.

It felt like I had spent a lifetime in the Underground. What did my grandmother's house even look like? What did my bed feel like? Did anyone miss me? Would there be cops waiting at my doorstep with my overly dramatic mother crying about her socially awkward daughter's quick hang up? It was hard to guess what would be waiting for me.

More than likely no one had noticed. Everything would be the way it was and work would be there in the morning. It was half tempting to stay in the Underground just for the lack of enthusiasm I had for the human world in general.

"Are ye comin' or not?" Mop snapped his fingers at me, pulling my focus to the little brown Fae. "Time's a wastin', and I'd rather not spend my best years lollygaggin' with ye."

"Impatient to get rid of me, huh?" I smirked as he shuffled his feet. If his skin had been lighter I'd swear he blushed.

"Well now, I wouldn't say that. I've grown kind of used to ye." He scratched the back of his head. "Don't ye wanna go home?"

I thought about it for a moment. Did I want to go home? Not really. What was there for me? No real job. No boyfriend. My family, I could admit, I would miss no matter how out of place I was in the family pictures.

"I don't know to be honest."

"Lady could stay." Trip tugged on my hand. "Lady could stay with Trip. Trip would let Lady sleep in Trip's bed."

I laughed at the excitement in his eyes. "Oh really? Then where would you sleep?"

Trip opened and closed his mouth as he thought about it. I giggled at the dumbfounded scrunch of his brow. Guess I wasn't staying with Trip.

"It's all right." I patted him between the ears. "I really should go home. But you guys could always come visit. You have to deliver my biscuits to Teeth for me, remember?"

"Or ye could do it."

My eyes snapped to Mop. "But wouldn't you guys get in trouble? I mean, look at all the trouble it took to get me to this point."

"Yea but ye have the faerie key now." He pointed to the key around my neck, causing me to hold it up to examine it.

"What about it? I have to give it back, don't I? I mean, it does belong to Alice." I waited for Mop's usual chastising growl, but it didn't come. Instead, he shrugged his shoulders not at all worried about my slip.

"Not unless ye be wantin' to, and that there key don't have no time limit like the rest of them. It was stolen from the reception desk the first time the girl was here."

I clasped the key in my hand. It made me feel better to know I could come back. It made leaving so much easier, yet I still didn't want to go.

"Trip doesn't want Lady to leave. Trip will miss Lady." Furry white arms wrapped around my legs, and his ears and tail drooped.

I held my hands up not wanting to touch the opalaught. If I did, I knew I'd start crying. I really didn't want that to happen. If there's one thing I hate more than crying women it is when I cry. I'm not a pretty crier. I get all splotchy and puffy, a runny nose, and then I'd start wailing. It was not an attractive picture.

Seeing my dilemma, Mop placed a hand on Trip's shoulder, easing the opalaught away from me. "Come on, Trip. Let's go back to the tea party. Hare will be wantin' to know how everything went. And Hatter should be back by now."

Trip's sad eyes filled with eagerness at the thought of seeing his cousin again. The very thought of going back to Hatter's gave me a headache. That was one place I wouldn't miss.

I mouthed a thank you to Mop who nodded his head.

"Ye take care of ye self, and we'll see ye again after everything dies down on this side."

I gave a curt nod. "I will and thank you for everything."

I watched as my two companions that I hadn't known for long, but had become endeared to me, made their way back down the orchard's path. My eyes followed them until they disappeared beyond the trees, and I could no longer delay what I had to do. What I needed to do.

I turned back to the door before me. It was identical to the one I had entered back in the Between. It had the same texture to the wood, the same brass doorknob; even the scars in the wood were the same.

I supposed it would only make sense for me to come out the same place I went in. Meaning, I would have to go through the Between again and meet that horrid two-headed bird. Gripe and Type.

Great.

I gripped the key in my hand and poised it to insert into the keyhole. The urge to stay roared in me even as the key touched the hole. Though, before I could slide it home, the key jerked from my hand and into the brush a few feet away.

I glanced between the door and where the key landed. The feeling that was urging me to stay changed to an urgent need to go to it. My feet moved on their own, and with each step closer to the key, the need increased until I found myself before the brush. I bent down, searching between the branches. I could see the key glinting in the dark. I reached my hand out to grab it, the brass key just out of my reach.

Just a bit further.

I got down on my hands and knees and inched my way into the brush. I pushed the branches away from my face, the leaves pressing against my arms as if urging me forward. With each inch into the foliage, the key seemed to be further and further away. Then, when I glanced back, I could no longer see the orchard. The branches had closed behind me, blocking out any chance of going back.

Something or someone wanted me to come this way. I could still feel the tugging on my stomach, telling me I had to keep moving. There was something waiting for me. What it was, I had no idea, but I knew deep inside it was important. A piece of me was missing and I needed to get it back.

The bushes seemed to go on forever. The further I pushed my way through the more there were. I was about to give up hope of ever getting the key, despite my intense need, when I happened to glance to the left and see a wooden sign. The majority of it was covered by a bush and was overgrown with vines. I ripped the vines away to uncover the wood beneath.

It had seen better days. The wood was worn and decayed, and there were grooves along the edges from where animals had gnawed on it. In the dim light, I could barely make out the faded words etched into the wood's surface.

'Enter at Your Head's Risk.'

Well, that wasn't ominous at all. I peeked back at the closed over path. I didn't really have a choice; I'd already come this far. If I did get caught and ended up back in the Shadow's Between...well, hopefully, the shadow man would be there to rescue me. I shook my head and laughed at the thought of the shadows saving anyone. It sounded crazy even by Fae standards.

Passing the sign, I crawled further into the tunnel of bushes. As I progressed further, my eyes locked onto the key in front of me, the small opening I had to move through seemed to expand up and out, until I was able to stand up from the ground. There were fewer branches now and stone walls peeked out from between where one bush ended and another began. The heels of my boots made a click-clacking noise as the ground faded from dirt to stone floors.

Though I hadn't seen anyone move the key, or an invisible force picking it up, the key was always a few feet ahead of me. I was beginning to wish I had taken Trip up on his offer to stay with him when my game of cat and mouse ended. I found the key right at my feet.

I bent down, my hand slow to reach out and take the key for fear of it moving again. My shoulders relaxed when the cool metal of the key pressed into my hand when I wrapped my fingers around it.

Finally.

Standing up, I looped the key around my neck as my eyes took in my new surroundings. The stone walls were bare of any green life forms, and they wrapped up and around the area. A hoot from my right jerked my eyes to my missing feathered friend. What was he doing here? I stared up at the ceiling where the stone curved up into a dome.

How did he get here? I glanced back to Mr. Blue Eyes and noticed the familiar large stones he was perched on. I had a feeling I had been here before.

"I didn't mean to. I didn't know what would happen." Alice's voice echoed in my mind as my eyes searched out the tree I knew would be there.

Staring up at the tree, it was not as huge as I had believed from my perch in the daydream. The tree was actually not much bigger than a one-story house. The large roots poking up from the ground were disproportionate to the height of the tree, as if they had grown out on their own accord. There was one thing about the tree that was the same.

The fruit.

Unlike in the dream where there was an abundance of fruit, a lone glowing fruit hung from one of the branches. The peach-like shape made the fruit resemble a glowing ball of light and it beckoned me forward.

My eyes stayed on the fruit as I once again found my feet moving on their own. The closer I got to the tree, though, the more I found myself drawn to something else in the roots. The need that had begun to settle in my belly flared to life.

There was something there. I remembered something. Something from the vision or maybe a memory? But how was that possible? I'd never physically been here before, had I?

I stretched my hand out, taking one step after another, each step becoming more urgent than the last. I fell to my knees, both of my hands spread out across the rough surface of the tree's roots. The magic inside me, which had not surfaced since the veil, began to raise its head, seeking out something that lay beneath the tree's base.

A body.

It was there, beneath the wood and stone, but hollow. An empty shell forever stuck in time. It was no use to my magic now. It couldn't fill the empty hole inside me. The one I somehow had always known was there but could never fill.

I sat back onto the ground, leaning back against the base of the tree, my eyes wandering to Mr. Blue Eyes who was watching my every movement. He tilted his head to the side, eyeing me as if to ask 'What are you going to do now?'

I wish I knew.

The magic in me was still simmering on the surface, waiting to be released. To where though? There wasn't anyone attacking me. I didn't have a clue what I was capable of let alone what I could do to dispel the magic that had built up in me.

My eyes swept away from the owl and across the rock-filled area before landing back on the lone glowing fruit I had bypassed earlier. Why was there only one? In the vision I had there were so many more on the tree. Had someone taken them? The tree did seem a bit more worn than before.

My magic tingled along my skin as I thought about the glowing fruit. My hand came up and beckoned the fruit forward. At first nothing happened. I furrowed my brow and coaxed the energy from below my skin to do as I bid.

Mr. Blue Eyes squawked an alarming cry when the fruit wiggled on its stem. Fighting the temptation to look at him, I kept my eyes on the fruit and willed it to me. It jerked in place as I stood to my feet. Gaining more confidence from my new stance, I gave a sharp cry of surprise when the fruit hurled itself toward me and into the hand I had held up to protect my face.

Well, at least I knew that worked.

"Pretty cool, huh?" I glanced over at the white-speckled owl. He huffed and shuffled his feathers as if to say to me 'big deal.'

"Screw you too, buddy," I growled, turning my back on him with the fruit in my hand.

It was a big deal to me. Magic was something I still hadn't fully accepted yet, let alone the idea of me doing magic. I smirked at the fruit in my hand. I could move objects with my mind.

I felt a bit giddy at the idea. Even more so because of the floating feeling that began to inch up my skin from where I was holding the glowing peach-like fruit. I turned it over in my hand and held it up to my face as I searched out the source of the light coming from inside it.

This was the fruit that granted Alice her powers and killed the Seelie Princess?

Like most things in the Underground, I had to be cautious until proven otherwise. Could the fruit grant my wish? Probably. Would it be exactly what I wanted? Not fucking likely.

Still, part of me whispered, what could it hurt? I couldn't go back the way I came, even if I had the key to get home. Home. That one word made the decision for me. I wanted to go home and this fruit could get me there.

Ignoring the warning bells going off in the recesses of my brain saying it was a bad idea, I brought the fruit to my mouth. Mr. Blue Eyes must have agreed because as my teeth sank into the skin of the fruit, and its juices flowed into my mouth, he began to squawk and hoot in vigor. As I swallowed the tangy flavor down, my head began to swim.

The magic of the fruit poured into me, making me drunk on power. I tried to focus on the thought of going home and my grandmother's house. The vegetable patch in the backyard and the lines of flowers all along the front lawn, but the images just wouldn't come. The only coherent thought in my mind was the word home.

I focused on that one word. Home. I willed the fruit's magic to take me home. To where I belonged. Of course, it wasn't a clear enough request, but it was the best I could do under the circumstances. It wasn't like I had any other home to go to.

I waited for the energy in me to do something. Transport me somewhere. When nothing happened, I peeked my eyes open and saw I was still in the closed-off grove. I began to think it wasn't going to do anything at all.

Then the images began.

A blonde-haired Fae, with a much kinder face then when I'd seen her in the ballroom, smirked at me as she teased. "You want to see him, don't you?"

See who?

"I don't care if you can't stand him. You have a duty to your kingdom." The White Queen's voice growled through my head, her icy blue eyes breaking through Gab's face.

"I'll never leave you."

My body enveloped with warmth at the words. A feeling of overwhelming love and devotion filled me as the UnSeelie Prince's face swam into view. Before I could register where the feeling was coming from more images poured in. Places I'd never been, thoughts and words I'd never spoken, and a deep gut-wrenching feeling of betrayal.

It was too much at once. My head was overloaded, and I knew I was going down even as a pair of arms caught me. The warm body holding onto mine barely registered, but the dark blue eyes broke through, and one word slipped from my mouth.

"Dorian."

HOME AGAIN

IT HAD BEEN raining that night. As cliché as it was, the Underground only had one rainy season. It lasted exactly one week and was there one minute and gone the next.

It was one of those days that I loved the most. I'd sit beneath one of the many fruit trees with Dorian as we talked about the future and what it held for us. Sometimes we'd feed each other the fallen fruit. The best times were when we'd just sit and hold each other. I loved the way he wrapped his arms around me and hold me tight. I'd breathe him in and forget everything else in the world. Even now my body yearned for his arms around me.

He'd been waiting for me in the orchard. We had a long standing date to meet on the second day of the rainfall. But I'd been running late that day, and when I got to our tree, someone else was already in those arms. The blonde human girl who had been popping in and out of the Underground since she was a little girl was holding on to my Dorian.

I had never really met her. She had always chosen to hang around the UnSeelie Court for Reaper knows what reason, so I didn't know her enough to give her a second thought.

But when I saw her there with Dorian, with her hands tangled in my dark prince's midnight tresses, and her petite form pressed against his as her mouth tasted what was once mine, I was overwhelmed with emotion.

Anger and hate filled me for the girl named Alice. In the same instance, I was filled with sadness and devastation for the man I thought loved me. And then pity and self-loathing overshadowed any other feeling. Why should I think I could be happy? To have love?

I was a fool.

No longer able to stand watching my life crumble before my eyes, I ran. My slipper-covered feet splashed in the puddles, soaking me to the bone. My hair matted to my face as the rain pelted down on me, but I didn't care. Nothing mattered anymore, and I only had one thought on my mind.

I wanted to get away. I wanted it all to stop. The pain. The pressure that pushed down on me and threatened to rip me apart. I wanted to die, but taking one's own life was hard when you were a Fae. Near impossible.

Iron was the only real sure way to kill us, and the Fae didn't leave it lying around just anywhere. I'd have to go to the human world to get some. I was on my way to the door when it called to me. The same, now familiar oaky voice that had plagued me for over a year.

When I happened upon the tree I didn't question what it was, the betrayal and heartache overrode my senses. I was too mesmerized by its fruit as it cooed to me like a new mother, welcoming me into its bosom.

I remembered biting into the fruit and the sweet liquid pouring into my mouth as I thought of my pain and the need for it to stop. But after that, nothing. There was nothing up until my earliest memory of my childhood as Katherine.

But that wasn't really my name, was it?

Remembering wasn't hard. It was all too easy to remember the life I had before. The person I was before. A person that had begun to creep out since the moment I was sucked into the rabbit hole.

I knew the human in me didn't like the person I was. The cool and calculating Fae who never wanted to fall in love, and when she finally let her walls down, her heart was obliterated. The human in me much preferred the awkward English Lit major who couldn't find a real job or a boyfriend. At least she was kind. At least she had choices.

Lynne.

That was my name. A name I hadn't heard in over a century. A name I had hoped to never hear uttered again. Not that anyone, save my mother, would remember it.

Except Dorian.

He remembered. I knew because as my consciousness floated back up, that was all I could hear. A deep silky voice that urged me to wake up. The voice of the man who I'd loved as a Fae. The man that even as a human, I still found myself drawn to.

I fought to keep my eyes closed, torn between wanting to see him, and dreading it. The last time I'd seen him as a Fae was with *her.* Alice. The feelings I expected to surface, the ones I had been running from, didn't appear. They were still there, just beneath the rampant pounding of my heart, but it was like it had happened to someone else.

In a way it had.

I wasn't the Seelie Princess. I was human. My body still felt the same. The aches and scrapes from my battles to get home still wracked my mortal form. If I could get through the Underground with all of its wonders and horrors as a mere mortal, I could certainly look my ex-fiancé in the eye.

The moment I shifted in place the hand holding mine tightened, and Dorian's voice became louder and more urgent.

"Lynne? Can you hear me? Are you all right?"

My eyes peeked open to meet the concerned dark blue of the UnSeelie Prince's eyes. The markings on his face were still there, but unusually inactive. My mother didn't forgive easily, and only the reappearance of her only child would make her willing to remove a curse once cast, which meant my mother must have been notified of my return.

Fan-fucking-tastic.

I eased up in the bed I was lying in, pulling my hand away from his to cradle my head. My world had become tilted and my stomach lurched at the aching in my head. Apparently shoving a lifetime's worth of memories back into your head was not something to be taken lightly.

"Lynne? Talk to me, please. Are you all right? How did this happen? Why do you still look like the human?"

I avoided looking at him, instead taking in my surroundings. I was in the room from the mirror, well my room. My breakfast table was still there, but the tea set and writing pad were gone. My vanity still stood next to a full-length mirror, but this time instead of looking out to Mop's and Trip's concerned faces, only my own looked back. My eyes lingered over the image of Dorian sitting next to me on the bed. His lips were still moving as he plied me with questions that only made my head pound harder.

Was I okay? No. How'd it happen? Magic, duh. Could I explain it more than that? No fucking way.

The last question, though I could kind of answer. Why did I still look like Kat? Well, because I was still her, or well me. And while my human body was limited, it was a far cry better than my Fae form. It was a dead and useless carcass that could easily be discarded. The stupid tree had at least done that right. When I had wished to die, I didn't know I needed specific instructions on what to do with my soul afterward. Who knew how long that tree held onto it before it shoved me into a human body?

"Lynne!" Dorian grabbed my shoulders, turning me to him and yelling out to a waiting servant when I didn't show any plans of responding. "Somebody call a healer!"

"Stop yelling. Geez. I'm fine." I smacked his hands away from me and stumbled from the bed.

"You are certainly not fine." He came up beside me, catching me before I face planted into the dresser. "You cannot even keep your feet under you."

"Yes, I can. It's just these damn..." I trailed off as I noticed I wasn't wearing boots. In fact, I wasn't wearing any of the clothes Chess gave me. Not that I was complaining, they were risqué for my tastes, Fae or human, but the silky white night gown I was wearing wasn't any better.

"One of the servants changed you," Dorian provided, leading me to sit back on the bed. "That human girl made a wreck of your clothes."

"I'm still that human girl, you know." I jerked my arm out of his and scooted away from him. "There's just more to me now."

I turned my face away from him and stared at my reflection in the mirror. My eyes had turned completely blue, and there wasn't a speck of red on my head. So much for going back to the way things were.

Dorian sat down next to me. As usual, his presence caused a tingle to buzz along my skin. "But how is this possible?"

He really wasn't going to give up, was he?

"Hell if I know." I sighed, throwing my hands up in the air.

The prince tried to inch closer to me to take my hands again, but when I tensed, he stood and turned away from me to face the window. Dorian didn't say anything for a while; his eyes stared out the window, giving me a chance to scan his profile from behind.

Seeing with Fae eyes was different than seeing with human eyes. I didn't just see him as a whole delicious package. Sure my eyes were drawn to the way his pants fit his backside, but whose wouldn't be? We never had an issue with being attracted to each other. The taut muscles in his shoulders, though told another story.

"I tried to find you afterward." His voice was tight as if he were trying to control his emotions.

I kept silent as he spoke. I knew we would have this conversation eventually; I just didn't think it would be right away. Right now. I wasn't even sure what was going to happen in the next five minutes let alone what to do about what happened in the past.

"The moment I figured out it was a trick. That Alice had..." he paused, caught up in his anger. He turned to me his jaw tight. "But you had already done it."

I couldn't meet his eyes as they bore into me. I tried to wrap my arms around myself to shield me from his accusatory glare. He knelt down before me, grabbing ahold of my hands. My eyes jerked to his as his voice melted from angry to desperate.

"Why, Lynne? Why did you not let me explain?" He dropped my hands and grabbed my shoulders, his emotions becoming more intense as I sat in silence. "I would have never cheated on you with another, especially not a human. I thought you knew that.”

His hands tightened on my shoulders. My eyes hardened as he spat out human as if the mere word were repulsive. He kept forgetting, I was still human.

My eyes hardened and I scowled at him. “In the Seelie Court emotions are only weapons that can be used against us. You know this, and still you ask why.”

My voice became quiet as I tried to retain my anger. “If you’d asked me back then why I did it, I wouldn’t be able to tell you, because I honestly didn’t know what I was feeling. Seeing you with her caused all reasoning to go out the window. I couldn’t see the bigger picture. I couldn’t think this isn’t something my Dorian would do. All I could see was her hands on you and you...you kissing her.”

His face and hands softened at my admission. “And now?”

My eyes burned at the hope in his eyes. He thought we could go back to the way we were before. Like we could just pick up where we left off. That everything would be all right again.

“I...” I sighed. This was hard. Harder than I thought it would be, yet easier in so many ways.

“Dorian,” I started again. It felt weird to say his name out loud. I didn’t know this person.

Not really. "You have to understand. The Lynne that you knew, the one you loved, isn't me."

"What do you mean? Of course you are." He tried to grab my hands again, but I moved them before he could. Touching would not make this any easier on either of us.

"I'm not Lynne. I'm Kat." I scratched the back of my head and looked up at the ceiling. "I mean, I have all of Lynne's memories. All of her feelings for you." I peeked up at him. My heart ached at the forlorn expression in his eyes. "But it's like its secondhand knowledge, like it didn't even happen to me. So you see." I gave an awkward chuckle. "You're virtually a stranger to me. I think it would be awkward, if not inappropriate, for us to go back to the way it was before."

"I see." Dorian stood up. The face that had been so open and full of hope had locked down into an expressionless mask. "If that is how you feel then there is nothing that can be done."

The part in my heart that was Lynne wanted to run after him. But it was like she was submerged in water and could barely be heard above my own feelings. Those feelings were telling me to keep my distance. I didn't know these people. I didn't know what they would do when they found out I couldn't be the Fae Princess they wanted me to be. So I sat there and watched as he moved toward the bedroom door, his shoulders stiff as he opened it.

"I will leave you to get settled. Your mother should be here any moment. Please feel free to call if you need anything." He glanced over his shoulder, his eyes hard and cold. "I am sure you can at least manage that."

The door slammed behind him, the sound resonating through the room. Had I been too blunt? Should I have lied and pretended everything was okay?

I shook my head to clear my doubtful thoughts. No. I did the right thing. It wouldn't have been right to lie.

"Well, that didn't go very well."

"Chess!" My head jerked to the mirror where the pink-haired feline was poking his head out.

Chess gave me a fanged grin as he stepped out of the mirror, the heels of his plum-colored boots sinking into the plush carpet. Gone was the golden outfit and back was his violet-and pink-colored ensemble. Only this time, I wasn't so distracted by the extravagant belts at his waist.

"So this is the palace? It looks so ordinary. Hmm." His tail picked up a bobble from the vanity and passed it to his hands as he chuckled. "Goes to show you, you can't judge a fish by the hook in its mouth. Look at you for instance."

He moved away from the vanity and approached my scantily clad form. I itched to move my arms over myself, but I knew from previous experience that would just encourage him. He leaned in until our faces were inches apart as his tail wrapped around my waist.

Chess picked up a piece of my blonde hair and brought it to his face. I could feel his breath against my cheek as he watched me. Unable to stop it, my face filled with heat at the intensity of the emotion in his eyes.

"If I'd known you were royalty, I wouldn't have teased you so much." He pressed my hair to his mouth. His voice became low and husky. "You'll forgive me won't you, your highness."

I tugged my hair from his claws, blushing harder as I muttered, "Yeah right, like being royalty would have stopped you."

Chess shrugged, placing his hands on my waist to pull me closer. "Probably not, but I'd have been more diplomatic about it."

"At least you haven't changed." I chuckled and then frowned remembering Dorian's retreating back.

"They are going to expect things from you. Things you might not be prepared for." He placed a claw under my chin, tipping my face up to his before letting me go with a shrug. "Well, what's a princess to do?"

"Do?" I took a step back from him when his tail released me to trail along my arms. "About what?"

"Your marriage of course!" His words and voice proclaimed his excitement, but I'd come to know the telltale signs of agitation by the way his tail and ears twitched in jerky movements. He wasn't all that happy with my parentage or my prospect of getting married. Not that I was either, but it was nice to know someone else was still on my side.

"I hardly doubt they'll want me to marry him after they figure out I'm not all Fae." I shook my head, not needing to explain who he was to Chess. "Besides, I like being human. I remember what it was like being the princess, and I don't think I could go back to being her. At least not be the princess again and stay sane."

"A rose is still a rose even hidden under different petals. I doubt they'll care if you want to be a dandelion. They'll still try and make you a rose." A far-off look filled his eyes. "Take it from someone who knows. You're a tool for their use. Nothing more."

A tool? Was that all I was? I knew my mother wanted to stop the shadows. It was the whole reason behind the marriage, well part of the reason. My heart ached thinking back to Dorian's expression as he slammed the door. But even without Dorian, I'd known what my mother had wanted, and I agreed to do it like a good dutiful daughter. But not this time.

Chess was right. If I stayed they'd want me to change. To be more Fae than human. To spend the rest of my life, as short as a mortal's life was, hiding my emotions. Then there was all the bowing and the etiquette, the never having a moment to myself, and always having to be on guard. Even when I was with Dorian. Especially when I was with Dorian.

I could never really let myself go, even in the rare moments of passion we'd shared. If I chose to marry Dorian, it would mean I would have to give up my human life. I would have to stay in the Underground and be their princess, and some day, when my mother retired, their queen.

I wasn't ready for that kind of commitment. The very thought of eternity caused panic to fill my chest. I couldn't marry Dorian. I was only 22 for Christ's sake. I had my whole life ahead of me. I wanted to be reckless and flounder for a few more years. Then, when I was pushing thirty, I'd buckle down and make a definite life decision.

There was also the question of my family. What to do about them? Should I at least stay and meet with my mother after all these years? I'm sure she had missed me even if her face would never say so. She had a permanent look of cool indifference whenever she was in front of the Seelie Court.

Oh, the Seelie Court. I had left so many people behind there. Would they be happy to see me? Even when they realized the girl they had teased in the ballroom was their friend? Gab would be happy no doubt, but the others were harder to guess. Fae friends were hard to come by and even harder to keep. Not like the human world.

And what of my human friends? Would they quickly forget me when I never showed up to work? And my human mother? We never got along, and she was always criticizing my choices, but she was still my mom. Not to forget the rest of my family. I couldn't do to them what I had done to those in the Underground.

While it had been over a century for the Underground, it was like yesterday for me. I didn't know how I was supposed to answer their questions. I had no doubt they would be like Dorian – desperate to understand – and I wouldn't be able to give them more than I had given him. Soon they would realize I wasn't the princess they had mourned all these years. I wasn't even sure who I was, not really. But I knew who I wasn't. I wasn't a princess, Fae or not.

"So, my lovely, what are you going to be? A rose or a dandelion?" He held his hand out to me, the offer as obvious as the nose on my face.

He could take me home. Get me out of here before they forced me into a choice I didn't make. Even in my state of panic, I could tell he really wanted me to take his hand. To choose the human world over the Fae, and maybe even a part of him that was too afraid to admit it, wanted me to choose him over the courts.

But could I do it?

Before my mind had been completely made up, my hand slid into his. As I stepped through the mirror, I didn't think about what I was leaving behind, but rather what I was returning to. Maybe, just maybe, even where I truly belonged.